EDINBURGH ESCAPE

BROTHERHOOD PROTECTORS INTERNATIONAL
BOOK FIVE

ELLE JAMES

TWISTED PAGE INC

ISBN EBOOK: 978-1-62695-651-3

ISBN PAPERBACK: 978-1-62695-652-0

ISBN HARDCOVER: 978-1-62695-653-7

For my son who loves Scotland as much as I do!
For my daughters who traveled through Scotland with me on quite the adventure gathering data and visiting locations that would help me to write this book.
Elle James

AUTHOR'S NOTE

Enjoy other military books by Elle James

Brotherhood Protectors International

Athens Affair (#1)

Belgian Betrayal (#2)

Croatia Collateral (#3)

Dublin Debacle (#4)

Edinburgh Escape (#5)

France Face-Off (#6)

Visit ellejames.com for more titles and release dates

Join her newsletter at

https://ellejames.com/contact/

EDINBURGH ESCAPE

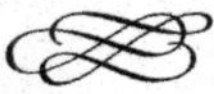

BROTHERHOOD PROTECTORS
INTERNATIONAL BOOK #5

New York Times & USA Today
Bestselling Author

ELLE JAMES

PROLOGUE

"TAKE POINT, ROOK," Callum McCall whispered into his headset. "Nae need tae barge in like a bull."

"I'm not barging," Rook responded, moving forward on silent feet, one building corner at a time, his green heat signature visible through Cal's night vision goggles.

As the newest man on the British SAS team, Rook was smart, light on his feet and as green as Nessie's toenails. The boy, in his early twenties, had only just completed the rigorous SAS training. This mission to Syria was his first assignment. Fortunately, he was eager and willing to take direction from the more experienced members of their team.

Rook took his position at the corner of a building and knelt, aiming his rifle forward to provide cover for Taff.

The team's Welshman, smaller, wiry and fast, pushed forward, leapfrogging past Rook to the next corner.

Cal held his rifle close to his chest and pushed away from the side of the building.

With Rook and Taff covering their forward movement, Smudge, Yeti and Bazza joined Cal, heading for the center of the small township.

The intel they'd been given indicated a particularly heinous ISIS leader was holed up in an old Greek Orthodox church at the town center. All they had to do was get in, get the leader and get back out. Easy, right?

Cal's lips twisted wryly. It was the easy assignments that proved to be anything but easy. One more street up and one over from Taff's position would be the targeted structure.

Cal motioned for the others to continue forward. Bazza took point, followed by Yeti. When Smudge neared the last corner, blending into the shadows, Cal hurried to catch up to him.

Dusk had long since given way to night, with the first stars blinking to life in the heavens above, barely visible between the rooftops.

So far, they had met with no resistance. Not a single sentry stood guard along the streets or the roads leading in or out of the little town.

Cal's gut knotted. It didn't feel right. If there were an ISIS leader somewhere in the town, they'd have guards monitoring roads leading in and out. They'd have people on the rooftops, armed and ready to shoot.

Instead, they'd made it all the way into the little town without any skirmishes.

Once he stood beside Smudge, Cal glanced around the corner of the building and frowned. No one moved. No guards at the door. No civilians moving around. It wasn't midnight yet. All night operations in small Syrian towns that Cal had been involved in had had at least one civilian roaming around in the late hours. And any operation they'd been involved in, that revolved around terrorist cells or enemy strongholds, had sentries.

There was no way they could walk right into a building and capture an ISIS leader with nobody challenging them.

"I'm going forward," Smudge said.

That sense of foreboding deep in Cal's gut increased tenfold. "No, let me," Cal said.

Smudge shook his head. "I've got this if you've got my six." Before Cal could argue with his teammate, Smudge slipped into the shadows of the building and darted across the street toward the building intel had identified.

Cal knelt at the corner, his M4A1 rifle pressed into his shoulder, his night vision goggles in place, searching for the green heat signatures of the enemy. Smudge was the only heat signature Cal picked up.

His teammate made it across the open space and pressed his back against the building they would eventually have to enter.

Taff slid in behind Cal. "I've got you covered."

Cal nodded, rose, looked both directions and toward the rooftops before running across the road. Smudge eased around the side of the building.

Soon, Yeti and Bazza joined Cal and Smudge at the building. Taff and Rook would remain nearby, providing coverage and early warning should enemy forces move in while the rest of the team breached the building, located and extracted their target.

Smudge appeared at the opposite corner of the structure from Cal. "The front is the only entrance," he whispered into Cal's headset. "I'm going in." Keeping to the shadows as much as possible, Smudge eased toward the front entrance.

From the opposite side, Cal moved toward the door, arriving at the same time as Smudge.

Cal reached for the doorknob. It twisted easily in his hand. As he pulled the door toward himself, Taff's voice sounded in his ear.

"Holy shit! Rook! Behind you! It's a trap! Abort!"

Before Cal could react, the world exploded around him. The door he'd just opened slammed into him, knocking him flat on his back. The entire front of the building crashed down on him, crushing the air from his lungs and making his world go black.

Minutes, hours, days later... Cal couldn't be sure how long he'd been out. Voices pulled him back to awareness. Blinking his eyes open did nothing to clear the darkness. Pain knifed through his temple. When he tried to move, more pain stabbed his thigh.

Someone was yelling, his voice slightly muffled by what Cal could only figure were walls. His hands moved beside him, touching hard-packed dirt. Where was he? What had happened? Where was his team?

He pushed against the dirt, trying to sit up.

The pounding in his head increased. He lay back again until it eased and then tried again. This time, he was able to push himself into a sitting position, the pain in his thigh aggravated with any movement.

He ran his hand over the thigh, his fingers coming into contact with something that felt like a shaft of splintered wood, jutting out of his leg. Just touching it sent waves of agony radiating across his nerves. Without thinking, he gripped the splintered edges and yanked it from his leg.

He clenched his jaw to keep from crying out as a jolt of pain ripped through his leg and blood spurted out of the wound.

Cal pressed his hand against his thigh to staunch the flow, the pressure easing the waves of pain if only for a moment. Releasing the pressure, he shrugged out of his tattered jacket and yanked his T-shirt over his head, briefly wondering what had happened to his armor-plated vest. Probably gone with his boots.

He tore the shirt into strips, wadded up a portion and pressed it against the wound on his leg, then snugly tied the other strips around it. All was accomplished in the dark, while he listened to the continuous shouts in another language somewhere outside the structure where he was being held.

Cal tensed when he heard words he understood, from a voice he recognized.

"Fuck you and the horse you rode in on." Though weaker than Cal was used to hearing, he knew that voice. His chest tightened.

Smudge had been a huge fan of old black-and-white western movies. He'd perfected an imitation of John Wayne's drawl and used it with that exact phrase to end arguments or when he had nothing else to say.

"You will tell us what we want to know," a heavily accented voice commanded.

Crackling sounded much like that of electricity arcing.

An anguished grunt pierced Cal's heart. They were torturing Smudge.

Cal tried to get to his feet. As soon as he put pressure on his injured leg, he fell back to the dirt floor. Not only did he have a puncture wound, but his ankle also wouldn't support him, shooting more pain up his leg.

But he couldn't do nothing. Not when his teammate was being tortured. Half-scooting, half-dragging himself across the dirt, he felt his way around the dark chamber, bumping into stone walls until he located what felt like a wooden door. He ran his hands over the surface, hoping to find a knob or handle. There was none, and no way he could open the door from inside.

Desperate to help Smudge, he pounded his fist against the solid wooden panel. "Leave him alone!" Cal yelled, knowing how futile his words would be, but hoping they might take him instead of Smudge. If he could just get out of the cell he was in, he might have a chance of saving his friend, his teammate, his brother.

Something hard hit the door, the force of the blow reverberating against Cal's hand. "Shut up!" a man yelled. Then he said something in what sounded like Arabic.

Moments later, another man yelled. "I told you, I don't know anything."

Rook. He was alive. The newest and youngest member of the SAS team. Baptism by fire on his first deployment. Was he to be the next one tortured?

"You will tell us what we want to know," the accented man demanded. "Or we will cut off your comrade's fingers one at a time."

"I don't know anything," Rook cried.

Words were spoken in Arabic.

A sharp whomp sounded, followed by a strangled grunt.

"Jesus!" Rook cried out. "I can't tell you what I don't know. I just follow orders."

"What were your orders?"

"Cover my team. That's all I knew."

Another Arabic order.

"Wait!" Rook yelled. "It's true. My only job was to cover my team. They didn't tell me why we were there. I don't know why."

Whomp!

"Mother fu—" Smudge's curse ended in a grunt of pain. "He doesn't know anything. He's just a kid. We wouldn't tell him anything until he proved himself. You know why we came. Obviously, someone told you we were coming. What more do you expect to get out of us?"

"The truth," his captor demanded. "Who gave you the order to come? Who did you come to find? Why shouldn't we kill you? You're nothing but infidels."

"And you're lying, murdering bastards," Smudge said. "You think you're fighting for Allah and that your sacrifices will buy you a place in heaven with forty virgins? Ha! They'll be forty male virgins and it won't be heaven, it'll be hell—"

A loud smacking sound cut off Smudge's words.

Cal slammed his fist against the door again. "Leave them alone!" he yelled. He traced the edges of the door with his fingertips, praying he could pry it loose by sheer force of will.

Someone said something sharply in Arabic.

Moments later, footsteps sounded outside the door behind which Cal lay. He pushed backward and to the side, wincing as he jolted his leg. He reached for the jacket he'd shrugged out of, twisted it into a long rope-like shape and positioned himself just inside the cell, lying on the floor with his back to the door.

The door creaked open. Dim light spread in a wedge across the floor and Cal.

A guard stepped into the cell and kicked Cal in the back.

Cal rolled onto his back, flung the jacket around the man's leg and yanked hard, sending him backward. He landed hard on his back.

Unfortunately, he hadn't come alone. A second man entered the cell and backhanded Cal with a meaty fist.

The force of the blow made Cal's head spin.

Before he could regain clarity, the man he'd knocked on his ass scrambled to his feet. The two men came at Cal.

When they reached for him, he swung his fist, connecting with one man's jaw.

The other guy backhanded him again.

Cal's head snapped to the side.

The man he'd punched in the jaw pounced on him, straddling his torso, his hands closing around Cal's throat.

When Cal tried to hit the guy, the other guard captured his hands and pinned them over his head.

The tighter the hands squeezed around Cal's throat, the darker the room became.

He must have blacked out. When his eyes opened, he was sitting in a chair, his arms secured behind his back, his legs strapped to the chair legs.

Smudge sat opposite him, slumped over, his face battered, his eyes swollen almost shut and blood dripping from the stumps where two of his fingers had been.

Bile rose up Cal's throat. His leg ached, but not nearly as much as the muscle at the center of his chest. He was out of the cell and powerless to do anything to help Smudge.

A moan drew Cal's attention to his side.

Rook stood between two other men. Or rather, he hung between the men, each holding him up by his arms. Bruises marred his cheeks, one eye was swollen shut and his lip bled. He lifted his head as if it weighed too much to keep up. "I didn't say...anything." His head lolled forward.

Cal jerked his hands against the ties that bound him.

A bearded man, dressed all in black with a black turban wrapped around his head, stood beside Smudge, his gaze fixed on Cal. "Tell us who you and your team are, where you're from, who gave you the order to trespass in our country," the man's lips twisted into a sneer, "and the names of your firstborn sons or your friend dies."

Cal recognized the man from the photo they'd been shown at the briefing. This was the ISIS leader they'd been sent to kill. He was known for his ruthlessness. He'd captured a squad of American soldiers who'd been sent into a small town to deliver food and medical supplies. One by one, he'd executed them and then dragged their bodies through the streets of that town as a warning to the citizens that this would be their fate if they allowed other Americans to sully their streets.

"Don't tell him anything," Smudge said, his voice rattling like gravel in a tin can. "Not a goddamn thing."

Cal stared at his friend, then shifted his gaze to the man demanding information. "Go screw yourself."

The terrorist's eyes narrowed. He pulled a curved dagger from a sheath at his waist, grabbed a handful of Smudge's hair and yanked his head back.

Cal threw himself forward, chair and all, falling into a silent, black void.

Falling...falling...in an endless downward spiral...

CHAPTER 1

AN INCESSANT CHIRPING sound pierced the silence, slowing Cal's descent before he came to a bone-shattering crash on hard-packed earth. The more the chirping continued, the closer he came to the surface of his abyss.

He lifted one eyelid, unwilling to confront the horror.

Light crept into the room, sneaking around the corners of curtains covering a tall window.

Cal opened the other eye and stared around the room, confused for a moment. He moved his arms. They weren't restrained. He stretched his legs. Only a twinge of pain and stiffness remained from the wound he'd received from the explosion. Gone were the chairs he and Smudge had been tied to. Gone were Smudge and Rook. The dirt floor was replaced by a soft bed with clean sheets and pillows.

Cal ran a hand through his hair, willing his heartbeat to return to normal and the recurring nightmare to fade.

The chirping sound ceased about the time he located his cell phone on the nightstand. He reached for the device and checked the caller ID of the missed call, his brow furrowing.

Hank Patterson, the head of the Brotherhood Protectors? The man had started the agency after he'd saved his wife, the megastar Sadie McClain, from a stalker.

Why was he contacting Cal? Had Ace Hammerson, the regional lead of the Brotherhood Protectors International division, asked Hank to convince Cal to join their ranks and become a glorified bodyguard, protecting rich clients from stalkers, jealous rivals or assassins? Cal had told Ace he wanted to think about the job offer. He wasn't sure he was cut out to babysit the elite, entitled wealthy individuals who'd never had to work hard a day in their lives. Who'd never faced death or watched someone they'd loved have their throat slit while being completely helpless to stop it from happening.

Cal stared at the name on the screen. Hank understood what it was like. He'd been a Navy SEAL in his former military life. He'd seen as many horrors as Cal. Yet, he'd managed to get on with his life, to push past the worst of humankind to dare to bring children into a world as fucked up as this one.

Cal frowned at the clock on the nightstand. Why was Hank calling in the middle of the night? The leader knew there was a seven-hour time difference between the UK and Hank's home in Montana. Of course, it would only be eight o'clock in the evening there.

Cal sighed. Not that he'd been sleeping well. The nightmares that had barely begun to fade had returned with a vengeance, reminding him of his last mission, of the lives lost mere seconds before they'd been liberated by a team of US Navy SEALs. Only two of the six-man team had survived. Rook and Cal. Taff had been shot a moment before the explosion occurred. Yeti and Bazza had died when they'd been crushed beneath the falling wall.

After their rescue, Cal had spent time in the hospital, his system pumped full of antibiotics to fight a staph infection picked up in the dirt and filth of the cell he'd found himself in when he'd regained consciousness.

Rook had overcome his physical injuries but couldn't let go of the emotional damage he'd suffered watching his teammate murdered in front of him. Rook had been placed on administrative leave, assigned to a mental health provider and put on suicide watch.

Cal had still been in the hospital when Rook had jumped off the Tower Bridge into the Thames, late one night. No one knew he'd done it until his therapist had called Cal the next day, asking if he'd seen Rook. He hadn't shown up for his appointment. When Cal said he hadn't seen him, the therapist had a police officer swing by his apartment in London for a wellness check. When Rook hadn't answered the knock on the door, the officer asked the building manager to let him in.

He'd found a handwritten note on the counter in the kitchen addressed *To Whoever Finds This.*

In the letter, Rook spoke of failing his team and costing them all their lives. He'd begged his dead brothers in arms for their forgiveness for letting them down. He'd asked that someone call his mother and let her know he wouldn't be home for Christmas as previously promised and to please tell her he loved her—and don't bother looking for him. The Thames didn't give back what it claimed.

They'd found Rook's body three days later.

Cal stared at the cell phone screen, his thoughts on Rook, Smudge and the others, guilt souring his stomach. *Why them and not me?*

The cell phone chirped again, startling Cal out of the trance he found himself falling into all too often.

He answered just to make it stop. "Yeah."

Instead of Hank's deep voice, a softer, gentler female voice sounded in his ear. "Is this Callum McCall?"

Cal frowned. "It is."

"Thank goodness. This is Sadie McClain, Hank Patterson's wife. Hank's here with me."

"Hey, Callum," a deep, male voice filled Cal's ear. "Hank Patterson here. Sorry to call you so late, but we wanted to contact you before morning. I know you haven't committed to joining the team, but Sadie has a big favor to ask of you. You can say no if you're not ready. We'll understand."

"Only, I hope you won't say no," Sadie said. "A close friend of mine is headed to London as we speak. She arrives around eight o'clock tomorrow morning. She plans to see a few sights in London before boarding the Caledonian Sleeper train to Edinburgh at ten-thirty tomorrow night."

Cal shook his head. "What does your friend have to do with me?"

"She's a preschool teacher from Montana. She's barely been out of the state and never left the country. I'm worried about her traveling alone. Especially since she's going to meet newfound relatives in Scotland. I don't want anything to happen to her or for anyone to take advantage of her."

"Again, I don't know what you want me to do about it?" Cal shoved a hand through his hair, sleep the furthest from his mind, the nightmare still lingering.

"What Sadie wants is for someone to follow her friend and make sure she doesn't get lost or that no one exploits, manipulates or abuses her, including her relatives in Scotland."

"Has she had a falling out with her Scottish kin?" Cal asked.

"Not that we're aware of," Sadie said. "She only just discovered she has relatives in Edinburgh after taking one of those online DNA tests. After contacting her half-brother, he invited her out to meet the rest of the family. She doesn't see where anything could go wrong or pose danger to her, but I'd feel a whole lot better if someone was looking out for her."

Cal sighed. "And you want me to be that someone? Why not someone she knows?"

"Everyone she knows is here in Montana. Most of them couldn't afford to travel to the UK, and my friend could barely afford her own trip and certainly couldn't afford to pay for someone else's," Sadie said. "I was supposed to go with her, but my baby isn't feeling well, and I couldn't leave him."

Cal pushed to a sitting position, his back against the headboard. "Why not one of the other members of Hank's international team?"

"There's a reason Ace was recruiting you," Hank said. "Every one of his team has a current assignment. He needs more protectors to handle the workload. You don't have to commit to being a member of the team immediately. You could consider this a one-off request to help Sadie's friend. We'd pay you, of course."

"Would you do this for me?" Sadie asked. "Please?"

Cal's first inclination was to say no. He wasn't ready to face the world. The recurring nightmares kept the deaths of every member of his team fresh in his mind, not allowing him to let go and move past the grief and feeling of failure. However, staying in the hotel room he'd lived in for the past couple of months wasn't helping him get on with life. Though he didn't want to get involved, a change of scenery might help. "How long will she be in the UK?" Cal asked.

"You'll do it?" Sadie asked, the excitement and relief evident in her tone.

"I will." How hard could it be? Following a woman around for a couple of weeks might help get him out of the rut he'd landed in when he'd left the military. And it would force him to go home to Scotland, something he'd avoided since Smudge's death. He might find the courage to go to Smudge's family home on the Isle of Lewis and let them know how brave their son had been and how much he'd meant to Cal and the rest of their team.

Well, maybe not. He wasn't sure he could face Smudge's mother. Why had they killed Smudge and not Cal? Could he have done more to stop them from slitting his friend's throat?

"My friend has to be back in two weeks to start

the new school year," Sadie was saying. "She planned on spending at least a week in Edinburgh to meet the blood relatives and see the sights there. Then she wants to see more of Scotland. She's not used to driving on the opposite side of the road, and she can't afford to hire a driver, so I assume she'll be doing most of her touring by train."

"Is she expecting someone to meet her at the airport?" Cal asked.

"No," Sadie said.

"Sadie's friend considers herself a strong, independent woman. She doesn't think she needs anyone to have her back."

"Everyone needs someone to have his or her back," Cal murmured. Too bad he hadn't had Smudge's and Rook's.

"Agreed," Hank said. "That was the first lesson we learned in BUD/S training. We look out for each other. Work as a team. Point is, she didn't want me to assign one of my guys to provide her with protection."

Cal shook his head. "Then why are you asking me to do it?"

"She doesn't have to know you're actually there to protect her," Sadie said. "I would feel better knowing someone is looking out for her. She's one of the nicest people I know, and I don't want anyone to hurt her."

"So, let me understand," Cal frowned. "You want

me to stalk your friend without her knowing I'm there to protect her?" His mind churned through the possible outcomes. "She might call the police if she suspects me of following her."

"I hadn't thought of that," Sadie said. "I did secure the room on the sleeper train adjacent to hers. The London-Heathrow airport is large. You could easily tail her there, and she'd never know. Same with the train going from the airport into London. And you'll both have to be at the Euston Station by ten-thirty to board the sleeper train. I can email or text all the information I have on her flight, the train and the address of her relatives in Edinburgh, along with a recent photo of my friend."

The thought of stalking a preschool teacher who'd never been out of her home country sounded about as boring as it could get.

Brilliant. He might be able to handle that, since he hadn't had the desire to do anything else since leaving the military. He hadn't really considered joining the Brotherhood Protectors. What good would he be in his current condition? Maybe easing into what sounded like a simple job would get him back on track or at least headed in the right direction. Falling into a bottle of scotch each night certainly wasn't the answer.

"Are you in, McCall?" Hank asked.

Cal sighed. He might regret it, but at least he would check out of the hotel and be forced to do something other than wallow in grief and an endless wallow of self-loathing. "I'm in," he said, already regretting his decision.

"Thank you," Sadie gushed. "I'll feel so much better knowing someone is looking out for her, especially since she thinks she doesn't need it."

"Send me the information and the photograph," Cal said.

"Thanks, Cal," Hank said. "She'll probably be fine with or without you along, but she jumped into this visit before we could run the data on the family. We know nothing about them, and neither does she."

"What's this woman's name?" Cal asked, his temple throbbing.

"Maggie," Sadie responded. "Maggie McKendrick. She's a real sweetheart. You're going to love her."

Cal almost laughed. He settled for a soft snort as he ended the call.

Love her? He seriously doubted that. Cal barely tolerated himself, having failed his team and having the audacity to live with the regret of not dying.

No, he couldn't love anyone. It hurt too much when you lost friends or loved ones to senseless bastards who placed no value on life except to use it to threaten others.

Cal prayed he didn't run into any trouble. He'd lost confidence in his ability to come to anyone's rescue, as he'd proved when Smudge had died at the hands of the ISIS leader. He'd been unable to do anything to stop the knife from slicing through Smudge's jugular. Even more disturbing, Cal hadn't been there for Rook when the young SAS operator had felt the only way to exorcise the demons in his mind was to execute himself.

Cal should have been there for the last member of his team instead of languishing in a hospital bed. He could have left sooner, limped his way across London and been there for Rook in his darkest hour.

The more he thought about it, the more he realized he was the wrong man for this job. He lifted his phone, prepared to call Hank and tell him he'd changed his mind. As he checked the screen, it lit up briefly and then went black. His battery had died.

He searched the hotel room for the charging cable. By the time he located it and plugged the cellphone in to charge, he'd talked himself out of a full-blown panic attack. He'd do the job.

How could he disappoint the beautiful Sadie McClain? The sweetheart of cinema really cared about her friend. A loud pinging sound made Cal jump.

The information Sadie had promised came through. Airline and flight schedule, the address of Ms. McKendrick's relatives in Edinburgh, the train ticket for the Caledonia sleeper train and the photograph of the preschool teacher.

He'd have no trouble identifying Maggie McKendrick with her mass of strawberry-blond curls, falling loosely down around her shoulders. Her eyes sparkled with laughter as she smiled for the camera. She was petite, with an almost elven face and pale skin, dusted with freckles across her nose. She was as unique as a woman could be.

Her genuine happiness tugged at the grief he hadn't been able to shake since that horrific day in Syria. If a photo of a woman had that kind of impact on him, he could only imagine what she'd be like in person. He could use some cheer and happiness in his life, although he just wasn't sure he could let go of the grief.

Not yet. It was too soon. Too raw.

The weight of his loss pressed him back into the bed, his head sinking into the soft pillow he should have enjoyed but didn't feel like he deserved. If he was to be at his best, he should go back to sleep so he'd be rested and ready to perform this mission.

As soon as he closed his eyes, images of his nightmare sent him right back to that chair across from Smudge, the moment before...

Cal bolted upright, grabbed the pillow from behind him and slung it across the room. He rose from the bed and paced, anger and adrenaline coursing through his veins. Sleep was overrated. He gathered the trousers and shirt he'd tossed on the floor the night before. One sniff had him flinging them across the room to join the pillow where it lay against the door. He'd been wearing the same clothes for a week. They could stand in the corner on their own.

Cal found his duffel bag on the other side of the bed and dug through everything he owned, searching for clean clothes. It was sad and a bit pathetic to think his life had been reduced to the contents of one duffel bag.

The only child of older parents, he'd lost his mum and dad years ago. Their home had been a rental flat in London. He'd seen no need to lease a place when he rarely stayed anywhere for long. Such was the life of an SAS operative. He owned a couple of sets of civilian clothing. When he'd been on active duty, he'd worn flame-retardant assault suits provided by the UK Ministry of Defence, their uniforms for combat. Joggers, T-shirts and trainers had been his mainstay when he hadn't been on a mission. He hadn't needed much. A pair of jeans, trousers, a button-down shirt, and a leather jacket summed the entirety of his wardrobe.

He missed the assault suits. They took the guesswork out of dressing. He found a pair of black trousers he'd worn to the funerals of his teammates, along with the black shirt and tie he'd purchased to go with them. He hated suit jackets, finding them too snug and confining. His teammates wouldn't have expected him to wear one to see them off. He'd worn his one shopping splurge, the black leather jacket he'd picked up on a rare layover in Italy after a mission in Africa.

Cal shook the trousers and shirt. When the wrinkles remained, he sighed and pulled the iron and ironing board from the closet and smoothed out the wrinkles as best he could. He couldn't show up in this woman's life looking like he'd just rolled out of a bed after pissing the night away.

His clothes somewhat wrinkle-free, he laid them out on the bed and entered the bathroom, turned on the shower and stripped out of his boxers. A glance in the mirror made him shake his head and rub his hand across the scruff of his beard. He hadn't shaved in a week. Hell, he wasn't sure where his razor was. After a couple of minutes searching, he gave up and studied his reflection. Short of going to the market just to buy another razor, he could let his beard grow. He'd worn a beard on most of his missions in the SAS. He couldn't remember why he'd shaved when he'd left the military. Most soldiers grew their beards after leaving the military. He hadn't been in his right mind for quite some time.

Cal stepped beneath the shower's spray and scrubbed his hair and skin as if by doing so, he was removing the dirt and grime he'd accumulated in that cell in Syria, hoping it would wash the dreams down the drain with the soap suds.

It never worked, but it had become a habit he couldn't quite shake.

By the time he'd washed his entire body, head to toe, the water was cooling. He stayed another couple of minutes, letting the cold water shock his system fully awake. Finally, he turned off the water, stepped out of the shower and dried off.

He dressed in the trousers, shirt and tie and glanced at the clock on the nightstand. He'd managed to pass an hour and a half since the call from Hank. That left three and a half hours until Ms. McKendrick's plane landed.

Too wound up to wait in his room, Cal slipped into his leather jacket and left the hotel. He walked the streets of London in the dark until he found a bakery that opened early with a promise of a scone and coffee. He sat at a small table inside, going over different scenarios of how he'd handle following Ms. McKendrick. He didn't like the idea of stalking her, but he didn't want to announce himself as being hired by Hank and Sadie. She might be offended and tell him to fuck off.

As the time neared, Cal returned to his room, packed all his belongings into his duffel bag, checked out of the hotel and hurried toward the nearest metro station. He hopped on a train heading for the airport, arriving thirty minutes before Ms. McKendrick's plane was due to arrive. One glance at the arrivals display had him hurrying through the airport. Her plane had landed early. If he hoped to intercept her before she left the airport, he had to hurry toward the doors she'd emerge from once she cleared customs.

With his duffel bag slung over one shoulder, he arrived in the baggage claim area at the exact moment, a pretty, petite woman wth strawberry-blond hair stopped near a carousel to speak to another woman, carrying a toddler.

He had no doubt she was Maggie McKendrick. Even with her hair piled high in a messy bun, there was no mistaking the reddish-gold color from the photograph. She smiled at the young mother and said something Cal couldn't hear.

The woman gave Maggie an answering smile and hurried toward the family bathroom, probably to change the baby's nappy.

Maggie carried a backpack over her shoulders and wheeled a small carry-on suitcase. She bypassed the baggage carousels, looking over her shoulder several times as she headed for the exit, a frown marring her pretty face.

Cal hurried to catch up, falling in step a reasonable distance behind her.

When she paused to study the signs, her brow furrowed.

Cal chose that moment to step up beside her. "Looking for ground transportation?"

She nodded and gave him a brief smile. "I am."

"Rental car, taxi or train?" he asked.

"The least expensive way to get into the city," she said.

"That would be the train," he nodded in the direction she needed to go. "It's that way. I'm heading into London myself if you want to follow me."

"That would be nice," she said and fell in step beside him. "Do you come to London often?" she asked.

"I've lived here off and on for the past fifteen years."

"Then you know your way around," she said.

He nodded. "Fairly well."

"But you weren't raised in London…?" she asked as they walked along the long corridor.

"Nae, lass," he said, laying on his thicker, Scottish accent. "Ah'm a Glaswegian, born and bred."

Her lips pressed together, and she shot a glance his way, a reddish-gold brow cocked. "Sorry?"

He chuckled and dropped the thick accent. "I was born and raised near Glasgow." He held out his hand. "Callum McCall."

As she took his hand, he was distracted by the jolt of electricity that speared through him at her touch. "Aye." He tipped his chin toward her. "And you?"

"I'm from the US." Her smile brightened as she pulled her hand free of his. "But I have relatives in Scotland. That's where I'm headed."

"Are ye, now?" He jumped in with both feet. "I am, as well, after spending the day in the great city of

London. It's been a while since last I was here." *All of thirty minutes.*

"That was my plan as well. I want to see as much of London as I can today. You know, all the touristy things like the London Tower, the Tower Bridge, Westminster Abbey, Big Ben." She raised her hands. "All the things I'm sure you've seen a dozen times and now find boring."

"On the contrary, I love seeing all those things, especially through someone else's eyes for the first time." He glanced down at her. "If you'd like, I could show you all those things." He held up his hands. "And no, I'm not asking you to jump in a car with me. I know the train, the tube and the stops you'll need to get where you're going." He shrugged.

Her brow furrowed. "I don't want to take up your time. I'm sure you have other things to do rather than play tour guide to a stranger."

"I wouldn't offer if I weren't sincere," he said. "I don't catch my train for Scotland until later tonight. It would be nice to see the city with company, rather than alone. Or I can point you in the right direction and leave you to it." He shrugged. "Your choice."

Whatever she decided, he'd be with her. Her decision would determine just how far away he'd be.

CHAPTER 2

Maggie McKendrick walked alongside Callum, mulling over his offer. She would probably have thanked him and refused if she hadn't had an altercation with a rude man moments before meeting the handsome Scotsman. She'd just come out of passport control and was tucking her passport into her purse when a big oaf of a man had slammed into her.

She'd staggered several feet and almost tripped over her roller bag before she'd righted herself. The man who'd rammed into her hurried away before she could call him out for being rude. What was wrong with people these days?

The woman with the toddler who'd been on the same plane with her had stopped to ask if she was all right. Maggie had assured her she was, but the incident had left her feeling less confident in her hasty decision to fly to London and take a train to Edinburgh. She probably should have taken a transfer flight from London to Edinburgh.

No. She refused to let some bumbling bully ruin her trip. This was her first time in the United Kingdom. Delaying her arrival in Edinburgh by just a day was a good idea. There was so much to see in London, and they had the mass transit to get her around without having to drive. It was a no-brainer to delay arriving in Edinburgh long enough to do a quick tour of London. She'd planned to buy a ticket for one of the hop-on-hop-off buses as soon as she found a place that sold them. But first, she had to get to London via the train.

Excitement resurfaced. She was in London! Or almost.

Who would have thought the results of a DNA test would lead her to the UK to meet relatives she hadn't known existed? She'd spent her entire life in Eagle Rock, Montana, only leaving long enough to attend college in Bozeman, to take a driving vacation to Reno and meet college friends in Spokane, Washington. She hadn't even been on a commercial aircraft until she'd boarded the plane in Bozeman the day before. If not for help from her friend Sadie, she wouldn't have known where to start when she'd made her flight reservations.

At first, Sadie had tried to talk her out of going, or at least waiting until Sadie could go with her. She'd reminded her that Maggie didn't know anything about her newfound relatives. She should wait until Hank could check them out. However, Maggie only had two weeks until she had to be back in the classroom with her preschoolers for the new school year. Her half-brother had invited her to the family home in Edinburgh. If she wanted to meet them, she had only a short window to do so.

Thankfully, Sadie and her husband Hank walked her through making the flight reservations. Hank had even offered to send one of his ex-military men along with her as her personal bodyguard at his own expense.

Maggie didn't make a lot of money, but she prided herself on paying her own way. She refused to accept Hank's offer and assured her friends she'd be all right. If she didn't feel comfortable around her half-brother, she'd find a hotel and continue with her plan to see more of Scotland a little sooner.

She hadn't slept much on the plane, finding it difficult to nod off while sitting upright in her middle seat in the economy section. She'd had a man with broad shoulders taking up the armrest on one side and a teenage boy on the other side who had watched movies all night long, shifting in his seat every few minutes in an attempt to get comfortable. By the time they'd landed in London, she was tired, running low on energy but not on determination. She could sleep on the train that evening.

When Callum had offered to show her the way to

the train, she'd been happy to follow. It wasn't like he was taking her down a back alley to sell her into the sex trade. They were surrounded by people. If she'd felt at all threatened, all she had to do was scream.

And he seemed so nice—and wasn't at all hard on the eyes.

When she'd shaken his hand, she'd been startled by the spark that had shot through her veins, dispelling any sleep-deprived grogginess. Since they'd be on public transportation and visiting public, tourist-heavy places, she'd never be alone with him. Why not take him up on his offer to show her around town?

"Thank you," she said. "If you aren't already regretting the offer, I'd appreciate the guided tour. I have all day, but I need to get to Euston Station this evening."

"Great," he said. "We can start with Buckingham Palace and work our way back to Westminster Abbey and Big Ben. If you aren't afraid of heights, we can hop on the London Eye for a spectacular view of the Thames and the city."

"Sounds wonderful," she said.

Callum showed her how to use her smartphone to pay for her train ticket and then escorted her onto the train, along with dozens of other people eager to get into the city.

Once they arrived in London, they stashed their bags in lockers at the station. Then they got on the tube to get closer to Buckingham Palace and walked the rest of the way.

Callum was full of information about the palace, the changing of the guards and the statue in front of the gates. As they walked toward Westminster Abbey, he told her some of the history of the church and famous people interred there, including Sir Isaac Newton, Charles Darwin and Charles Dickens.

"Isn't it Stephen Hawking's final resting place as well?" Maggie asked, remembering some of the information she had read recently.

"Indeed," Callum said. "A brilliant man, Mr. Hawking."

Maggie caught sight of Big Ben, the clock tower, standing high above a long, huge building.

"The House of Lords and House of Commons meet in Westminster Palace." Callum tipped his chin toward the clock. "Big Ben is actually part of Elizabeth Tower, also attached to Westminster Palace."

"You must have spent a lot of time in London to remember all of this," Maggie said.

"We learn much about the history of the United Kingdom in school."

"Is Edinburgh very different from London?" Maggie asked.

Callum chuckled. "Very. For one, London is much larger and more cosmopolitan. Edinburgh, with its Gothic architecture, transports one to another time.

It's quite lovely yet has many of the amenities found in London. On a smaller scale, of course."

Maggie couldn't wait to see it for herself. She'd researched online and found the photographs amazing. She could imagine it would feel like stepping back several centuries in time. Talking with Ewan Drummond, her half-brother, hadn't given her any clue as to whether her newfound family was happy or dismayed at discovering a long-lost sibling. Nor had it given her any idea of where their home fit into the city of Edinburgh. Would it be near the old town or in one of the more modern suburbs?

"You say you're on your way to visit relatives in Scotland?" Callum asked as they walked along the Thames toward the Tower of London.

"I am," she said.

"In Edinburgh?"

"Yes."

"I'm sure they'll love showing you around the city," he said.

"I hope so," she murmured.

"You don't think they will?"

She shrugged. "I don't know. I haven't actually met them in person."

Callum glanced down, his brow dipping low. "Yet they're your relatives?"

"It's not like I've ever been to Scotland before," she said. "As far as I know, they've never been to Montana." And they hadn't known about her until she'd connected with Ewan through the ancestry application after receiving her DNA results. Callum didn't need to know all that. He'd probably think she was a ridiculous romantic for searching out relatives she'd never met.

Maybe she was. After losing her mother the previous year, Maggie had felt the void. For as long as she could remember, it had been her and her mother. No grandparents, siblings or cousins that she knew of. Her mother had never spoken of her father. When Maggie had been old enough to be curious, her mother had told her he was dead. Her grandparents had died before Maggie was born. Her grandfather had been an American soldier who fell in love with her grandmother while stationed in England. He'd brought her grandmother and mother to live in Montana after he left the military.

Sadly, he'd died of pneumonia within the first year there, shortly after Maggie's mother was born. Her grandmother returned to her native Scotland, where she'd raised Ayleen, Maggie's mother. When Ayleen's mother had passed away, Ayleen returned to Montana, where her father was from, pregnant with Maggie. To this day, Maggie's birth certificate had a blank space for the name of her father.

Based on the DNA results, Maggie's father was Ewan Drummond's father as well. She wondered if Ewan's father knew Ayleen had given birth to his daughter. Ewan had mentioned his father had recently passed away, which made Maggie sad she hadn't had the chance to meet him. Still, learning she had a half-sibling made her feel less alone in the world.

"If you don't want to go inside St. Paul's Cathedral, we can move on to the London Tower," Callum was saying.

"What?" Maggie glanced up, her cheeks heating. "Sorry. I was thinking. What did you say?"

"I asked if you wanted to go into St. Paul's. There's a long line for tickets and it's lot of steps up to the top, but worth the view."

She smiled. "I'd love to go inside, but viewing it from outside will have to be enough for this short tour of London. I still want to see the Tower of London and the Tower Bridge—and I'm getting hungry."

"I know a great pub that serves an amazing roast chicken not far from here," Callum suggested. "We could eat first and then walk over to the Tower of London."

"That would be nice," Maggie said. "I didn't realize how tired I'd be after the flight over."

Callum nodded. "It takes a couple of days for your internal clock to synchronize with the different time zone. Maybe you'll regain some energy with a hearty meal."

He led the way to the pub, an old building that

had been carefully refurbished, retaining the charm of centuries past.

The waiter led them to a table in the corner.

Maggie ordered a glass of Cabernet Sauvignon.

Callum ordered a pint of beer. "Are you interested in the roast chicken?" he asked. "It's more than enough for two people."

"Sounds good," she said, glad she didn't have to scour the menu for something familiar that wasn't a hamburger or fish and chips.

She sipped her wine, staring across the table at the handsome Scotsman. "So, what do you do besides acting as a tour guide to clueless tourists in London?" Her cheeks heated. "I mean, what's your occupation?"

He stared down into his beer. "I recently left the military. Since then, I haven't quite settled on what's next."

Maggie frowned. "That has to be hard, coming from a very regimented lifestyle. My friend's husband was in the military. I've met some of the men he works with, all former military. They all say the same thing. It's hard to go from military life to the civilian world. Some don't handle it well at all. I guess that would account for the high suicide rate among former military folk." She blinked. "Not that I'm suggesting you're headed down that path. You seem to have your head on straight, even if you don't know what you want to do next."

"I'm not sure about having my head on

completely straight, but I'm getting there." Callum took another swallow of beer. "What about you? Do you have a job back in the States?"

"Nothing as dangerous and exciting as being in the military," she said. "I'm a preschool teacher."

Callum's warm chuckle made Maggie's heartbeat flutter. "I imagine being surrounded by small children could be dangerous. Is it much like herding cats?"

Maggie grinned. "It's not so bad. They're all super sweet. The hardest part of the job is letting them go at the end of the school year. I get too attached to my littles." She drew in a breath and let it out. "Then a whole new class comes, and I fall in love with all of them."

Callum shook his head. "It takes a special person to teach. Especially when children that small probably have never been in a classroom before."

"They're like little sponges, soaking in all the knowledge. When you think about it, from the moment babies are born, they learn so much. How to laugh, roll over, walk, all the words they acquire and so much more. Children are amazing."

"Do you have children of your own?" he asked.

Maggie laughed. "No, I don't. But maybe someday." She shrugged. "I'm not in a hurry." She would like to have a man in her life before she ventured into motherhood. Not that she was totally against being a single mom. It was just that having a partner would be easier. They could share the effort and the love.

"I would think working with small children every day would make you not want to have any of your own." Callum cocked an eyebrow.

"My mother and I had such a close relationship. We were more than mother and daughter. We were best friends." Her voice softened. "I miss her every day. I want that kind of relationship with a daughter or son. Only I'd have more than one. I was an only child. I would have loved having a sibling to hang with or lean on during tough times."

"Like losing your mother?" Callum asked quietly.

Maggie's vision blurred. She blinked several times before nodding. "Yes. Thankfully, I have some amazing friends who were there for me." She pasted a smile on her face and stared across the table at Callum. "What about you? I didn't even think to ask if you're married and have children. Are you? Do you?"

He laughed and shook his head. "No, on both counts."

"Never married?"

Again, he shook his head. "Didn't think it would be fair to marry some poor girl and then leave her alone for three hundred and sixty days a year. Other guys tried and ended in divorce and hard feelings. Some had kids split between them. I don't wish that for any child."

"Do you have brothers or sisters?" Maggie asked.

Callum nodded and glanced away. "I had a brother."

Maggie's heart squeezed hard in her chest. "Had?"

"Richard and I were as close as brothers could be. We raised enough hell in our town, we had quite the reputation. We got into quite a few scrapes, but we always looked out for each other." He drew in a deep breath, his gaze shifting to an empty corner of the pub.

"What happened to Richard?" Maggie asked and then held up a hand. "Don't answer if it's too personal or painful."

His gaze returned to her. "It's okay. It was a long time ago. He was a year younger than me. When I joined the British Army, he was still in school. I was so busy learning how to be a soldier and then training for Special Forces, I didn't realize my little brother had fallen into a bad group of lads. He got into drugs and dropped out of school. When his girlfriend dropped him, he committed suicide by overdosing on the drugs he was taking." Callum shook his head. "By the time I learned he was in a downward spiral, it was too late."

"And you feel responsible," Maggie said softly.

For a long moment, Callum stared at a corner of the room without speaking. Then his gaze returned to hers. "I should've checked on him. I should've been there for my brother."

Maggie reached across the table and touched his hand. "You couldn't have known what would happen."

He stared at her hand covering his, though he seemed miles, or maybe years, away. "I could have, if I'd stayed in closer contact. A phone call, a conversation with my parents. Anything. But I did nothing. I was too wrapped up in my own world to worry about my brother."

Maggie curled her fingers around Callum's hand. "You couldn't have known. And you can't spend your life beating yourself up over your brother's choices. More than likely, he wouldn't have wanted you to do so."

Callum nodded, straightened and glanced at his wristwatch. "We'd better get going if you want to see the Tower of London, the bridge and get to your station on time."

Maggie didn't push the issue of Callum's brother and the fact he wasn't to blame for Richard's death. She might have felt the same. Instead, she pasted a smile on her face and strode out of the pub, determined to be cheerful and positive as they continued the tour Callum was surely regretting by now.

As they stood in line for tickets to see the Tower of London, Maggie asked Callum about his favorite sports team. They got into a discussion about American football versus European football. Callum explained the sports of rugby and cricket. By the time they got tickets to get inside the Tower, the afternoon was sliding into early evening and they had little time to spend inside, viewing the Crown Jewels, the Bloody Tower, known for torture and executions and the Green Tower where Anne Boleyn had been executed.

By the time they left, Maggie was ready for something lighter, not so heavy and depressing. Outside, with the sun low on the horizon, casting a lovely glow over London and the Tower Bridge, she breathed in a grateful lungful of air.

"That was depressing," she commented.

Callum chuckled. "London is full of history, not all of which is in the least cheerful."

"Hopefully, Scotland will be a little more uplifting," Maggie murmured, once again nervous about meeting the family she'd never known existed.

Callum walked with Maggie across the bridge, stopping to enjoy the sunset and the reflection of light on the River Thames. When she asked, he gladly agreed to take a picture of her with the Thames behind her. She took a moment to send the photo via text to Sadie McClain. "It's times like these that I wish I could send pictures to my mother. Although I'm not sure how she would've felt about them. Whenever I asked her if she'd like to go to Scotland and visit her old stomping grounds, she'd always shake her head. *Why go so far when I have everything and everyone I need right here in Montana,* she'd say."

Maggie drew in a long breath and let it out slowly. "She was content to stay in Montana, and she did until her dying breath."

"And you?" Callum leaned against the railing along the bridge. "Were you content to stay in Montana?"

"I was." Maggie looked out over the Thames. "As long as my mother was still alive. I loved her so much."

"And now?" he persisted.

"Other than my friends, I have no family holding me back. I think I'd like to see more of the world outside the state lines of Montana."

"Won't your wee ones miss you?" Callum asked.

A smile curved Maggie's lips. "I would miss the littles. Their innocence and excitement lift me up." She really did love working with the small children in her preschool class.

For a long moment, Maggie stared out at the setting sun, glinting off the calm waters of the Thames. If she had all the money needed, she might consider traveling the world, seeing all the countries, visiting different cultures, tasting foods and life so foreign to Eagle Rock, Montana.

After a long silence, Callum straightened and glanced at his watch. "We should get you to your train station before your train leaves. Where did you say ye'll be leavin' from?"

"Euston," Maggie said. "But you don't have to go

with me. I'm sure I can figure out the tube, now that you've shown me how."

Callum shook his head. "I wouldn't be much of a gentleman if I didn't see you there safely." He glanced down at her. "Ready?"

She fell into his deep, brown eyes, forgetting for that second they were relative strangers.

A lock of his dark hair dipped low over his forehead.

Maggie fought the relentless desire to brush it back with her fingertips. She fought and lost, reaching up to sweep the hair back. It refused to stay and fell over his forehead again.

Callum raised his hand and ran it through his thick, dark hair, a smile twitching at the corners of his lips. He pulled his cell phone from his pocket. A moment later, he held it up. "The nearest underground train entrance is across the bridge and a block over. We'll head back to the station where we left our things in the lockers then on to Euston Station." He held out his arm.

Though she was in no hurry to end their time together, Maggie curled her fingers into the crook of Callum's elbow and walked with him across the bridge and to the nearest tube entrance.

They paid their way through the turnstiles and stepped onto the next train headed to where they'd stashed their bags. Then they hopped on another train to Euston Station.

Surrounded by so many people, Maggie couldn't think of anything to say. She stood beside Callum, her tongue tied, her thoughts spinning through options of comments she could make, but didn't want to, given the density of commuters in the rail car.

When they arrived at Euston Station, Callum exited the train car, held out his hand to Maggie and helped her to alight onto the platform as well.

Minutes later, he stood with her in front of the attendant directing her to the waiting room for the train heading for Edinburgh that night.

Another couple approached the attendant.

Maggie stepped back and stared up, letting them get situated with the attendant. She turned and stared into Callum's eyes. "Thank you again for the guided tour of London. If you're ever in the States, let me know. Depending on where you land, I could take you on a tour of my hometown, Eagle Rock, Montana. That'll take about five minutes." She gave him a weak smile, knowing how lame her words sounded. "Well, I guess this is goodbye." Maggie held out her hand.

Callum engulfed her slim fingers in his and squeezed gently. "I don't think it's goodbye. I'll see you soon is much more positive." He raised her hand to his lips and pressed a kiss to the backs of her knuckles. "Thank you for spending the day with me. It was quite lovely."

Maggie stared down at where his fingers still held hers. "It was a lovely day." A day made infinitely better with Callum in it. Her heart pinched hard in her chest. This couldn't be their last goodbye. She might never see him again. For someone she'd just met, it hit her harder than she'd expected.

The fact that she might not see him again made her do something she'd never have dreamed of doing in a million years. Maggie rose on her toes and pressed her lips to his in a brief kiss, as terrifying as it was electric. Rather than bringing closure to their short time together, the gesture only made her want more.

As she lowered her heels toward the ground, his arm came up behind her, lifting her and pressing her body against his. His mouth descended on hers in a hungry, sensuous kiss that left her breathless, her blood raging through her system, molten hot.

When he set her back on her feet, he stepped back. "You'd better go." His voice was husky, as if he was just as affected by the kiss as she was.

Maggie pressed a hand to her mouth and nodded. Words were beyond her. She met his gaze once more, then turned and hurried away in a swift walk. She had to focus on not breaking into a run, convinced that if she stayed another moment in the man's presence, she'd beg him to come with her, make love to her and show her all the treasures of Scotland.

For a lone female who hadn't been far from her small town of Eagle Rock, Montana, how pathetic would it be to fall for the first Scotsman to kiss her?

CHAPTER 3

CALLUM PROBABLY SHOULD HAVE TOLD her he would be on the same train with her. Why he'd withheld that information, he wasn't sure. He told himself it was because he didn't want her to think he was a stalker. The only way to convince her of that fact would be to tell her the truth, that he'd been hired to protect her.

After she disappeared into the waiting room where the sleeper car passengers gathered, he turned to the attendant. "I'll be on the Caledonian sleeper train to Edinburgh, as well."

"Name, please," she said, staring down at the paper printout of the guests who'd booked passage on the train.

"Callum McCall," he responded.

She ran her finger down the list of names and stopped at his. "Ah, here you are." She gave him his car and room assignment. "You're welcome to wait in the lounge until boarding at ten thirty." The middle-aged brunette waved her hand in the direction Maggie had disappeared.

"Thank you, but I prefer to be out here."

Her eyebrow rose. "It'll be over an hour until you can board."

He nodded. "Thank you." Rather than argue with her, he walked toward the lounge. Instead of entering, he stopped beside the door and peered through the doorway into the room beyond.

Maggie had taken a seat at a round table with a family of three: mother, father, and their teenage son. Already, she was talking animatedly with them, smiling, her eager excitement to be in a different country hard to resist.

Callum watched for several minutes before leaning his back against the wall and relaxing. She was safe, surrounded by other passengers. After twenty minutes, the train eased into the station, coming to a stop.

Passengers disembarked and hurried toward the exit. The cleaning crew went to work, quickly preparing the cabins for the guests who would be sleeping on the trip to Edinburgh that night. As soon as they were finished, one of their staff reported to the attendant that they were ready to board.

Callum eased back into the shadows and watched as the passengers flocked out of the lounge and went in search of their cars, Maggie among them. He followed at a distance as she walked along the platform until she arrived at their assigned car.

When she turned to step onto the train, she glanced in his direction.

Callum lowered his head and slid into the shadows.

Maggie hesitated a moment, her brow dipping low. Then she gave a slight shake of her head and entered the car.

He watched as she walked past the windows on the narrow corridor and stopped in front of one of the doors. Using her key card, she opened the door to the compartment and shoved her roller bag in first. Once she'd stepped inside and closed the door, Callum made his move.

Quickly boarding the train car, he hurried along the same corridor, stopping at the door before Maggie's. He waved his key card over the scanner. It didn't work. He tried again. This time it worked. As he pushed through the door, Maggie's door creaked open. Callum managed to get inside before Maggie emerged. He left the door cracked just a little. Not enough she could see inside, if she was looking that direction, but enough where he could hear her movements.

Footsteps sounded in the corridor. Heavier. Possibly a man's.

Callum tensed, ready to spring into action if the man posed a threat to Maggie.

"Oh, good," Maggie said. "Are you one of the train stewards?" Maggie called out.

"Yes, ma'am," a deep voice answered. A man dressed in the Caledonia uniform stopped in front of Callum's door.

"The toilet in my cabin won't flush," Maggie said.

"Let me look at it." The steward moved past Callum's door.

Maggie eased past the man, coming to stand in front of Callum's door.

He peered through the narrow slit he'd left open, admiring the pretty American's coppery hair and trim figure. At least what he could see of it. He wished he'd told her he'd be on the same train. He could have invited her to the dining car for a nightcap and extended their time together. Then he could keep an eye on her out in the open, rather than playing a ridiculous game of hide and seek.

Now, if he chose to let her know he was in the same car, she'd think it too much of a coincidence, even stalkerish.

"It's all sorted, lass," the man said.

Maggie left her position in front of Callum's door. "Wonderful," she said. "Thank you so much."

"My pleasure. If you need anything else, you can always find one of us in the dining car throughout the night."

The steward didn't walk by Callum's door this time. Instead, he continued down the corridor to the end of the car.

Callum eased his door open wide enough to catch a glimpse of Maggie going into her compartment.

When the door clicked shut behind her, Callum glanced in both directions and went back into his small room, which had bunks on one side and what passed for a bathroom on the other. A tiny sink attached to the outer wall beneath the only window looked out over the train station platform.

More tired passengers passed by, rolling suitcases or carrying backpacks. As the scheduled departure time neared, the ground crew hurried stragglers along.

Eleven-thirty came and went, but the train remained on the platform. Callum left his door open slightly, monitoring the passageway, alert and ready to respond.

He didn't feel comfortable closing his door, especially while they remained at the station. Anyone could board the train at any time. Not that he had any reason to be suspicious. They'd gone through the entire day without incident. Sadie McClain could be worrying for no reason. Maggie might be naïve and unworldly, but she was intelligent and observant.

Callum stretched out on the lower bunk, propped against the far wall, his gaze on the narrow gap he'd left by propping the door open.

A few minutes before midnight, the train started moving, easing slowly out of the station and eventually picking up speed. They were scheduled to arrive in Edinburgh at seven-thirty in the morning. If all went well, Maggie would get a good night's sleep, swaying gently with the train's movement. She hadn't come back out since she'd waylaid the steward to fix her toilet. Considering she'd probably gone thirty-six hours without much sleep, she'd likely fallen asleep even before the train had departed the station.

Eventually, Callum's eyes drooped, and he fell into a light slumber. While he dozed, he listened, alert enough to detect any unusual noise. The steady hum of the train lulled him deeper into sleep.

The nightmare returned, taking him back to Syria, the mission, the explosion and then the dark, foul-smelling cell. This time was different. When he woke in the interrogation room, it wasn't Smudge tied to the chair across from him. Callum stared across at the bright copper hair and petite facial features of Maggie McKendrick. His gut clenched, and his pulse leaped into overdrive.

"No," he said through gritted teeth, straining at the ties binding his wrists. Maggie wasn't supposed to be there. How had they captured her?

When the guard grabbed a handful of her hair and yanked it back, exposing the pale, slender line of her throat, Callum surged forward, chair and all. He almost toppled over but managed to remain upright.

No, this wasn't right. Maggie didn't belong there. He hadn't even met her.

It's only a dream.

If it was only a dream, why did the knife the man holding Maggie's hair look so damned real?

The only way out of that chair, the only way out of that dream, was to wake. If he didn't wake up soon, he'd bear witness to yet another senseless death.

Wake up.

The man holding Maggie's clump of hair placed his knife against her throat.

Wake up.

Callum jerked awake and sat up, crashing his head against the bunk above him.

Pain shot through him, causing him to lie back against the pillow and let his eyes adjust to the semi-darkness.

He wasn't in that horrible place where Smudge had died. The bed beneath him and the bunk overhead reminded him that he was on a train back to his native Scotland, a long way from Syria.

He frowned. The train wasn't moving. Had he slept long enough for them to arrive in Edinburgh? A quick glance at his watch made him shake his head. They'd only been moving for three hours. They had four more to go. The train wasn't scheduled to stop anywhere along the west coast line until they reached their destination in Edinburgh.

The sound of a door creaking open in the corridor made Callum roll out of the lower bunk and rise to his feet.

Maggie passed his door, dressed in soft shorts that looked like pajama bottoms with a light jacket wrapped around her top. She'd pulled her riotous curls up into a loose, messy bun on top of her head, and she was makeup-free and even more beautiful than she'd been all day. She followed several others out onto a station platform.

Why had the train stopped?

If he followed her too closely, she'd eventually turn around and see him.

Callum waited until she turned the corner at the end of the railcar. As soon as she disappeared out of sight, he sprinted to the end of the corridor and peered around the corner.

She'd already passed through the exit doors and stepped out onto the platform among other passengers gathered around one of the stewards, filling them in about a delay.

A sign on the station's wall identified the station location as Crewe.

Callum slipped up behind one of the taller men, needing to hear the steward speak.

"Unfortunately, a very large tree fell on the electric lines ahead, causing enough damage the entire west coast train route has been shut down further north. We're to return to London as soon as we receive clearance. Please understand that many other trains are in similar situations, and they will also have to be redirected to London. It will take time. From London, you can show your ticket to other train lines. They'll honor it to get you to Edinburgh at no cost and take you there on the east lines unaffected by the downed tree. Or you can get a full refund for your tickets for tonight's passage on the website."

"Do we have to go all the way back to London?" a man asked.

"You can choose to disembark here and take some of the smaller trains across to the eastern line. It won't be as straightforward as taking the train from London to Edinburgh, but it can be done," the steward said. "If that's your plan, you'll need to gather all your belongings and vacate your cabin in the next twenty minutes. We are not certain how long it will take until we receive clearance to start our journey back to London, but when we get it, we'll be on our way."

"We've already come three hours north; I'll take my chances crossing over to the eastern line," the man who'd asked about alternatives said, then spun and returned to the train.

The steward left the crowd and moved further along the line of cars to meet with others just coming out of the train.

The clump of passengers began to disperse, some

talking about going back to bed, others looking at their smartphones for alternate train connections.

Callum circled the crowd, staying out of Maggie's line of sight, wondering if she'd choose to go back to London or try to make it the rest of the way to Edinburgh on her own.

She stared at her cell phone for a long time, scrolling through what Callum assumed were options.

The group of passengers thinned, leaving her standing alone.

A man emerged from the train, wearing a hat pulled low over his forehead and a dark trench coat with the collar pulled up around his neck.

Callum's eyes narrowed.

The man glanced left, then right. He didn't carry a suitcase, and he wasn't in a hurry until he moved toward Maggie.

With her focus entirely on her cell phone, she didn't see him until he was almost upon her.

Callum dove for the man, but not soon enough.

The guy in the trench coat wrapped his arm around Maggie's neck and dragged her toward the edge of the platform.

She dropped her cell phone and grabbed the man's arm in an attempt to loosen his hold around her neck.

Callum jumped on the man's back and caught him in a neck lock similar to the one the man held

Maggie in. Only Callum applied enough pressure long enough that the attacker let go of his prey, dropping her over the side of the platform onto the track below. Then he reached over his shoulder in an attempt to grab Callum and flip him over his shoulder.

Callum held his ground. Almost as large as the other guy, he wouldn't easily be flipped over the man's shoulders. He dug in his heels and held on, leaning back with all his might.

The attacker must have realized he wasn't going to outmaneuver Callum; he quit trying to flip him over his shoulder and went limp. Either that, or he really had lost consciousness.

Callum refused to loosen his arm around the man's neck, now taking on all of the big guy's weight. He staggered several steps but remained unrelenting.

A whistle sounded down the line of cars as a steward warned the train would be leaving soon.

Callum had to rid himself of the oaf and get Maggie off the tracks soon, or she could be crushed when the train started moving.

With the steward too far away and facing the opposite direction to see what was happening, Callum couldn't rely on him to help.

Callum dragged the man backward, away from the tracks. Once he was out of view of the steward or anyone else who might be watching, he loosened his hold on the man's neck.

Immediately, the man jerked free and swung around, his fist bunched and ready.

Callum kicked him in the groin.

As the man doubled over, Callum brought his fists together and slammed them into the man's nose, sending him staggering backward. He hit the wall and slid downward, his nose gushing blood.

Callum gave him one last glance and dove for the train and the track below.

Maggie pulled herself up to the edge of the platform.

When Callum bent over the edge of the platform, Maggie shrank back.

He held out his hand. "It's me," he said. "Callum."

Her brow furrowed as she stared up at him. "What are you doing here?"

His lips twitched on the corners. "Saving you from an attack."

"What happened to the man who attacked me?"

Callum tipped his head toward his rear. "I gave him an old-fashioned Scottish sedative. He's sleeping it off."

"Is he alive?" she whispered.

"I didn't stick around to determine whether he was still breathing," he said. "I was more concerned about getting back to you. Give me your hand and let me help you off the track and onto the train. It's about to leave the station."

"But—" her gaze darted from left to right, searching past him for danger.

"He is well and truly out, but I'm just not sure for how long." He glanced over his shoulder at the man still slumped against the wall. If he was dead, they needed to leave before someone found him and the entire train station shut down. If he was alive, he could wake soon and go after Maggie again.

Maggie's hand slid into his, her slim fingers warm against his palm, sending sparks through his nervous system.

Callum's attention swung back to the pretty red-haired American, and his fingers tightened around hers. With a swift but gentle tug, he pulled her up onto the platform.

Off balance, she pitched forward into his chest.

Naturally, his arms came up around her, pressing her body against his.

Big mistake.

Her soft curves melted into his hard planes, and the sparks generated from holding her hand sent fire raging through his veins and south to his loins. He held her longer than was necessary for her to regain her balance. Funny, but she wasn't in a hurry to push him back.

He'd spent the day getting to know this beautiful, quirky woman on a mission to meet a family she'd never known. Either she was incredibly stupid or desperately searching for roots.

Callum had lost his brother, but he had family scattered all around Glasgow: his parents, grandparents, aunts, uncles, cousins and friends who were as close as family.

Maggie had admitted it had been just her and her mother until her mother had passed. He could only imagine how hopeful she'd been when she'd found a group of relatives through DNA testing and an ancestry application.

He hated to see her cheerful, optimistic personality take a hit if her newfound relatives were complete bastards and shunned their pretty kin.

As she clung to him, he drew in a deep breath. She smelled like fields filled with fragrant heather. Heady, wild and incomparable.

He leaned forward and brushed a feather-soft kiss against her silky curls. It wasn't much, but she couldn't feel it, thus making it easier for him to get away with it without suffering a stinging slap to his face. They hadn't even known each other for a full twenty-four hours. If having him appear suddenly to save her from an attacker wasn't suspicious enough, stealing a kiss would surely be a reason for her to distrust him and steer clear.

Maggie was the first to step away. Her pale cheeks flushed a bright pink as she tucked a stray curl back behind her ear. "I thought you were taking another train," she said.

Callum's gaze shifted away from hers. "I never said what train I was getting on."

Her brow wrinkled. "Was I that uninspiring during your London city tour that you didn't want to spend another moment with me?" She wrapped her arms around her middle. "All you had to do was tell me you weren't interested, and I wouldn't have bothered you. I'm a big girl. I can handle rejection."

"On the contrary," Callum sighed. "I enjoyed spending time with you in London."

Her brow dipped lower. "Then why didn't you tell me you'd be on the same train with me?"

He gave her a tight smile and made a decision. "Because I was only supposed to follow you and keep you safe, not spend the day sightseeing with you in London."

Maggie's eyes rounded. "You were supposed to keep me safe? Why?" she demanded. "Wait. Who sent —" Suddenly her eyes narrowed, and she pinned him with her stare. "Hank and Sadie sent you."

It wasn't a question.

"They did," Callum admitted.

The steward at the other end of the column of cars blew his whistle. "Last call if you're exiting the train, it leaves in five minutes!" he yelled.

"Are you going back to London on this train?" Callum asked.

"I was looking at the train schedule for another way to get to Edinburgh when I was so rudely attacked. "I'd rather continue than go all the way back."

"Then you'll need to gather your belongings before the train leaves."

"And change out of my pajamas," she murmured with a twist of her lips.

"I don't know. With the jacket, I thought you made an impressive fashion statement." He winked, cupped her elbow and guided her back on board the train. "We can continue our discussion after we get to our next platform."

"Damn right, we will," she said, though she let him usher her to her cabin. She paused at the door, her brow dipping. "Where were you staying?"

He tipped his head toward the door beside hers.

Maggie pressed her lips together. "How did you manage to board without me knowing?"

"I was in super-stealth mode," he said with a sly smile.

She huffed, scanned her card on the reader and pushed the door open. "Give me a second to change and pack."

"Remember, you have less than five minutes before the train leaves."

"I only need three," she said and closed the door between them.

Callum ducked into his cabin, grabbed his backpack and slung it over his shoulder. He was back in the corridor a moment later, where he waited, spending the short time scrolling through the train schedule app and searching for an alternate route that would get them to Edinburgh quicker than going three hours back to London before heading north again for four more hours. He found a train leaving in fifteen minutes, purchased two tickets and noted the location of the platform in less than two minutes.

True to her word, Maggie emerged from her cabin at exactly three minutes, having exchanged her pajama shorts for jeans and her slippers for boots. She pushed her roller bag ahead of her and followed Callum off the train and onto the platform.

His gaze went immediately to where he'd left the man who'd attacked her.

He was gone.

"What's wrong?" Maggie stepped up beside him, her brow lowering.

"I guess he lived," Callum's lips tightened. "Stay close to me."

Maggie hooked her hand through the crook of Callum's elbow. "Do you think he'll attack again?"

"I don't know, and I sure as hell don't want to find out." At three-thirty in the morning, he'd bet it hadn't been a random attack. He also wondered whether the tree on the track had been the result of a natural disaster or sabotage. Either way, leaving the train might be the best option. Maggie wouldn't be following her scheduled travel itinerary.

"Come on." He took her empty hand. "I found a

route that will get us to Edinburgh. It leaves in ten minutes. We need to get to the correct platform before the doors close."

Maggie matched his pace as they descended the steps from the current platform, hurried along the central corridor and then back up to the one they needed. Once they'd boarded the train and found empty seats with a table between them, Callum stowed her suitcase on the shelf above them.

Maggie sat across from Callum, her eyes narrow, her jaw set in a firm line. "Okay, now that we're back on track, tell me how you got roped into playing babysitter to a stranger?"

"I prefer the term bodyguard."

She waved her hand dismissively. "Whatever."

Callum could tell by the stubborn set of her chin she would accept nothing but the truth. "Hank and Sadie were concerned about you traveling alone to Scotland and about the new relatives you know nothing about."

Maggie held his gaze for a long moment before her expression softened. "They're my surrogate family and so very good to me, but I told them I didn't want a bodyguard."

"Considering what just happened on the other platform, they might have been right to assign one without your knowledge."

"I wanted to prove to them, and more importantly

to myself, that I was capable of traveling alone." She sighed. "I guess I was wrong."

"Not necessarily," Callum leaned his elbows on the table. "Under different circumstances, you might have been fine. If that wasn't a random attack, someone either has it in for you, or doesn't want you to make it to Edinburgh."

"Or both," she said softly. "I just want to meet Ewan. I want to see if there's any resemblance between me and my half-brother. I have my mother's facial features and build, but..." she flicked a strand of her hair, "she had blond hair, not red. Her eyes were blue. Mine are green. I want to know where I came from and who I resemble. If nothing else, I'd like to know what medical issues I might have based on heredity."

Her heartfelt words did little to convince Callum that she didn't need him. "Have you considered that your unknown family might look at you as a threat?"

"Why? I've never threatened anyone. Ever."

"But you've come all this way to meet your relatives shortly after the patriarch of the family passed. That would make me suspicious. Why surface now, if not to claim an inheritance?"

"I contacted Ewan Drummond as soon as I found the connection on the ancestry app. I emailed him, asking questions about his father. He told me he'd died. He didn't tell me when. When I told Ewan I was disappointed that I wouldn't get to meet him, he laughed and said it was just as well. He sounded like he hadn't been very close to his father. We emailed a few more times, and then he invited me to his home. Since I'm free during the summer and have money in the bank that my mother left me, I accepted. I was so excited to learn I had a sibling."

"Half," Callum corrected.

"Half is better than none," she said softly. "Up until I made that connection on the app, I had no siblings, no parents, grandparents or cousins. You wouldn't know how that feels because, as you said, you've got loads of family." She lifted her shoulders and let them fall. "I'm not going to claim any inheritance. I just want to meet my half-brother. What danger could there be in a casual meeting? It's not like they're going to throw me into a dungeon or push me off a cliff."

"What about dropping you onto a train track?" Callum pointed out.

Her shoulders drooped. "You don't think it was a random attack, do you?"

Callum shook his head. "My instinct says no."

Her lips firmed. "I'm still going. I want to meet Ewan. He sounded so nice in his emails. Maybe once he knows I'm not after any inheritance, whoever feels threatened will calm down."

Callum didn't respond. He had the feeling the attack on the platform was a warning.

Maggie crossed her arms over her chest. "I'm still

going. I've come this far, it would be ridiculous not to." She pulled her bottom lip between her teeth. "The question is, if you were sent to protect me, how do I explain why I showed up to the family home with a bodyguard in tow?"

"You don't tell him I'm your bodyguard," Callum said.

"If not a bodyguard, what do I tell them?"

"That I'm your travel companion," he said. "Or you could say I'm your boyfriend or fiancé."

Color flooded into her cheeks. "They'd expect us to show some signs that we're an item."

"I'm a good actor." Callum grinned. "And I can give a very convincing kiss."

The color in Maggie's cheeks flamed a bright red. "Uh, hopefully...that won't be...necessary."

Callum shrugged. "We can play that by ear. You tell them what you want. But if you plan on staying at their home, I'll need a plausible reason to join you there. Otherwise, I'll be wandering around the home, like a stalker. They might call the local police and have me hauled off to jail. Then you're on your own, completely at their mercy."

For a long moment, Maggie sat in silence. Finally, she nodded. "Before I commit, I want to talk with Hank and Sadie."

"We can do that," he said and pulled out his cell phone and selected Hank's number.

CHAPTER 4

CALLUM PUT his phone on speaker and turned the volume up.

Maggie leaned forward, her fists clenched in her lap, her breath arrested in her throat.

The ringer only ran once before a familiar voice answered, "Callum, Hank here, did you find Maggie?"

"Yes, sir," Callum replied.

Maggie released the breath she'd held like a balloon deflating. Hank Patterson's words confirmed what Callum had told her. Hank and Sadie had sent this man to protect her. She wasn't sure what made her angrier, the fact that they'd gone against her wishes or the fact Callum had befriended her, not because he felt drawn to her, but because it would make it easier for him to do his job.

She was the job.

"Is that Callum?" Sadie's voice sounded in the background on Hank's line.

"It is," Hank said, his voice a little faded as if he'd turned away from his phone. "Say hello."

"Hi, Callum," Sadie's voice sounded sweet and clear.

Maggie couldn't be mad at the petite blond movie star who'd been her friend since childhood.

"How's our Maggie?" Sadie asked. "Were you able to follow her from the airport all the way to the sleeper train? Wait. You should be on the sleeper train now. What is it, four o'clock in the morning there?"

"Yes, ma'am," Callum said, his gaze connecting with Maggie's. "Only we're not on the sleeper train. I have Maggie here with me. We left the Caledonian in Crewe."

"Maggie's with you?" Sadie asked. "Maggie, sweetie, are you all right?"

Maggie's lips twitched. "I am, thanks to your stealthy bodyguard you sent to keep tabs on me."

"What happened?" Hank asked.

Callum gave Hank and Sadie a brief recap of the sleeper train stop in Crewe because of the downed tree on the electric lines, the passengers getting out to hear what the train's attendant had to say and, finally, the attack on Maggie.

"Maggie, are you sure you're all right?" Sadie asked, her voice clipped.

Maggie's heart warmed at the concern in her friend's tone. "I'm fine. Callum came to my rescue."

"Oh, thank goodness," Sadie said. "I was worried about you going on your first-ever trip abroad. I was afraid you'd get lost or turned around. I didn't think you'd be attacked. Though you never know what can happen with a lone female traveling in a foreign country or even here in the States."

"I guess I should say thank you for going against my wishes," Maggie said, her lips twisting into a wry grin. So, he hadn't befriended her because he liked her. He'd been there when she'd needed help. She'd have to get over the disappointment of having her little bubble of attraction burst. She was alive because of the man sitting across the table from her.

"I'd say I'm sorry for going behind your back," Sadie said, "but that would be a lie. I care about you. I can't believe someone attacked you in the train station. I'm glad Callum is with you. You're going to keep him, aren't you?"

Maggie laughed. "He's not a puppy I get to keep."

Callum smiled, the gesture making Maggie's heart flutter. He truly was a handsome man, even more so when he smiled. And his accent made her pulse quicken every time he spoke.

Get a grip, woman. He's a hired protector. You're a preschool teacher from Montana. At the end of her two-week trip to Scotland, she'd head back to Eagle Rock. Callum would remain in Scotland.

"You know what I mean," Sadie said. "Are you going to let him provide your protection for the entirety of your stay in Scotland?"

"I'm not sure about the entire stay, but we agreed he should come with me to meet my half-brother," Maggie said.

"Good," Sadie said. "Hank has some information on the Drummonds you might want to hear."

Maggie tensed. "What kind of information?"

"Swede did some digging and found that Ewan Drummond, the eldest son of Lord Douglas Drummond, was to be the sole heir to the Drummond estate. However, Lord Drummond changed his will near the end of his life, splitting the estate equally among his surviving children."

Maggie's heart beat faster. "I have another half-brother?"

"It appears so," Hank said. "Bryce Drummond, age five, is Lord Drummond's second son by his second wife, Fiona Drummond."

"Five?" Maggie blinked. "How old is Ewan?"

"Ewan is thirty-one. At the age of twelve, he was shipped off to a military boarding school. He spent some time in the British military and became a part of the SAS. He deployed several times to Afghanistan. He left the military after being injured in battle. Ewan didn't return to the family home until after his father passed."

"Thanks for letting me know more about my half-brothers," Maggie said.

"Something else you should know," Hank said. "Were you aware that your mother was Ewan Drummond's nanny before she moved to Montana?"

Maggie's heart skipped several beats. "She was?"

"She worked for him for a year and then moved to Montana," Hank said.

"Wait." Maggie's brow furrowed. "You say the little boy is from Lord Drummond's second marriage. What happened to his first wife?"

"She died in a horseback riding accident. She was thrown by her mount," Hank said.

Maggie pressed a hand to her chest and asked, "When?"

"Around the time Ewan was in Afghanistan," Hank said softly.

Maggie's heart sank to the bottom of her stomach. "So, he was married when my mother got pregnant with me." Her vision blurred. All the years she'd wondered who her father was, her mother had kept the secret to herself for a reason.

Her mother had had an affair with a married man.

"Maggie?" Sadie's voice sounded through the speaker.

"I'm okay." Maggie pinched the bridge of her nose. "Just processing."

"Are you sure you still want to meet your half-brother?" Sadie asked.

Maggie stared down at the cell phone as if she could see her friend, not the device. "Ewan had access to my information on the Ancestry site. He knows I'm three years younger than he is. Which means he knows I'm the result of his father's extramarital affair. Why would he invite me to his home?" She looked up, her gaze connecting with Callum's.

"Good question," Hank said.

"That could explain the attack," Callum offered. "If she's of Drummond bloodline, could she inherit a portion of the late Lord Drummond's estate?"

"Possibly," Hank said. "I'll have Swede look through Lord Drummond's will for the exact wording. In the meantime, Maggie, you might reconsider your visit to the Drummond estate."

"My plans haven't changed." Maggie lifted her chin. "I'm even more determined to meet these people. If they're behind the attack, I want to know."

"It could be dangerous," Sadie said.

"I'll be with her." Callum reached across the table for Maggie's hand.

She placed hers in his open palm, his warmth helping to dispel the sudden chill spreading through her body.

"Will you be enough?" Hank asked. "Do you need backup?"

"I'll contact Hammer if we need help," Callum assured Hank.

"Swede is still looking for more information," Hank said. "We'll keep you informed."

Callum nodded. "I appreciate that."

"And, Callum," Hank paused. "Welcome to the Brotherhood Protectors."

Callum frowned. "Sir, I hadn't agreed to join when I took this assignment."

"And now?" Hank prompted.

Callum met and held Maggie's gaze. "I'm in."

A flash of heat rushed through Maggie. Or was it the heat in Callum's gaze transferring to her? Whatever it was, she'd felt it, and it confused her.

"Maggie, stay safe," Sadie said.

"Stay with Callum," Hank urged. "He's prior SAS, highly trained and capable of defending you."

Her lips twisted. "I witnessed that first hand." She really should have pulled her hand free of Callum's, but her hand in his made her feel grounded, safe, protected. "I'll keep him around."

"We'll be in touch," Hank said. "Out here."

Callum ended the call and stared across the table into Maggie's eyes. "I guess we're going to meet the Drummonds."

Maggie snorted softly. "I feel incredibly stupid."

Callum's fingers tightened around hers.

"I was so excited to discover I had a half-brother that I didn't bother to look at the timeline. I could be walking into a shitshow with me as the main, unwanted attraction."

His mouth curved. “It will make for an interesting vacation story to regale your teacher friends with upon your return to Montana.”

“I’m sure.” Maggie stared at the window, though she couldn’t see the landscape in the darkness. Instead, she studied her face reflecting back at her. No wonder her mother had never spoken of her father. She’d had an affair with a married man. No matter how hard she tried to imagine her mother engaging in anything so sordid, she couldn’t reconcile the act with the kindhearted woman who’d been her best friend since she could remember. Ayleen McKendrick had never hurt a soul. Now, as she looked at her reflection, she wasn’t as keen to know where she’d gotten the red hair and green eyes that had dark circles beneath them.

Maggie closed her eyes, wondering if she should abandon this quest, tuck her tail between her legs and go back to Montana. Then again, her mother hadn’t raised a quitter. She’d come this far. If someone didn’t want her to arrive at the Drummond estate, she wanted to know who that was and why. Then she’d give them a piece of her mind, let them know she didn’t want any part of the cheater Lord Drummond’s estate or anything to do with relatives who had lured her to Scotland just to hurt her or scare her away for good.

“Why don’t you stretch out on the seat?” Callum’s deep voice penetrated her internal battle.

She opened her eyes and stared into Callum's dark brown gaze. "Are you sure you want to go with me to meet my relatives?"

He nodded, still holding her hand. "I'm with you, lass, but you look like you're ready to pass out."

"Is that code for I'm a wreck?" Maggie yawned. "Maybe I will close my eyes for a few minutes."

"We have an hour until we change trains. I'll wake you before we stop. Then it's another hour after that."

She wrinkled her nose. "Maybe we would have been better off on the sleeper train back to London."

"That would have put us after noon getting to Edinburgh. This way we'll be there as the sun rises. We can check into a hotel and sleep for a few hours before we go to meet your half-brothers."

"Sounds like a plan." She yawned again. "In the meantime, an hour nap sounds good." Rather than stretch out on the seats, she lay her head on the table, her cheek resting on their joined hands.

Seconds later, Callum whispered in her ear, "Maggie, my bonnie lass, wake up."

Something brushed across her temple as softly as a kiss.

Maggie blinked, lifted her head and stared into Callum's dark eyes so close to hers. "I just closed my eyes."

He grinned. "You've been sleeping for an hour. We have to change trains, or I'd leave you to sleep longer. I'll need my hand long enough to retrieve your luggage from overhead."

Maggie glanced down at their joined hands. Had he sat there the entire time holding her hand while she'd slept for the past hour? She released his hand and sat up straighter, feeling like she'd had too much alcohol to drink when she hadn't had any.

The train slowed to a stop.

Callum rose, pulled Maggie's carry-on bag from the overhead shelf, slung his backpack over one shoulder and her backpack over the other. "Ready?"

She pushed to her feet, amazed at the amount of effort it took. When she swayed, Callum slipped an arm around her waist and steadied her.

"We'll need to hurry. These trains don't stay long in the station," Callum ushered her to the exit and onto the platform. They descended a set of steps, marched along a corridor and up another set of stairs. Maggie felt like a zombie, barely able to focus on placing one foot in front of the other. All she wanted was to lie down and sleep.

Once they were on their train, Callum settled her in one seat, stowed her suitcase overhead and dropped into the seat beside her. "Now, you can sleep."

She leaned her head against the window and closed her eyes.

The train left the station, the rumbling motion

lulling her to sleep, though the glass was cold and hard, not a pillow or a comfortable bed.

Callum shifted beside her. "You can lean on me if it's more comfortable."

"What about you?" she murmured. "Aren't you tired?" The hard window annoyed her to the point she sat up and tipped toward Callum, her cheek finding a softer resting pillow against Callum's shoulder.

"I haven't been traveling for two days without sleep," he said. "I'm fine."

"Thank you," she said and slipped into an exhausted sleep.

The next time he tried to wake her, the train was slowing.

"We're here," Callum said.

"Where?" she whispered.

He chuckled. "Edinburgh. Let's get out of the station. I texted a friend who lives nearby and has a flat in Old Town. He'll let us use his place to sleep for a few hours rather than try to find a hotel. If we hurry, we'll catch him before he goes to work, and he'll let us in."

"Okay," Maggie nodded but didn't move.

"Are you awake?" Callum whispered.

"I'm awake," she said.

Something soft brushed across one of her closed eyelids.

"Mmm, that's nice," she said, not at all ready to open her eyes.

The same soft touch swept across her other eyelid.

Curious as to what could possibly feel so good, she opened one eye to Callum's mouth coming closer.

His lips pressed lightly against her forehead. "Wake up, sweet Maggie," he whispered.

For a moment, she basked in the tenderness, the haze of exhaustion slowly dissipating.

By the time she came fully awake, Callum smiled and pushed to his feet. "Feel any better?"

Maggie's head spun a little at the realization that Callum had kissed her forehead. And, if she wasn't mistaken, both her eyelids. Was kissing part of the standard operating procedures for a bodyguard to wake his client? If so, could she ask him to repeat the process?

Wait. What was she thinking? Heat flooded her cheeks.

Suddenly wide awake, she sat up straight. "I'm much better," she lied and pushed to her feet.

Awake? Yes. Confused? Extremely.

Able to move about on her own, she didn't take the arm he offered. Instead, she followed him off the train and through the station.

"We can take the shortcut or the long way around," Callum said as they left the station.

"Shortcut," she said.

His brow wrinkled. "I warn you, there are a significant number of stairs."

The sooner they got where they were going, the sooner she could get a real shower for the first time since she'd left Montana. The shower-toilet combo in her cabin on the sleeper train didn't count. "I'll take my chances."

Minutes later, on the hundredth step, Maggie was second-guessing the shortcut.

"Do you need to stop for a breath?" Callum paused a couple of steps above her, barely breathing hard despite the fact he carried her case, her back-pack and his backpack. "I'm sorry. We should've taken the long way around."

"You warned me," she wheezed. "I'll be all right once we reach the top. Please tell me we're close."

He grimaced. "We're about a third of the way up."

Maggie swallowed a groan. "I'm hiring a personal trainer as soon as I get home."

Callum chuckled. "Seriously, you should stop and catch your breath."

"No way," she said, moving past him, "I'll lose my momentum."

He fell in step with her and stayed at her side the rest of the way to the top. Once there, Maggie bent over, a stitch in her side, sucking air into her lungs. After a minute, she straightened. "I thought I was in reasonably good shape from chasing four and five-year-olds around the classroom and playground. I was sorely mistaken."

He took her hand. "Come on, it's not much further."

Callum came to a stop in front of a building that had probably been standing since medieval times. He glanced over at her. "The good news is that this is his building. The bad news is there are more stairs involved."

Maggie stared up at the beautiful old building, thankful it wasn't more than four stories. "I can do it. Lead the way."

Callum held the door for her.

Maggie crossed the threshold into a small entryway with doors on either side and a staircase leading upward.

Callum took the lead and started up the steps. When he stopped on the first floor, Maggie could have kissed him.

A door opened in the middle of the hallway, and a big man with a barrel chest stepped out. "Cal, old man, glad you made it. Come in. Come in."

Cal laid a hand against Maggie's back and guided her toward the man dressed in a traditional plaid kilt.

"Still playing pipes for the tourists?" Cal held out his hand.

"It's a living and better than being target practice for the Taliban, wouldn't you say?" The man gripped Callum's hand and pulled him into a hearty hug, pounding his back hard enough Maggie winced. When he stepped back, he turned to Maggie. "And who is this bonnie lass with ya?"

"Angus Graham, this is Maggie McKendrick," Callum introduced them.

Angus took Maggie's hand in his big, meaty one. "Nice to meet you, Maggie McKendrick." His gaze went from Maggie back to Callum. "Your wife? Fiancée? Girlfriend?"

Heat filled Maggie's cheeks as she quickly shook the man's hand and let go. "None of the above."

Angus's eyebrows rose. "If that's the case, there's a chance for me." He lifted his chin and patted his broad chest. "I'm a lot more man than the likes of young Callum."

Maggie shook her head. "I'm sure you are, but I'm not here for long."

"Ah, a Yank, are ya?" Angus smiled. "I'd like to spend the day listening to your accent and watching the sun glint off your hair, but duty calls." He opened the door behind him and waved them inside. "Make yourselves at home. If you're still around this evening, we can find something to eat. Nothing much in the fridge but some cheese. There's bread on the counter."

"All we need is a shower and a couple of hours of sleep," Callum said. "Ms. McKendrick has an appointment to keep. We may or may not be back afterward."

Angus nodded. "Just let me know." He gathered a set of bagpipes, settled a beret on his head and waved a hand. "It was good to get your text. Last I heard, your entire team was hit. I thought you might be dead."

As Maggie watched the interaction between Angus and Callum, she was shocked at the sudden change in Callum's demeanor.

Her bodyguard's jaw tightened. "I'm still here," he said, his tone flat, emotionless.

A moment before, he'd been smiling and seemingly happy to see his friend. And just like that, a shadow fell over his face, giving it a grayish tinge.

The mention of his team had done that to him.

Maggie wondered what had happened. If Angus had assumed Callum was dead, were there others who hadn't survived whatever hit they'd taken?

"Make yourselves comfortable. If you run into any trouble, you know what to do."

Callum met and held Angus's gaze. After a moment, he nodded. "Aye. It's good to see you, old man." He reached out and clasped Angus's forearm.

"Take care," Angus said and turned to shake Maggie's hand. "A pleasure to meet you, fair Maggie." Angus left the flat, closing the door behind him.

Maggie turned to Callum, wanting to ask him what Angus had meant when he'd said, *You know what to do*. She also wanted to know what had happened to him and his team.

His face set in tight, unapproachable lines, Callum moved away from the door and dropped their backpacks on the floor.

Maggie would have to wait to ask her questions when Callum wasn't so distant. Instead, she moved around the small flat. Though the kitchen was small, it had a full-sized refrigerator and a table with two chairs. The living room had a single sofa against one wall with end tables on either side. A television rested on a stand against the opposite wall. She walked down the short hallway. Two doors led into bedrooms, one larger than the other. Behind a third door was a bathroom with a toilet, sink and shower.

When Maggie returned to the living room, she found Callum in the kitchen, peering into the refrigerator. "There are two bedrooms. I assume the larger one is Angus's."

"You can sleep in the other." Callum tipped his head toward the sofa. "I'll be okay on the sofa. You can be first in the shower, while I find something to eat."

Too tired to argue, Maggie grabbed her roller bag and backpack and headed for the bathroom. As she stripped, her mind replayed all that had happened since she'd landed in London, her thoughts revolving around the man in the other room—her bodyguard who'd saved her from the attacker in Crewe and then kissed her awake like a lover, not a hired protector.

She turned on the water, waited for it to warm

and then stepped beneath the spray, hoping the water would wash away her confusion along with the grungy feeling of travel grime. It didn't.

Standing naked, a few very short steps away from Callum, only added to her confusion. Yes, there was a door between them, and he'd probably faked his interest in her while playing tour guide through London, but her interest in him was all too real. So real the water sliding over her sensitized skin made her wish Callum would join her in the shower and run his hands over the same places the water touched.

With the tips of her fingers, she traced a path from her neck, over the swell of her breast and downward to the juncture of her thighs. A moan rose up her throat.

"Everything all right in there?" Callum's voice sounded through the closed door, shaking Maggie back to reality. She turned the faucet to cold. "Yes. Everything is fine. Just fine," she squeaked as the cold water hit her skin, chilling her desire into submission. She was a job. Nothing more.

But if there could be more...

CHAPTER 5

CALLUM STOOD on the other side of the bathroom door, his hand on the doorknob, his pulse pounding through his veins. When he'd heard the water come on, he'd gravitated toward the door, imagining Maggie standing beneath the spray, naked, her fiery curls hanging down around her shoulders and over her breasts.

When she'd moaned, Callum's cock had throbbed, fully erect, hot and thick. He'd almost shoved the door open and joined her in the shower.

And what would that get him?

A slap in the face would be the least of his problems. She'd likely scream like a banshee and demand he leave her and the flat. Then she'd be on the phone to Hank, asking for a replacement protector, one who wouldn't attack his client in the shower.

The beauty had enough problems without him

adding to them. He released the doorknob and returned to the small kitchen, determined to keep his distance from Maggie. It was one thing to let her sleep in his arms on the train and to kiss her eyelids and forehead before she was completely awake. Pangs of guilt still reverberated through him. He'd been out of line to do even that. Molesting her in the shower was out of the question. He'd never taken an unwilling woman. Women usually came to him willingly.

Hands off was the best way to handle Maggie McKendrick. Her day had been traumatic enough and would be even more so before it was over.

Callum gathered the bread and cheese and went to work, preparing sustenance. They hadn't eaten since the day before. His belly rumbled in protest. Maggie had to be hungry as well. Thoughts of the red-haired beauty made him pause in the middle of cutting slices of cheese. He still reeled from the sudden and intense surge of desire that had almost overwhelmed him. Since his return from Syria, he hadn't felt that kind of desire. Hell, he'd never felt desire of this intensity ever. Not with any woman he'd dated.

Why now?

Why her?

Because she was spunky. She was optimistic, embracing new experiences with open arms. Everything he wasn't and hadn't been for a long time. He found himself wanting to run his hands through her glorious copper curls and down the length of her body, touching every inch of her silky skin as if by doing so he could erase all the ugliness and brutality he'd witnessed during his time in the military.

Her green eyes twinkled with excitement and curiosity, reminding Callum that life went on even after he'd lost so many friends. She made him feel as if he could breathe again, as if the weight of his losses that had been pressing against his chest had lifted just a little. She'd lost her mother recently, yet she'd eagerly boarded a plane and flown to a foreign country, hoping to connect with people who shared her DNA. Innocently hopeful of finding family. Naively assuming they might want her to be part of theirs.

Callum couldn't fault her enthusiasm and her desire for connection and love. It was who she was. As he'd sat so still on the train, with her in his arms, he'd realized what he was missing and what she provided.

Maggie brought light into the darkness of his soul.

An image of the big man who'd attacked her at the train station flashed through his mind, dimming that light. If Callum hadn't been there, that man could have killed her with his bare hands or thrown her on the train tracks for the train to do the job.

Maggie was a sweet, kindhearted school teacher, for God's sake. She deserved to have a long, happy life filled with love, laughter and children, with her bright red hair and sunny disposition. The more Callum learned about her relatives, the more he was convinced someone didn't want her to make it to the Drummond estate—or worse, wanted to ensure she didn't claim any inheritance left by the late Lord Drummond. Perhaps she'd be better off returning to Montana. Unfortunately, Callum wasn't certain her troubles would be over if she retreated. She'd still be a target as long as she was alive.

His jaw clenched, and his shoulders straightened. It was his duty to do everything in his power to keep her alive. He had to find the one, or ones, responsible for putting her in danger.

Callum's cell phone vibrated in his pocket. He dug it out and read the name across the screen.

Ace Hammerson.

"This is McCall," he answered and put the call on speaker so that he could continue to prepare food while he listened and talked.

Without preamble, Ace said, "Hank and Swede filled me in on what's going on with Ms. McKendrick. I have Peter Atkins, one of our protectors based out of London, on standby in case you need him. You might know him from your days in the SAS."

Callum was impressed by how well the Brotherhood Protectors communicated with each other—another reason to sign on with them. "I do. We deployed together back when I was fresh out of training. He's a decent sort. I'll keep him in mind."

"Do you have a plan going forward with Ms. McKendrick?"

"I do," Callum said. "I'll accompany her to her meeting with the Drummonds under the cover of being either her boyfriend, fiancé or travel companion. Where she goes, I'll go."

"Good," Ace said. "Given the information Swede found, the Drummonds might have invited her there for nefarious purposes."

"My thoughts as well. Especially, considering she was the product of an affair between her mother and Lord Drummond."

"Drummond's sons might harbor resentment toward Ms. McKendrick."

"Well, one of them is only five years old, but you're right. I'll be with her at all times, monitoring the situation. If anyone show signs of aggression, I'll get her out." He couldn't imagine they'd openly attack Maggie, but he wasn't taking any chances.

"Roger," Ace said. "Glad to have you aboard as a Brotherhood Protector. Besides Swede, we have our own technical support, a computer guru here in Zurich. Dmytro is a jack-of-all-trades who has contacts throughout Europe and the UK. You need weapons, he's the one who can set you up. Air transport? He's your man. He can fly airplanes and helicopters, or knows people who can do it for him. Ms. Monroe, our blue-haired cyberpunk technophile, can bleed information out of the tightest firewall. Between Swede and my crew here, we'll have everything you need to know about the members of the Drummond clan. Hopefully, by the end of the day. I'm sending contact information for Atkins, Dmytro and Monroe now."

"Brilliant." A text message pinged on Callum's cell phone. He checked the incoming message and saved the data to his contacts. "Received. I'm not sure how long we'll be at the estate. If I have it my way, we'll only be there an hour, at the most."

"Either way, send us a GPS coordinate," Ace said. "If you two go missing, we'll know where to start the search."

"I don't plan on going missing, but I'll send that location in case I need backup."

"You're not in Afghanistan, Iraq or Syria battling Taliban or ISIS," Ace said. "But what you do as a Brotherhood Protector is important and often dangerous. Granted, bodyguard duty isn't always glamorous and is often boring, but we've learned that just when you think it's easy...it's not."

Callum's lips twisted. He'd already learned that lesson at Maggie's expense. He wouldn't be caught off guard again, if he could help it. "Understood."

"We're here for you twenty-four-seven. Stay safe. Hammerson out," Ace said and ended the call.

Callum's blood heated as movement drew his attention to the kitchen entrance.

Maggie stood there with her hair wrapped in a towel, wearing the short pajama bottoms she'd had on when she'd stepped off the train to find out why they'd stopped mid-journey. Instead of the jacket, she wore the matching top to the shorts in a soft pink.

The pajamas normally wouldn't be considered sexy, more like something a college coed would wear in a dorm room. To Callum, they left enough to the imagination to set his blood on fire.

"Who's Hammerson?" she asked, forcing him to drag his gaze from her legs to her makeup-free face with her auburn eyebrows framing her green eyes.

"My boss," Callum responded. With physical effort, he turned back to the bread and cheese he'd cut and placed them on a plate. "Hungry?"

"Starving," she said, and crossed the room to take the plate from him and set it on the small table in the corner of the kitchen. "Is there anything to drink?"

Callum opened the fridge and grimaced. "Beer." He moved the bottles around. "More beer." In the back, he found another bottle and held it up in triumph. "How are you with sparkling water?"

"I don't know. I've never had it. But I'm sure it's better than beer before noon. I'd like to have a clear head when I meet Ewan."

"Sparkling water it is, then." He grabbed one of the bottles of beer and carried his finds to the table, where he set them down. Then he held out a chair for Maggie.

She slid into the seat, her shorts riding up high enough to reveal more of her thighs.

Callum twisted the top off the bottle of beer and downed a long swallow before sinking into the seat across from Maggie.

She had unscrewed the cap on the water bottle and took a tentative sip. Her lips curved into a smile. "It tickles like a soda without the flavor. I have friends at the school who swear by sparkling water, only they prefer the flavored kind." She took another sip. "I like it."

"You and most of the people in the UK and Europe. If you don't want the bubbles, ask for still water."

"I'll remember that." Maggie plucked a piece of the bread from the plate and laid a slice of cheese on it. "How does Hammerson fit in with Hank?" She bit into the bread and began to chew.

Callum selected a piece of bread and cheese before answering. "As you know, Hank Patterson is the founder of Brotherhood Protectors. Ace Hammerson, a former Navy SEAL, is the leader of the International branch based in Zurich, Switzerland. He approached me after I left the SAS, asking if I would join the Brotherhood Protectors International. Apparently, they're expanding."

"They hire people trained and experienced in

special forces operations," Maggie said. "I've met quite a few of the members of the team based in Montana. They're smart, skilled and honorable. I'd trust any one of them with my life."

"And you can trust me to do my best to keep you safe."

"I know Swede. He's got amazing computer skills. If Hammerson's team is half as good, we'll know everything there is to know about the Drummonds, down to their shoe size and what they had for dinner the night before." She grinned. "Well, maybe not what they had for dinner. It's too bad we won't have all the intel before we meet with Ewan this afternoon."

"Can you delay the meeting?" Callum asked.

"I could, but after what happened in Crewe, I'd rather face the snakes in their den than be surprised on the streets of Edinburgh." She shrugged. "If they are truly snakes. There is a chance the attack was a random, crazy dude who saw an opportunity to do bad things to a clueless woman standing alone on a platform." She smiled weakly. "I should've been paying attention."

"I should've been beside you, not hiding in the shadows."

"You were there when I needed you," she said. "That's what counts. Now, have you decided if you'll be my travel companion, boyfriend or fiancé when we arrive at the Drummond estate?" She shook her head. "Hard to believe my relatives live on an estate. I imagined I'd meet my half-brother at some quaint little thatched-roof cottage, not a Lord's estate." She tipped her head, her brow puckering. "Since Ewan's father, mine too, has passed, does that make my half-brother a Lord?"

Callum couldn't help but smile at Maggie's rambling train of thought. "I believe Ewan, as the oldest son, will assume the title, barring any issues with the crown. As for what role I'll play, I think it's best if I arrive as your fiancé. That way, they won't question why I came along. A boyfriend might not be as committed to traveling so far."

"But you're obviously Scottish," Maggie said. "They might ask how we met and why you didn't fly with me from Montana?"

"You have a valid point," Callum said. "We need to agree on a story."

"First off, when and where did we meet?" Maggie asked. "Since this is my first time out of the States, you would have to have come to Montana. You could have come on vacation after you left the military and stayed in Eagle Rock, where I live. We met at the Blue Moose Tavern."

He cocked an eyebrow. "Blue Moose Tavern?"

Maggie nodded. "It's where everyone goes to get a decent meal and a beer."

"Why did I pick Eagle Rock, Montana?"

"It's got some of the best fly fishing in the country."

He shook his head. "I've never been fly fishing."

"You came to Eagle Rock to learn how." She frowned playfully. "Work with me here."

"Okay. Let me get this straight." He dipped his head toward her. "After I left the military, I went to Eagle Rock, Montana, because an American I met during special operations in Afghanistan told me how peaceful it was to go fly fishing there. I stopped at the Blue Moose Tavern for a meal and a beer. I was instantly smitten by a fiery-haired beauty and never took a fly fishing lesson."

Maggie smiled. "Now, you're talking."

He went on to say, "It wasn't love at first sight for you. I had to woo you over the two weeks I was there with flowers and chocolates."

She shook her head. "I don't like flowers, they remind me of funerals, and they die. And I'm not a chocolates kind of girl. I'm more impressed by actions than gifts."

"When a drunk got too friendly with you, I stepped in and told him to leave my girl alone. When he didn't, I escorted him out of the building."

"Good. I like that."

"Did I break his arm?"

She tilted her head. "No. You didn't have to. You were firm but kind."

"Then I put him into a taxi so he wouldn't drive home drunk."

Maggie laughed. "The town of Eagle Rock is

really small. We don't have taxis there. But Sheriff Barron showed up in time to take him to the jail where he could sleep it off."

"Why didn't he take him home?"

"Sheriff Barron didn't trust him to stay home. He was safer in the jail cell, sleeping it off. And the town was safer with him in the cell."

A smile pulled at Callum's lips. "You know this guy, don't you?"

Maggie nodded. "Ed Knowlton. Ever since his wife died, he comes to the Blue Moose on Saturday night, drinks too much and wants a female hug, usually from someone who doesn't want to give him one. Sheriff Barron always shows up to haul him to the jail, where he lets him sleep it off."

"Sounds like a lonely man," Callum noted.

"He and his wife, Lois, were high school sweethearts. It broke his heart when she died." Maggie tapped a finger to her chin. "We have how we met. How did we end up engaged?"

"I walked you home that night and asked you out for coffee the next morning."

"A safe place to meet and get to know each other," Maggie said. "Afterward, we walked through town, talking all the way."

"I took you on a picnic," Callum added.

"We ate cold fried chicken by the lake and talked about American football versus Scottish football."

"By the end of my vacation, I was madly in love

and couldn't imagine leaving you behind, so I proposed."

"I, too, had fallen so deeply that I accepted your proposal. That's when I got the DNA results."

"I had to return to the UK to wrap things up before I could make a permanent move to Montana."

"You'd move to Montana for me?" She smiled. "I'm honored."

He gave her a wink. "Anything for my beautiful fiancée."

"Before you could come back to Montana," Maggie said, "I got the invitation to visit Ewan. You met me at the airport in London, which you really did, and here we are."

"When's the wedding?" Callum asked.

"It's all so new to us, we haven't set a date yet," Maggie said. "I have to find a venue, get a dress, order flowers and a cake. I put it off until after I met my half-brother."

Callum clapped his hands. "We have a cover story." He glanced at his watch. "When are we supposed to be at the Drummond estate?"

"At three o'clock this afternoon."

"You have the address?"

Maggie pulled up the address Ewan had given her on her cell phone.

Callum entered it into his map application and requested directions from their current location. "It will take us twenty minutes to get to the estate by motor vehicle."

Maggie nodded. "I'd planned to rent a car at the train station." She smiled. "Do you mind driving it? I have to admit my sense of adventure was strained at the thought of driving on the opposite side of the road. I was especially nervous about getting out of Edinburgh."

"I can do that." He drank the last of his beer.

"Do I have enough time to grab a short nap?" Maggie yawned. "I'm running on fumes."

Callum nodded toward the guest bedroom. "Certainly. Rest easy."

Maggie frowned. "What about you?"

"I'll sleep on the sofa out here, if I feel the need."

Maggie ate the last bit of her bread and cheese and chased it with the sparkling water. "Thank you for preparing this. I was hungry." She stood and stretched.

Callum rose at the same time. "I'll clean up. Go. Rest. I'll wake you well before we have to leave."

"I just need a couple of hours lying down, and I'll be good to go." She yawned again as she left the kitchen and padded barefoot down the hallway to the guest bedroom.

Callum gathered the dishes, washed them in the sink then dried and placed them in the cabinets where he'd found them. When he was done, he grabbed his shaving kit and headed for the bathroom where he showered, shaved and brushed his teeth. He emerged refreshed and ducked his head into the guest bedroom.

Maggie lay on her side, her hand tucked between the pillow and her cheek. She'd removed the towel from her hair and draped it over a chair. Her hair, still damp, lay in dark copper curls around her face and shoulders, and her russet eyelashes made dark semi-circles below her eyes as she slept.

Callum couldn't look away. More than that, he struggled to resist reaching out to brush his fingers along the soft curve of her lips.

He realized that, like the story they'd concocted, he was smitten with this school teacher. Sadly, he wasn't in a good place in his head to start a relationship with her or anyone else, for that matter. She deserved a man who didn't have horrific nightmares that plagued his sleep, who didn't often wake swinging. He'd be afraid he'd hurt her. Already haunted by the fact he hadn't been able to help Smudge or Rook, he would never be able to forgive himself if he inflicted physical harm on a defenseless woman.

After one last glance, he backed out of the room and pulled the door closed.

Too keyed up to sleep, he paced through the flat, stopping at the windows overlooking the entrance and the street below. He stood to the side, careful not to expose himself to anyone who might be looking up.

Tourists moved along the sidewalks heading for the train station or the Royal Mile, eager to see more of the city or the Scottish countryside. The city was a vibrant blend of modern amenities and a stunning mix of architectural styles, including Celtic, Gothic, Renaissance and Romanesque. For a city established over nine hundred years ago, it had stood the test of time with grace and beauty.

Four men in dark clothing came into view, weaving swiftly between tourists as if they were on a mission.

Callum tensed as they neared the street-level entrance to the building housing Angus's flat. When they arrived in front of the building, they paused, looked around and then entered.

Callum cursed and spun away from the window. As he sprinted for the guest bedroom, he cast a glance at his backpack and her suitcase on the floor in the living room. He didn't have time to hide them, and it probably didn't matter. They already knew Maggie was there. Somehow, they'd followed them there.

When he burst through the door, he called out in an urgent whisper, "Maggie. Wake up."

Maggie's eyes shot open. She focused on him and sat up straight. "What's wrong?"

"Four men entered the building below. I think they're on their way up here."

She leaped to her feet. "Is there a back door we can go through? I don't recall seeing one."

Callum shook his head. "No, but Angus has a safe room hidden behind a wall in his bedroom." He spun and stepped back out into the hallway.

The sound of footsteps clumping up the stairs made Callum's heart beat faster as he led the way into Angus's room with Maggie close on his heels. "Close the door," he ordered.

Maggie shut the door. "Lock it?"

"No. We don't want them to know we're here."

Two of the walls in Angus's room were a soft French gray. The third wall was a feature wall of rich, dark wood, with four bands of gray stone stretching from floor to ceiling, giving the room a distinctly masculine and modern look.

Callum ran his fingers along the stones. The button was there somewhere. Angus had shown it to him the first time he'd visited his old friend after he'd renovated the flat.

A loud thump reverberated through the closed door of the bedroom. They were trying to break down the door to the flat.

As Callum's finger rolled over what appeared to be just another stone in the feature wall, the far side of it sank in. He pushed harder. The latch released. Callum swung the entire band of gray stone mounted on a solid metal sheet, opening it like a door. When the gap was wide enough for a person to squeeze through, he grabbed Maggie's arm and shoved her into the narrow enclave, barely large enough for two people to stand side by side.

Another loud thump sounded from the other room, followed by the crack of splitting wood.

Callum slipped into the space beside Maggie and pulled the metal door shut, easing the metal latch into the clasp.

He felt, more than heard, the thump of heavy footsteps entering the room on the other side of the feature wall.

A soft hand reached for his. He raised it to his lips, pressed a kiss to the backs of knuckles and whispered, "You'll be grand. I'll make sure of that."

CHAPTER 6

MAGGIE CLUNG to Callum's hand, her breath lodged in her throat. How had those men found her? She'd been hyper-aware of her surroundings and the people around her since the attack at the train station in Crewe---except when she'd fallen asleep on the train beside Callum. Knowing he worked for Hank as a Brotherhood Protector, there to see to her safety, she'd trusted that he had been on alert for trouble as well.

She prayed that the wall of stone and metal separating them from the men on the other side of the room would be enough. She hadn't been able to detect the button Callum had depressed to open the secret panel. He'd had to feel for it to locate it. Surely the men wouldn't think to look behind a wood and stone wall.

The space was tight, giving them just enough room to stand. Sandwiched between the metal door and the back wall. All they had to do was wait for the men to leave. How long would they look around before they vacated the premises? Another thought followed that one, making her bite her bottom lip. What if they decided to stay, assuming she and Callum would return for their belongings? They might be stuck in that tiny space indefinitely. Did it have ventilation? Would they run out of air? Her pulse pounded so hard against her eardrum, she could barely hear the movement in the other room.

Callum gently squeezed her hand, bringing it up to his lips again to kiss the backs of her knuckles.

Maggie drew in a deep breath and let it out slowly, letting the words he'd whispered so softly sink in.

You'll be grand. I'll make sure of that.

If the men found their hiding place, Callum would come out fighting. And so would she. One man couldn't take on four.

Maggie's mother had been adamant about self-defense. She'd driven Maggie to Bozeman once a week for months to have her trained. She'd never wanted her daughter to be at the mercy of any man. She almost laughed.

The first time she'd been attacked, all that training had flown out of her mind. It hadn't helped that the man had been so very much larger than her and that she'd been caught by surprise. But that was no excuse. She should have been able to break free long enough to get away.

Lesson learned.

She couldn't let that happen again. Maybe she could use her self-defense training to fight alongside Callum.

These thoughts, along with a multitude of scenarios, ran through her mind like a horror film on fast-forward.

The thumping footsteps reverberating through the wooden floor faded. Silence and stillness stretched on for one minute...two...

After what felt like an hour, the latch on the metal door suddenly clicked.

Callum tensed and released her hand.

As the tall, metal door swung open, Callum sprang out and grabbed the man on the other side in a chokehold.

Maggie came out, ready to kick, punch and bite if necessary. When she saw a man's bare knees and pleated kilt, she touched Callum's arm. "Callum, it's Angus."

He must have realized who it was at the same moment. He immediately dropped his arm from around his friend's neck.

Angus staggered forward, his face red, his hands rising to his throat. "I see your reflexes haven't slowed a bit." His gaze shifted to Maggie. "For a moment, I was worried they'd gotten to you before you could get to the safe room."

"Sorry, old man," Callum said.

"Better to come out fighting." Angus stepped back, staring around the bedroom.

Maggie gasped.

It had been trashed.

The navy comforter had been ripped into several pieces, the cream sheets were in shreds and the mattress had a long, jagged slash down the center. Ripped from the wall, the lamp that had been on the nightstand lay shattered on the wooden floor. The nightstand drawers had been flung across the room.

"Oh, Angus," Maggie said. "I'm so sorry."

"Dinna worry yourself," Angus said. "These are only things. What's important is that you two are safe."

"I thought you wouldn't be back until later this evening," Callum said.

"That was my plan until I received a call on my mobile from my neighbor on the second floor asking if I was having a party." His lips pressed together. "I figured if there was enough noise in my flat to bother eighty-five-year-old, half-deaf Mr. Campbell, I might need to join the party. I called the police and arrived when they did. Four men exited the building at that exact moment. The police gave chase, and I came up to look for you."

Callum gripped Angus's forearm. "I owe you."

Maggie moved toward the broken lamp, feeling the need to set the place to rights.

Callum's hand shot out, grabbing her arm. "Don't get any closer to the broken lamp. You'll cut your bare feet on the shards."

"Leave it," Angus said. "That can wait until later."

Callum placed a hand at the small of Maggie's back and guided her toward the bedroom door. "What concerns me most about this incident and the one at the train station in Crewe is how they found you. I've been watching for anyone following us. I've seen no indication that someone has been lurking nearby. Not in London, not on the train and not on our way from the train station to when we arrived at Angus's flat."

Maggie walked with Callum into the living room, her heart sinking into the pit of her belly. Here, too, they'd destroyed every piece of furniture. Every drawer in the kitchen lay in splinters on the floor, the contents scattered. Across the wall in the living room, words had been painted in blood red.

GO HOME BITCH

Maggie pressed a hand to her mouth, her eyes filling with tears. "I'm so, so sorry," she whispered.

Angus wrapped an arm around her shoulders. "They're just things. I have insurance that will set this place to rights."

Callum disappeared into the guest bedroom and

came out carrying Maggie's backpack. He unzipped the top and dumped the contents on the floor.

Maggie frowned. "What are you doing?" She bent to gather her belongings.

"You said someone bumped into you at the airport," Callum said. "They might have planted a GPS tracking device on you." He sifted through her charging cords, makeup kit and her change of clothes, including a lacy black pair of panties.

Maggie snatched the panties from his hand and wadded them into her left hand. With her other hand, she sifted through the items.

When they didn't find anything that might resemble a GPS tag, Callum unzipped the side pockets and emptied them as well.

A small round piece of metal that looked like a coin rolled across the floor.

"Son of a b—" Maggie muttered.

Callum straightened and stepped toward the device.

"Wait," Angus said. "Don't smash it. Let me deal with it." He bent to retrieve the tag. "I'll be right back. Might be a minute as I want to speak with the police when they return."

Angus left the flat. His footsteps rang out on the stairs leading down to the street.

"How did I not know that was in there?" Maggie shook her head.

"Because when that man bumped into you at the

airport, he probably slipped it into your backpack. You were rightfully angry about his rudeness and were more focused on the man, not your backpack."

Maggie shivered and wrapped her arms around her middle. "And they've been following me ever since." The chill of the room raised goosebumps on her arms and bare legs. She dug in her backpack for slacks and a sweater, then ducked into the bathroom to change out of her pajamas and into something more substantial. After she stuffed her pajamas into her backpack, she brushed her hair and teeth, then left the bathroom.

Suddenly restless and greatly paranoid, she crossed to the window overlooking the street below. "What's Angus going to do with the disk?"

Callum came to stand behind her. He laid his hands on her shoulders and pulled her back against him and out of view of anyone who might look up and spot her.

The heat of Callum's body warmed the chill that had crept through her when she realized she'd led the bad guys to them. Not only could they have kidnapped or killed her, but they could also have hurt Callum in the process. What if Angus had come home and surprised the four men during their raid on his flat? He, too, could have been injured or killed for allowing Maggie to stay there temporarily. As it was, they'd trashed his home. All because she'd dared to come to Scotland to meet her half-brother?

Angus stood on the sidewalk below, glancing in both directions.

A garbage truck rumbled up the street. It stopped, and two men leaped off, grabbed trash bins and emptied them into the back of the truck.

Callum's friend lifted the lid of a rubbish bin perched on the sidewalk, tossed something, closed the bin and moved back as the garbage truck came toward him.

The guys on the back of the truck jumped out, grabbed the bin, emptied it into the garbage truck and set the empty bin on the curb.

As the truck moved on to the next trash container, two Scottish policemen joined Angus. They bent over, hands on their knees, dragging air into their lungs, winded from chasing the burglars. Since they'd returned on their own, the intruders had obviously gotten away.

Maggie sighed.

For several minutes, Angus spoke to the police, and then he waved toward the entrance.

The two policemen disappeared into the building, followed by Angus. Their footsteps echoed on the wooden steps as they ascended to the third-floor flat.

Maggie spun toward the policemen as they stepped through the door.

"Freeze!" the younger officer shouted, his face fierce and set in hard lines.

Heart pounding against her ribs, Maggie backed

away, hands in the air, shocked they'd come in acting like Maggie and Callum were the bad guys.

Callum moved between her and the exuberant policeman, his hands also in the air.

The officer's frightening scowl melted into a broad grin. "Always wanted to say that."

"Not funny," Callum muttered.

The older policeman clapped a hand on the younger officer's shoulder. "Stand down, McGregor." To Callum and Maggie, he said, "Ignore the whelp. He's still wet behind the ears. We need to look around for a few minutes and dust for prints to document the intrusion for our report."

Angus had entered the flat and hovered by the door. Maggie and Callum joined him to stay out of the way. The officers questioned them, though they didn't have much to add as they'd been hiding and out of sight while the burglars ransacked the rooms. The young police officer snapped photos of the damage and the writing on the wall.

Maggie shivered and leaned into Callum for warmth. He wrapped his arm around her and pulled her close, holding her there until the police finally left them alone.

"I slipped the tracker into the rubbish bin," Angus said. "Whoever has been following will now follow the truck through Edinburgh. It might buy you a little peace."

Maggie and Callum helped Angus clean up what

they could and set the furniture to rights. They couldn't fix the mattress on his bed or wash the paint from the wall, but they did what they could.

"Don't worry about it," Angus said. "It's just paint. I can take care of it.

"But your bed—" Maggie felt so bad about what had happened to the man's place when all he'd done was offer them refuge.

Angus waved a hand. "I have a friend who sells mattresses and can have a new one here before the end of the day."

"I'll pay for it," Maggie said. "My mother left me a small trust fund when she passed. I can wire the money once I get back to Montana."

Angus was shaking his head before she finished speaking. "The men who broke in did this. Not you. Besides, that's what insurance is for."

Callum laid a hand on Angus's shoulder. "You're a good man."

"We take care of our brothers," he said, meeting Callum's gaze.

Callum's eyes clouded as he nodded solemnly. "Or watch them die."

Angus's brow furrowed. "We do the best we can, given the circumstances."

"Sometimes our best isn't good enough."

"And sometimes, there's nothing you can do to change the outcome," Angus said. "When that happens, you have to live in the present and leave the past behind."

Maggie bore witness to the exchange, knowing nothing about what had happened that inspired their words, but she could feel the pain and regret that obviously weighed heavily on Callum's mind and memories.

Callum broke eye contact and glanced down at his watch. The moment passed.

"If we leave now, we can pick up a rental car at the train station and make your meeting with Ewan Drummond." He shot a glance toward Maggie. "Can you be ready to go in five minutes?"

"I'm ready now," she said.

Callum's gaze went to Angus. "Thank you again. I'm not sure what will happen when we meet with Drummond."

"When I first planned to come to Scotland, I'd hoped to stay close to where my half-brother lived and spend a little time getting to know him." Maggie shrugged and grimaced. "Now, I don't know. If it's all incredibly awkward and...who knows?...dangerous, I might just move on, see some of Scotland and go back home to Montana." She sighed. "When Ewan invited me for a visit, I thought it was no big deal. I was excited to know I had a brother."

Callum's gaze softened. "Let's meet the man, and we can decide what to do from there. If we end up leaving the same day, so be it."

Callum clasped Angus's forearm and pulled him in for a hug. "Stay safe, my friend."

"And you," Angus responded. "I'm here, if you need backup."

"Be careful what you offer," Callum said. "I might take you up on it."

Angus clapped Callum hard on the back and stepped back. "I'm counting on it."

Maggie hugged Callum's big friend. "Thank you, Angus. If you ever come to Montana, you're welcome to stay with me."

"Now, you be careful what you offer. I might just take you up on it." He winked and kissed her cheek.

"I'd be honored."

Maggie slung her backpack over her shoulder. When she went to collect her roller bag, Callum beat her to it. With his backpack over one shoulder, he lifted her suitcase and led the way out of the flat and down the stairs to the street below.

He stopped at the entrance, blocking her from stepping out until he'd checked both directions. "Stay close to me."

That's exactly where she'd be. After the four men had broken into the flat, Maggie didn't want to go anywhere alone. What would they have done had they found her?

She didn't know and didn't want to give them the opportunity to find out.

They walked the few blocks and turned to take a

long staircase downward. Had it only been a few hours earlier that they'd climbed up those same stairs? Maggie shook her head. It felt like a lot longer than hours.

At the train station, they found the rental car companies and arranged to rent a mid-sized sedan. Callum refused to let her pay for it, insisting it was part of the protection service provided by Brotherhood Protectors.

Maggie didn't argue. She'd settle up with Hank and Sadie when she returned to Montana. Her thoughts and focus were on the meeting with Ewan Drummond. In her mind, she'd pictured a joyful embrace with a long-lost brother where they'd sit around sharing stories of their childhoods. He'd tell her about their father and any aunts, uncles or cousins she'd never known about.

Now, a sense of dread had her second-guessing her impulsive rush to meet this half-brother who probably resented her because she was his father's bastard child, spawned out of an illicit act of adultery, now coming to stake a claim on his inheritance.

Maggie's stomach roiled as she slipped into the passenger seat, marveling at how strange it felt to be on the left side without a steering wheel in front of her. So many changes. Too many revelations. She almost wished she didn't know so much. Then again, the more she knew, the better prepared she'd be.

Callum slid into the driver's seat. Before he

started the engine, he reached across and took her hand. "We don't have to go to the Drummond estate if you don't want to. I can shift into drive and keep going as far as you want to go."

Her fingers curled into his palm. For all her bravado and insistence that she didn't need anyone to go with her to meet her half-brother, Maggie was so very glad Callum would accompany her to the estate. "As tempting as that sounds, I came to meet Ewan," she lifted her chin. "Since my presence in Scotland has stirred up some trouble, I want to know why and who has a problem with me."

"Very well." His fingers tightened around hers for a moment, and then he released her hand. "Next stop is the Drummond Estate." He started the engine and pulled out of the train station.

Maggie clasped her hands together in her lap, her gaze on the road ahead, barely taking in the amazing architecture lining the streets of Edinburgh.

During the thirty-minute drive through the city and out into the countryside, a knot formed in the pit of her belly. Twice, she opened her mouth to tell Callum she'd changed her mind. Twice, she closed her mouth and remained silent while her mind screamed ahead, imagining dozens of directions this meeting could take. Unfortunately, none of those directions seemed good.

As they pulled off the main road and paused at an ornate stone and iron gate, Callum glanced across to

Maggie and said, "You'll be grand. I'll make sure of that."

Maggie let go of the breath she'd been holding for too long and said, "Don't forget, we met in Montana."

His answering smile helped push back the overwhelming sense of doom. With Callum, she could do this.

CHAPTER 7

A CAMERA MOUNTED on the corner of the stone column looked almost incongruous to the gate that could have been older than Callum's great, great-grandfather. Many of the stone structures and buildings in Scotland had been passed down from generation to generation for centuries.

When he was young, Callum had dreamed of buying one of the old, stone mansions that had fallen into disrepair and rebuilding it to its former glory. Life in the military hadn't paid much, but he hadn't needed to spend much. Most of his pay had gone into investments that had grown in value over the years. He could potentially do it now, but hadn't had the heart to get on with his life when his teammates' lives had ended.

Callum drew in a breath, focused on the present and lowered the window. He reached out and pressed the button on the metal box set back in the stone structure.

"State your name and purpose," a staticky voice said.

"Callum McCall, accompanying Maggie McKendrick for her three o'clock appointment with Ewan Drummond."

"Proceed to the main house," the voice said.

The wrought iron gate slowly swung open.

Callum drove the rental car through the entrance and followed a winding road lined with towering trees on either side. A seasoned combat soldier, he instinctively studied the deep shadows.

Maggie had been attacked twice now. If the Drummonds were behind the attacks, he'd need to be on his toes and ready should more of the men in black appear.

They passed a small stone cottage on the right, probably what had once been the gatekeeper's quarters.

The trees overhanging the road gave a dark tunnel-like effect, blocking out much of the cloud-muted daylight and giving the feeling of dusk.

When they emerged from the tunnel of trees, the estate opened up onto a manicured lawn with garden patches tastefully scattered around stately trees or the graceful arches of ivy-covered arbors.

The crowning glory was a gray stone manor with cylindrical turrets on the corners and rows of arched windows across the front. Stone steps led up to a giant black wooden door.

Callum drove the car up to the circular drive and around a fountain, squirting water out of the mouths of stone fish. Petunias in shades of pink, purple, red and white spilled out of stone flower boxes ringing the fountain.

Maggie pressed a hand to her chest and stared up at the mansion, her eyes growing rounder as Callum parked. "This is an estate?" she whispered. "It's more like a castle."

The door opened. A man in a black suit emerged and descended the steps in time to open Maggie's door.

Callum left the driver's seat and quickly rounded the hood of the car, ready to run interference between Maggie and the man holding her door.

As Maggie got out, the man in the suit stood ramrod straight. "Ms. McKendrick, my name is Gregory. I'm the butler. Welcome to Drummond Manor." To Callum, he said. "You may leave your keys in the vehicle. I'll have our chauffeur move it."

A long black car rolled up beside their rental and a tall man with dark hair and heavy eyebrows unfolded himself from the driver's seat.

Gregory looked past Maggie and addressed the driver. "Alastair, Lord Drummond has postponed his trip to Edinburgh. You may take the car back to the garage. Then you can come back and park our guests' vehicle in the garage."

Alastair's brow dipped low as he studied Maggie and Callum. Without saying a word, he gave a brief nod, climbed back into the car and drove away.

He waved a hand toward the door. "If you'll follow me, Lord Drummond is waiting for you in the sitting room." Without waiting for her response, he pivoted on his heel, marched up the stairs and opened the door.

Callum joined Maggie, rested a hand at the small of her back and walked with her up the steps and across the threshold. Whatever happened, he would be there for her.

As Callum passed Gregory, the butler asked, "Your name, sir?"

"Callum McCall," he responded.

The butler led them across a cavernous marble foyer and into a room with a Victorian-era settee and matching chairs with intricately carved wooden legs, curved backs and floral upholstery. Beautiful tapestries and ornate paintings covered the walls.

A man wearing tailored slacks and a brown tweed blazer stood with his back to the door, leaning his arm against a white fireplace with gold trim and delicate porcelain figurines decorating the mantel.

The butler cleared his throat and announced, "Ms. McKendrick and Mr. Callum McCall to see you, sir."

The man in the tweed blazer turned, and immediately, Callum recognized the striking resemblance. He could only be Ewan Drummond, Maggie's half-brother.

Maggie gasped.

"Ms. McKendrick." He crossed the room, a crooked smile pulling at the corners of his lips. "If I'd had any doubt about your lineage, all my doubts have been dispelled." He held out both hands to her.

She placed her hands in his, her eyes round, tears welling.

Callum stood close, ready to step between them if Maggie's half-brother threatened to hurt her.

Ewan chuckled. "Startling, isn't it? The gene for red, curly hair is incredibly strong among the Drummonds as far back as anyone can remember."

Maggie blinked, and a tear slipped down her cheek. "I'm sorry. I'm not usually so emotional." She stopped. "No. Actually, I am," she said and gave a shaky laugh. "It's just that all my life I wondered where I'd gotten my red curly hair and green eyes. My mother had blond hair and blue eyes. She was taller, slender and athletic. I looked nothing like her, and she never told me anything about my father. I assumed he was dead. Until—"

"—the DNA test and the ancestry app," Ewan concluded. "Well, it's nice to know I have a sister." He squeezed her hands and released them, turning to Callum, a hand outstretched. "Ewan Drummond."

Callum took the man's hand. "Callum McCall." The man had a firm handshake.

Ewan's eyes narrowed. "Callum McCall," he said as if rolling the name over in his mind. "Sounds familiar." He tipped his head to the side. "Did you attend the Duke of York military school?"

Callum shook his head. "Nothing so high-brow. I'm a product of Glasgow Gaelic School."

Ewan smiled. "A Glaswegian, are ya?"

His chin rising proudly, Callum nodded. "Aye."

Ewan's gaze softened. "My battle buddy through all of my deployments was a Glaswegian. Saved my arse several times. I'd give my life for that man."

Callum's brow dipped. "You served?"

Ewan nodded. "Entered the British Air Force straight out of school and served in the SAS. Left three years ago after catching some shrapnel. My running days were over." He patted his left leg. "And you?"

Callum's lips twisted in a wry grin. "SAS."

Ewan's eyes widened. "Cal McCall. I thought I'd heard that name. Your team spent more time in Syria while we were cleaning up in Afghanistan. We probably ran into each other somewhere in our careers."

Callum nodded. The man's red hair did seem familiar. Many of Callum's memories of his time in SAS revolved around his team, most of whom were now gone.

"Ewan, are you going to introduce us to your guests?" a woman's voice sounded behind Callum.

He and Maggie turned toward the sound to find a tall, slender woman with platinum blond hair and brown eyes standing at the entrance to the sitting room. She wore a tailored pantsuit, classic heels and a pearl necklace.

"Ah, Fiona, come meet my sister, Maggie McKendrick." Ewan waved the woman forward.

As Fiona moved further into the room, something moved behind her. She turned and glanced down at a little boy with bright red curls. "It's okay. I won't let anyone hurt you," she said softly.

The little boy slipped his hand in hers and stared at Maggie and Callum, his eyes round and wary.

"Maggie, Cal, this is Fiona Drummond, my beautiful stepmother." Ewan crossed to the woman and child and swung the boy up into his arms. "And this little guy is my brother, Bryce."

The boy grinned and wrapped an arm around Ewan's neck.

"Bryce, my boy, come meet your big sister, Maggie." Ewan carried the boy over to Maggie and set him on the floor, squatting beside him.

Maggie's eyes widened and filled with tears. She slowly knelt beside the little boy to get on his level and held out her hand. "Hello, Bryce. It's nice to meet you."

The child took her hand and shook it, his face

solemn. "Pleasure to meet you," he said, his voice soft and the words so grown up for one so small. When she released his hand, he reached up and touched a strand of her curly red hair. "It's like mine."

She nodded. "Yes, it is." Maggie looked up at Ewan. "And like his."

"I thought sisters were smaller," he said.

Maggie laughed. "I once was small like you. Then I grew."

His brow puckered. "You sound funny."

"I grew up in a place called the United States. Do you know where that is?"

He nodded. "My teacher showed me where the United States was on a map. It's really big."

"Yes, it is," Maggie said. "People talk funny there. Like me. I'm a teacher back where I come from with students just like you."

"I like my teacher," Bryce said.

"I bet she's nice." Maggie straightened and held out her hand to Fiona. "It's nice to meet you. Your son is very nice."

Fiona's eyes narrowed as she looked down at Maggie's hand. She looked back up without taking the proffered hand. "Why are you here?" she asked, "and who is this man?"

"She's here because I invited her," Ewan said.

Maggie nodded.

"And I'm Callum McCall," Callum said, "her fiancé."

Fiona's frown moved from Maggie to Callum. "A man dies, and the vultures circle."

"Now, Fiona," Ewan said. "Maggie and I found each other on the ancestry app. That DNA test I sent off got a match. We exchanged emails, and I invited her to meet the family here in Scotland. Besides, it's just like Master Bryce said, I always wanted a sister. Isn't that right, my man?"

Bryce nodded and looked up at his mother. "Can we keep her?"

Fiona snorted and glared at Ewan. "You're going to confuse the boy."

"Not at all," Ewan smiled at Maggie and Callum. "She's family, and I say she's welcome to stay as long as she likes."

Fiona opened her mouth as if to argue with her stepson and then closed it again. "As you wish, Lord Drummond."

"I didn't come to stay," Maggie assured Fiona. "I only came to meet my brother..." Her gaze went to the little boy, and she smiled and added, "Brothers."

"How long will you be in Scotland?" Ewan asked.

Maggie bit her lip, looking from Ewan to Fiona. "I have two weeks. I'd planned on doing some sightseeing."

"You can use the manor as your base and travel out from here. There's a lot to see on day trips. No need to get a hotel when we have ten rooms available," Ewan said. "I insist."

"If the woman doesn't want to stay, she doesn't have to," Fiona said.

Ewan met Maggie's gaze. "I would be honored if you stayed. I want to get to know you." He shifted his gaze to Callum. "Of course, the invitation is for you and your fiancé."

Maggie glanced up at Callum.

"It's up to you," he said softly. "You'll be grand, either way."

She smiled and turned back to Ewan. "Maybe for a couple of days?"

Ewan grinned. "It's settled." To Fiona, he said, "Could you let Cook know we have two more for dinner. I had Mrs. Jones prepare the blue room for them." He turned to Maggie. "I assumed you two would want to be together."

Maggie opened her mouth.

Before she could respond, Callum said, "Thank you. We would, wouldn't we, my love?"

Maggie snapped her mouth shut and nodded.

Ewan strode out into the foyer, calling out, "Gregory, could you bring in our guests' luggage and take it to the blue room?"

Bryce reached out for Maggie's hand. "I'm glad you're staying. Do you want to see my horse?"

Maggie took the boy's hand in hers. "I would love to see your horse."

"Not now, Bryce," Fiona said. "Let her get settled."

Bryce frowned and then nodded. "Yes, mother."

"Go get washed up for dinner," his mother said.

"Yes, mother."

As the child walked by his mother, Fiona ran her hand over his curls and smiled down at her son. "You can show her your horse later," she said softly.

He glanced up at her and smiled, then hurried away to do her bidding.

The soft look Fiona had given her son vanished as she turned back to Ewan. "If you'll excuse me, I'll inform Cook of the change in dinner plans."

"Thank you," Ewan said.

After Fiona left the room, Ewan faced Maggie and Callum. "We're all still getting used to life without Lord Drummond in residence. I haven't been back here for years. I'm sure Fiona doesn't mean to be testy or rude, but she's had a lot to process with the death of her husband, the return of his prodigal son and Bryce's medical issues."

Maggie's brow puckered. "What's wrong with Bryce?"

Ewan frowned. "He's never been a really sturdy child, from what I gather. Fiona said he started feeling sickly a few months ago. The doctors can't find anything wrong with him. He gets ill at times, is often lethargic and has difficulties concentrating on his studies with the tutor."

"I'm sorry to hear that," Maggie said. "He's such a sweet little guy."

"I was surprised he wanted to show you his

horse," Ewan said. "He hasn't wanted to go outside much over the past few weeks."

"I really would like to see his horse." Maggie smiled. "I love to ride. My friend Sadie and I used to ride all over the countryside when we were teens. We still go riding when she has the time."

"I'm sure we can find a suitable horse for you," Ewan said. "Alastair, our chauffeur, also manages the stables. We have ten horses to choose from. He can arrange for you to ride one."

"That would be very nice."

Ewan turned to Callum. "Do you ride?"

Callum nodded. "I have in the past. It's been a while."

"I understand," Ewan said. "After I left for boarding school and joined the military from there, I had little time to ride. Since I've been back, I've been out every day."

"How long have you been back?" Maggie asked.

"I came for my father's funeral." His eyes narrowed. "I wanted to see for myself that the old bastard was dead."

Maggie's eyes widened. "I take it you and your father did not get along."

Ewan snorted. "That's putting it mildly. I was glad he sent me away to school. Otherwise, I would have run away and joined a gypsy camp or stowed away on a ship to America. Instead, I found my purpose, if only for a while, in the military."

"What was my—your father like?" Maggie asked.

Ewan's lips pressed into a tight line. "He could be charming with his peers and beautiful women. To his family—" He shook his head. "Let's just say he wasn't as charming, honorable or loyal."

Maggie's brow furrowed. "I'm sorry."

"For what? You didn't make him who he was. He did that all on his own. I wouldn't have come back, but his solicitor insisted I needed to be present at the reading of his will. If not for my sake, then for Fiona and Bryce." He drew in a deep breath. "You see, he left the estate to his surviving children. Fiona will be allowed to live here as long as she doesn't remarry, but she has no claim on the assets whatsoever. He had her sign a prenuptial agreement. She gets nothing if she leaves. I think, since I walked away from my father, his autocratic and abusive ways, that she believed he would leave his fortune and estate to Bryce alone. She wasn't too happy that I came back into the picture." Ewan forced a smile. "But you didn't come to hear about the dysfunction of our family."

"On the contrary," Maggie said. "I came to learn all about you and my father. Bryce is a lovely bonus. I have two brothers." Her brow furrowed. "It didn't occur to me until I was already in Scotland that I was the product of an affair between your father and my mother," she grimaced and added quietly, "while he was married to your mother."

Ewan's lips pressed together. "I'm sure she wasn't the first or the last. My mother knew he was never faithful to her. She turned a blind eye and pretended they had a stable marriage. When I asked her why she didn't divorce him, she said she didn't care if he had affairs as long as she could do as she pleased—and his affairs kept him out of her bedroom."

"But my mother was your nanny," Maggie said, her frown deepening.

"Yes, she was. One of a number of nannies I had until I left for military boarding school at the tender age of eleven. As a matter of fact, I've been going through his finances, bank accounts and employee records. When you popped up on the ancestry app, I went back through employee records and found Ayleen McKendrick."

Maggie touched a hand to her chest. "My mother."

"I vaguely remember a pretty blond-haired nanny who lived here at the house when I was around five years old. She read stories to me at night when I was afraid to go to sleep. She had the softest voice that made me feel warm and loved, something my father and mother never did."

Maggie smiled. "My mother read to me every night before I went to sleep. You're right. She had the most beautiful voice. It soothed and felt like a warm hug."

Ewan nodded. "One day she was there, then she was gone. When I asked my mother where my nanny had gone, all she said was that she'd gone away. The next nanny had brown hair and wouldn't read to me. She had a hard voice and didn't seem to care. I missed the pretty blond-haired angel."

"She was a beautiful person, inside and out," Maggie said softly. "I find it hard to picture her having an affair with a married man. She didn't even date and never married. I asked her if she'd been so in love with my father that no other man could capture her heart. She shook her head and walked away. She never would tell me about him. I assumed he was dead. It was easier for me to believe than that he'd abandoned us."

"Trust me," Ewan said. "You're better off for not knowing him. He wasn't a nice man. Your mother was right to get away from him." He squared his shoulders. "But where are my manners? I'll have Mrs. Jones show you to your room so you can freshen up for dinner."

Callum took Maggie's hand and followed Ewan out into the spacious marble foyer. Two sweeping staircases curved upward on the left and the right to the floor above.

A gray-haired woman in a black dress approached them from the hallway that led between the staircases. The dress resembled something a housekeeper from the Victorian era might wear, featuring long, narrow sleeves, a high collar, a narrow, belted waist and a skirt that draped to the floor, paired with serviceable black shoes. The woman had pulled her gray hair straight back from her forehead and secured it tightly in a bun at the nape of her neck. Her stern expression softened briefly when her gaze landed on Maggie.

"Mrs. Jones," Ewan addressed her, "this is my sister, Maggie McKendrick and her fiancé, Callum McCall. Could you please show them to the blue room? I'd do it myself, but I need to speak with Alastair about one of the horses that has developed a limp."

The woman dipped her head. "Yes, Master Ewan —" she stopped herself and corrected, "Lord Drummond."

Ewan gave Maggie a crooked smile. "You see? We're all trying to get used to all the changes since my father's passing. Mrs. Jones has been with the Drummonds since before I could remember. And old habits die hard." He turned his smile on Mrs. Jones. "Thank you, Mrs. Jones."

Mrs. Jones led the way up the curving staircase on the right, moving quickly and efficiently. When she arrived at the top, she turned right and passed through an archway, turned left and walked toward the rear of the manor, passing several doors before stopping in front of one on the right. She twisted the doorknob, pushed the door open and stood back. "Your room."

Maggie entered first, her eyes wide, her mouth forming an O. "Oh, my," she murmured. "It's lovely."

Callum followed her into a room with high ceilings, walls painted blue with gold-trimmed massive tapestries depicting women in gardens filled with flowers and small cherubic toddlers playing at their feet. A large bed dressed in a cream and blue silk comforter stood against the middle of the far wall, with towering posts at all four corners.

Mrs. Jones passed through the room to a door on the left and pushed open a door leading into a bathroom. "You have a private bath and a balcony. If you need additional towels, soaps or toiletries, let me know. I'll be up later to service the room and turn down the bed." She walked back to the center of the room. "Do you need anything now?"

Maggie shook her head. "Ewan said you've been here longer than he can remember." She paused. "Would you happen to remember a young nanny with blond hair and blue eyes. Her name was Ayleen McKendrick."

Mrs. Jones pressed her hands against her belt, her face poker straight, her lips pressed tightly together.

"It's okay if you don't," Maggie hurriedly said. "I'm her daughter and, well, I just want to know what her life was like when she lived here in Scotland."

Tears welled in Mrs. Jones' eyes, and one slid silently down her cheek. She quickly brushed it away. "I remember Ms. Ayleen well."

Maggie's face brightened. "You did? Meeting people who knew her when she was young makes me feel closer to her than I have since she passed."

Mrs. Jones pressed a hand to her mouth. "I'm so sorry. She was such a wonderful girl. Effie and I grew up together in the village down the lane. Ayleen was like my own child." Another tear slipped out of the corner of her eye. She didn't bother to brush it away. "Such a tragedy when Effie died in an automobile crash on her way back from Edinburgh. Ayleen was away at university in London."

Maggie nodded. "Mother told me she was devastated. She'd lost her father when they were living in Montana three years earlier. Without her father in the States, her mother returned to Scotland, where she'd been raised."

"Effie and Ayleen moved in with me." More tears flowed down Mrs. Jones's cheeks. "I cried when Effie died and held Ayleen through the funeral. I tried to make everything all right for her. I got her on here at Drummond Manor. For a while, we were muddling through. When she told me she was leaving to go back to Montana, I begged her to stay. She said she couldn't, that she was pregnant and had to go somewhere she could raise her baby where she felt safe. I loved Ayleen like my own. She was such a lovely young lady."

Maggie wrapped the older woman in her arms,

her own tears spilling down her cheeks. "She was the best mother. I loved her so very much."

Callum stood back, resisting the urge to either run from the room or wrap his own arms around both ladies in a group hug. All the emotion they were exhibiting and the grief they obviously felt echoed how he felt about losing his brothers in arms, emotions he hid, because that was what was expected of him. He envied the women's ability and freedom to express their feelings unguardedly.

Callum didn't run or join the hug. He stood ramrod straight, his grief firmly bottled inside with no release valve to let it out. He suspected the nightmares were the result.

After a few minutes, Maggie straightened and held Mrs. Jones at arm's length. "Thank you, Mrs. Jones, for sharing your memories with me. It makes me glad I came."

Mrs. Jones pulled a handkerchief from a pocket in her skirt and dabbed at her eyes. "I only heard you were coming today," she said. "Otherwise, I would have told you not to come."

Maggie's eyebrows rose. "Why?"

Mrs. Jones glanced past her and Callum toward the open door and lowered her voice. "There have been strange occurrences around here."

Callum frowned. "What do you mean by strange occurrences?"

"Accidents." She moved closer. "One day, a week ago, the tree swing on the old oak on the east lawn fell, branch and all, while Master Bryce was playing on it."

"Oh, no," Maggie exclaimed. "Was Bryce hurt?"

Mrs. Jones shook her head. "His little bum was sore for a day, but nothing else. Daniel Boyd, our former chauffeur and horse trainer, put that swing up when Master Ewan was his brother's age. The tree showed no signs of rot. The branch shouldn't have broken. Master Bryce doesn't weigh more than a couple of stones. Not nearly enough to break a sturdy limb. Then the railing on Master Ewan's—sorry, Lord Drummond's balcony broke free as he leaned against it one evening last week. He came close to falling but didn't. Apparently, the wrought iron was rusted through where it attached to the wall. Lord Drummond arranged to have the balcony repaired and an arborist to inspect the old oak tree. Sadly, the swing was destroyed and had to be disposed of."

"That's terrible," Maggie said. "But I'm glad no one was hurt."

Mrs. Jones nodded. "We almost lost Lady Fiona and Master Bryce when the brakes malfunctioned on her car. If they hadn't already slowed to allow another car to pass on the motorway, the crash could have been deadly. Lady Fiona was able to downshift with the gears enough to roll to a stop on the hard shoulder. Scared us all, especially Lady Fiona. She retired to her bed for two days. Master Bryce had no idea how close he came to losing his life."

Maggie's gaze met Callum's.

Mrs. Jones touched Maggie's arm. "Either the estate is cursed or someone is playing a dangerous game. You should stay somewhere else."

Callum gave her a slight nod. "Thank you, Mrs. Jones. We'll be on the lookout for trouble."

The older woman nodded, her gaze on Maggie. "I would hate to lose you, Ms. Maggie. You might not have your mother's looks, but I sense you have your mother's kindness in ya."

Maggie took the woman's hand and held it to her cheek. "Callum is prior SAS. He'll protect me."

"It's difficult to protect someone when you don't know the enemy," Mrs. Jones said.

"Don't worry. We'll manage," Maggie said.

"I pray you do, my dear. I pray you do."

Maggie hooked a hand through the crook of Callum's arm and leaned into him. "It's nice to meet you."

Mrs. Jones left them in the middle of the bedroom and closed the door behind her.

Maggie immediately faced Callum. "Is it too much of a coincidence that these three incidents happened so close to the attacks at the train station and Angus's flat?"

Callum's lips thinned into a tight line. "I don't believe in coincidence. Someone has it in for the Drummonds, and that appears to include you."

CHAPTER 8

MAGGIE'S GUT KNOTTED. "So far, Fiona, Bryce and I have all been attacked." Her eyes narrowed. "The only person in the Drummond family who hasn't been targeted, that we know of, is Ewan. Do you think he's behind the attacks?"

Callum gave a slight shrug. "He stands to gain the most. If all of Lord Drummond's children are knocked out of the running, he'll inherit everything."

"I can't imagine Ewan doing that. He seemed so nice and welcoming." Her heart sank. "Could he have brought me all the way here, just to cut me off physically?"

"Maybe. If he cared at all, why didn't he warn us about the incidents?" Callum asked.

Maggie lifted a shoulder and let it fall. "Because he didn't want to scare us away? I don't know."

"If he has placed a target on your back, he made it

easier to aim by asking you to stay." Callum reached out and cupped her cheek. "He has better access to you on his own territory, which he knows better than anyone."

"Though I don't like the idea of being on guard at all times, we need to be here and flush out the one responsible for the accidents and attacks." Maggie shoved a hand through her hair. "The thought of someone trying to kill that little boy makes me sick to my stomach. We can't abandon him." Her face softened. "He's a cute kid. I also hate that he's been sick. Makes me want to wrap him in my arms and take him back to Montana, where he'd be safe and the doctors there might figure out what's wrong with him."

"I don't think Fiona will let you do that," Callum said.

Maggie nodded. "She did appear to care about her son. I'll give her that, as long as it wasn't all for show."

"She was in the car when the brakes went out. I don't think she would've sabotaged it herself. And I don't think she would climb a tree to damage the branch to make it fall."

A frown pushed Maggie's brow downward. "I'm glad we came. Now that I've found my brothers, I'd like them to be around for a while."

"As long as the older one isn't behind the problems," Callum amended.

"Right." She squared her shoulders and brought

her fists up like a prize fighter. "I'm in for the fight. How do we flush out the person responsible?"

"I'd rather take you back to Edinburgh or on to Glasgow, where I might have a better chance of keeping you safe."

She shook her head.

Before she could say anything, he held up his hand. "But I know you won't go for that. I guess we'll be accepting Lord Drummond's hospitality."

"Good. Then we'd better get dressed for dinner. In a place like this, I imagine they're a little more formal than jeans and T-shirts. Afterward, I want to look around and talk to the others who live and work here. Mrs. Jones might just be the tip of the iceberg of information about the people who've come and gone from Drummond Manor. There might be others who know more of the Drummond secrets and are willing to spill."

Callum's lips curved in a deliciously sexy smile, making Maggie's heartbeat flutter. "Look at you being the sleuth."

"Damn right." She lifted her chin. "I don't take being attacked twice lightly."

"Whoever is behind all this has figured out you won't be easily acquired. They only sent one guy on the first attempt."

"And four on the second." Maggie shivered. "Think they'll send an army when they try again?"

Callum frowned. "I might need to get Ace to send

backup. Or at least position someone closer than London."

Maggie nodded. "Might be a good idea."

"You can have the bathroom," Callum said. "I'll change out here."

Hefting her backpack onto her shoulder, Maggie wheeled her roller bag into the spa-like bathroom with shiny white porcelain floors, a soaker tub large enough for two people and a shower that could easily fit a basketball team. As she stripped out of her jeans, her gaze went back to the tub.

Her pulse quickened at the thought of that tub—and sharing it with Callum. What a shame it would be to let such a beautiful tub go unused. And what a missed opportunity if she didn't share it with the man she found incredibly attractive. She'd never seduced a man before. Heck, she'd never been in a bathtub with a man. At that moment, she seriously considered asking him to join her.

Of course, it would have to be after dinner.

Her breathing grew ragged. Though she didn't have a sexy nighty to parade around in to catch his eye, she did have a pair of racy black panties and her black lace bra. Or she could just be naked in the tub and ask him to bring her a towel.

Holy smokes! What was she thinking?

She shook out the only dress she'd brought on the off chance she went to a fancy restaurant. Sadie had loaned it to her. She'd worn it in one of her movies.

Maggie would never have purchased something as expensive and seductive. But when she'd tried it on in Sadie's bedroom, she'd fallen in love with the emerald-green fabric that clung to her body like a second skin, accentuating the swell of her hips and breasts. It brought out the green in her eyes, making them sparkle.

She hung the dress on a hook on the wall and pulled out her toiletries bag. She rarely wore a lot of makeup, but the dress needed at least a little drama on the eyes and a statement lipstick. Sadie had shown her how to emphasize the green in her eyes and how to apply eyeliner for maximum effect. Maggie had spent a little time practicing before leaving for Scotland, just in case she had the opportunity to attend a play in London or Edinburgh.

Once she was satisfied with her makeup, she pulled her hair up and secured it in a loose bun, allowing a few curls to escape and frame her cheeks. She added pearl drop earrings and a matching necklace, completing her preparation for the last stage of her transformation...Sadie's incredible dress. She lifted it off the hook and stepped into the garment, sliding it over her hips. The material caressed her skin, cool and delicious. She slipped her arms into the thin straps and pulled them up over her shoulders. When she'd tried on the dress back in Montana, Sadie had been there to help her with the zipper.

Maggie reached behind her back and pulled the

zipper up as far as she could, stopping about four inches short of finishing the job. The bodice dipped low in front, making it impossible to wear her bra with it. She didn't really need a bra, but she did need help getting the zipper all the way up.

Holding the bodice against her chest, she hurried to the bathroom door and swung it open.

Her breath caught in her throat.

Callum wore black trousers and a black long-sleeve shirt, open at the collar. He'd combed back his dark hair, but a lock swept down over his forehead, giving him a dangerously sexy look.

His gaze swept her length from the top of her bun to the hem of her dress, his eyes flaring. "Brilliant," he said. "You're absolutely stunning."

Heat warmed Maggie's cheeks. "Thank you. You're not so bad yourself."

He dipped his head in acknowledgement.

"I'm almost ready," Maggie said. "But I could use some help with the zipper." She turned her back to him.

For a long moment, he didn't move.

Maggie was about to turn back around when footsteps sounded behind her and fingers brushed against her skin.

A spark of electricity raced across her nerves, sending delicious shivers down the length of her spine.

He moved the zipper up, excruciatingly slowly, his knuckles skimming her back all the way.

Her breath lodged in her throat, and her pulse quickened.

He could just as easily slide that zipper down if she asked him.

If he wanted to.

The truth was that she didn't know what he wanted or if he was interested in anything other than providing her protection.

When the zipper reached the top, he released the tab.

Maggie almost cried out in disappointment that it was over.

Then hands closed around her bare arms, and warm breath caressed the side of her neck where it blended into her shoulders. Lips brushed across her skin there.

She trembled, her knees turned to jelly, and she sank backward into Callum.

"I can't resist," he murmured, his words tickling her skin.

And she couldn't fight her overwhelming desire for him.

"As beautiful as that dress is on you..." he whispered, "I want to take it off."

She turned in his arms and stared up at him. "Would they come looking for us if we don't show up for their dinner?"

His gaze bore into hers. "Do you care?"

Maggie shook her head.

Callum touched a finger beneath her chin, tipped her face upward and at the same time lowered his mouth to hers.

He claimed her lips with his, at first gently, caressing, worshipping.

Maggie's hands climbed up his chest and wrapped around the back of his neck, dragging him closer. When his tongue traced the seam of her lips, she opened to him.

The kiss deepened. His hand slid around her and cupped her buttocks, pressing her hips to his.

When the evidence of his desire pressed into her belly, Maggie's breath caught in her throat, and her pulse raced so fast, it made her dizzy.

The kiss went on. All thoughts of half-brothers, attacks or trains disappeared behind a haze of lust.

A knock sounded on the door, and a woman's voice called out, "Ms. McKendrick?"

Maggie fell back to earth. She reluctantly stepped back, pressing a hand to her flaming cheeks.

Callum stared into her eyes. "I should say I'm sorry. I shouldn't have done that."

"Please don't," Maggie said. "I wanted it."

For a long moment, he met and held her gaze.

Another knock sounded on the door, "Ms. McKendrick, I've come to show you to the dining room."

Maggie recognized the voice. "That's Mrs. Jones."

"I'll get it." Callum headed toward the door.

Pressing her hands against her heated cheeks, Maggie spun away from Callum and sucked air into her lungs.

That kiss.

Holy smokes! Callum was right. They shouldn't have done it.

Now all she could think about was doing it again.

And again.

The door creaked open behind Maggie.

"I came to escort you to the dining room," Mrs. Jones said. "If you're ready, you can follow me."

Maggie smoothed her hands over the dress and squared her shoulders. She pasted a smile on her face as she turned toward the older woman. "Thank you, Mrs. Jones. We're ready." She crossed the floor, hooked her hand through the crook of Callum's arm and followed Mrs. Jones out of the room.

The housekeeper led the way down the stairs and into the hallway between the twin staircases, which led to the rear of the house. They passed through a room with a massive display of spears, bayonets and old wooden rifles arranged in artistic sunbursts across the walls. At the other end of the room, a corridor led into a dining room with a table long enough to seat twenty guests. Five settings had been laid out at one end, with a frightening number of forks. Maggie had no clue how to use most of them.

A massive chandelier, dripping with hundreds of crystals, hung over the table, casting light over the porcelain plates and glinting off the shiny silverware. The room was beautiful, stately and way out of Maggie's economic sphere.

Mrs. Jones left Callum and Maggie in the dining room as Ewan and Fiona entered the room behind them.

"Excellent," Ewan said. "Just in time to take our seats. Cook has a traditional Scottish dinner prepared for tonight of haggis, neeps and tatties."

Maggie tilted her head. "I've heard of haggis but not neeps and tatties."

"Haggis is a combination of meat, oatmeal, onion and spices." Fiona entered the dining room and stood to the right of the head of the table. "Neeps are smashed turnips, and tatties are mashed potatoes."

"Will Bryce be joining us?" Maggie asked.

Fiona shook her head. "When he isn't feeling well, he takes his evening meals in his room."

Maggie felt bad for the little guy and wished she could help him get well soon. She'd always had her meals with her mother, not confined to her room. She could imagine how lonely he was. She'd find his bedroom after dinner and check in on him.

Mrs. Jones served the dishes, placing steaming plates in front of each person.

The butler went from person to person pouring wine.

Once they were all served, Ewan lifted his fork in his left hand and cocked an eyebrow as if to say, *You may begin*. "Please, enjoy."

Maggie gathered her fork and knife, holding them in the same manner as Ewan, sliced off a sample of haggis and took a tentative bite. She'd heard that those who tasted haggis either loved it or hated it. She popped the morsel into her mouth and chewed, savoring the spices. It was like nothing she'd ever tasted.

"What do you think?" Ewan asked.

She nodded. "I like it."

Her half-brother laughed. "Good on you. Most tourists dislike our traditional meal."

Maggie dipped her fork in the turnips and tried them as well. They didn't have much flavor, but she ate them anyway. The tatties, or potatoes, were light and fluffy.

She glanced toward Callum, who'd quickly eaten everything on his plate. With a grin, she asked, "Taste like home?"

He nodded. "Some of the best I've had. I must thank the cook."

Maggie took a couple more bites, chewed and swallowed. "I understand there have been some disconcerting incidents here at the manor."

Ewan's lips twisted. "I suppose you heard about the brakes and the tree swing."

"We did," Maggie said. "I'm happy no one was

badly injured."

Fiona shivered. "I'm not sure I'll be driving again anytime soon. I was lucky I was able to stop when I did." She held up a hand. "I'll leave the driving to Alastair."

Maggie glanced from Fiona to Ewan. "Alastair?"

"Our chauffeur and stable master," Ewan said. "His family has been with the Drummonds as far back as the eighteen hundreds. Alastair took over after his father passed away. We don't have as many horses as they did before motor cars were invented, so the chauffeur's duties fell on the stablemaster. Alastair has Johnny, the groom, who helps clean stalls and exercise the horses. But if you need a driver, Alastair is our chauffeur."

"Thank you, but we rented a car," Callum said. "I prefer to drive myself."

Ewan nodded. "I feel the same. I prefer to have control of the vehicle."

A loud noise echoed through the hallways, coming from near the front of the mansion. Shouts followed, moving closer.

Ewan and Fiona exchanged a glance before he pushed back his chair and stood. "Please, excuse me."

He hadn't made it out of the dining room before a stout man with a barrel chest and heavy dark brows entered the dining room.

The butler hurried in behind the man, trying to grab his arm.

"Touch me again, and I'll knock your lights out," the belligerent man said.

Ewan waved a hand. "It's okay, Gregory. I'll take care of him."

"Damn right, he will. My cousin doesn't throw family out like the trash, do ya?"

Gregory, the butler, backed away, a frown settling across his brow. He didn't leave the room but stood his ground, ready to interfere if the newcomer got out of hand.

"Rory," Ewan waved a hand toward the table. "We're in the middle of dinner. Would you care to join us?"

Rory's gaze swept across the plates of half-eaten food, and he wrinkled his nose. "You're having haggis? Why? You have enough money now that you don't have to eat that rubbish."

Ewan gave his cousin a half-smile. "We happen to like it. You're welcome to join us. I'm sure Cook can provide an alternative you'll like better."

"I don't need your food," Rory said. "I came to talk with you, the new Lord Drummond, about that business opportunity I mentioned a few days ago."

Ewan cocked an eyebrow. "As you can see, we're at dinner. If you want to talk about business, you'll have to wait until we've finished. Better yet, you can schedule an appointment with me during the day."

Rory's frown deepened into a scowl. "I need an answer now."

Ewan's chin rose, and his eyes narrowed. "I told you that I had to think about it. I want to have our solicitor look into the details and run a background check on the other people involved. That takes time. Now, if you aren't joining us for dinner, I'll have to ask you to leave."

"If I say the business is legit, it's legit. You don't need to waste money you could be investing in it on a bloody solicitor or anything else. I'm family. You should trust me."

Ewan cast a glance at the people seated at the table. "Please excuse me while I take care of this." He advanced on Rory, hooked his arm and started to usher him out of the dining room. "Let's take this matter to my office."

MAGGIE FELT BAD FOR EWAN. This man, Rory, cousin or not, had been rude in front of Ewan's guests. Ewan was trying to handle it without upsetting the people at the table.

Callum tensed beside her. Maggie had no doubt he was ready to back Ewan if the intruder got more violent.

Rory jerked his arm free. "We'll talk here. You have the money now that you're the high-and-mighty Lord Drummond. You might not need it, but I do. You can afford to help a cousin out."

"I'm not in the habit of throwing away money on a blind investment," Ewan said.

"I should've known you wouldn't help any more than your father. You're a stingy old bastard, just like him. The only way anyone got money out of your old man was to sleep with him."

"Let's take this discussion into another room." Ewan reached for Rory's arm again.

Rory swatted Ewan's arm and stalked toward Maggie.

Her heart in her throat, Maggie got halfway out of her chair, ready to stand her ground or move in the opposite direction.

Suddenly, Callum stood, blocking Rory's path to Maggie.

CHAPTER 9

RORY GLARED AT CALLUM. "Now that Lord Drummond is dead, all his bastard children are coming out of the woodwork for a piece of his estate." He tipped his chin toward Maggie. "She's a case in point." He turned toward his cousin. "You've known me all my life. How long have you known that bitch? An hour. Maybe two. She could've lied about her lineage. How do you know she wasn't lying about having the same father as you?"

"DNA doesn't lie," Callum said. "Call her a bitch again, and you and I will have a problem."

Ewan nodded. "She's my sister, and this discussion is over."

"The hell it is. You'd give an equal share of your father's fortune to her, a product of your father's affairs? He cheated on your mother! You're a fool. And all I ask is enough to invest in a legitimate business. She'll take the money back with her to wherever the hell she's from. What happens if more illegitimate spawn show up with their hands out? Will you squander your entire fortune on all of them? Because, believe me, your father was a randy bastard who cheated on your mother every chance he got. She was a fool to stay with him. His second wife is equally foolish. What did he leave her? Not a damn thing. She might as well have been his whore instead of his wife."

Ewan punched his cousin in the face.

Rory staggered backward, blood dripping from his nose.

"Shut up, Rory." Ewan advanced on him, poking a finger into his chest. "You do not talk that way about my family. My father might have been a bastard, but he didn't give money to relatives with gambling addictions."

Rory pinched his bleeding nose. "You don't know what you're talking about." His gaze went past Ewan to Callum, who edged closer. "I'm not addicted to gambling. I quit."

"Not soon enough, was it?" Ewan planted a hand on Rory's chest. "Who loaned you money so you could play?"

"Who said someone loaned me money?"

Ewan snorted. "And they want it back with interest, don't they?" He shoved his cousin again. "How much, Rory?"

Rory raised his fists.

Callum stepped up beside Ewan.

"How much?" Ewan repeated.

Rory's gaze shifted from Ewan to Callum and back. "None of your bloody business."

"You made it my business when you walked into my home demanding money." Ewan crossed his arms over his chest.

"Just twenty-five thousand euros." Rory sneered. "A pittance compared to what you inherited."

"The problem with paying off your debt is that you'll just do it again. You went through your mother's entire inheritance in less than two years."

"The casinos cheated me out of my money."

Ewan shook his head. "Yet you kept going back until you lost every last cent."

"I did not."

"I've been in contact with your brother, Robert. I know everything. I wouldn't invest in any business with you. And I won't pay your debt. Your mother let you live with her to help her in her old age, and how did you repay her? Your brother put your mother in assisted living after you sold her house out from under her."

"She didn't need a house that big," Rory said. "I did her a favor by selling it."

"And yet she didn't see a cent from that sale. You spent it all in a casino. You have a lot of gall coming to me asking for money. You make me sick. Get out of my house."

Rory stood straight, his chest puffed out. "You don't know what I was up against then and now. These people played rough. They threatened to kill me."

"Did you ever consider your mother would've been better off if they'd gone through with their threat?" Ewan lifted his chin and stared down his nose at his cousin. "Get off my property and don't bother to come back. And you can tell your people they won't be getting any Drummond money. You'll have to find another way to pay your debt."

"You have to help me," Rory said. "We're family."

"You aren't part of my family." Ewan nodded toward his butler. "Gregory."

Immediately, Gregory stepped forward and grabbed Rory's arms from behind.

Rory exploded in fury, jerked free of the butler's hold, spun and landed a punch to Gregory's midsection.

Callum dove for Rory, knocked him down and pinned him to the ground.

Maggie leaped from her chair, grabbed a candlestick holder from the table and ran toward the two men. Callum had Rory under control, but she stood over them, ready to use the candlestick holder if Rory managed to get loose.

Callum's chest swelled at her fierce stance. The woman was tough and not afraid to join the fight.

"Let go of me!" Rory shouted. "You don't know who you're dealing with. If they don't get what they want, they go after anyone else in the family. They'll come for you, Ewan. And Bryce. Even the girl. They knew she was coming. They knew she stood to inherit a portion of the estate. They know everything."

"Because you told them." Ewan tipped his chin toward Callum. "Let him up."

Callum held Rory down for a moment longer. "Try to hurt anyone, and I won't go that easy on you next time." He got to his feet and reached for Rory's arm. Ewan grabbed his other arm. Between the two men, they hauled Rory to his feet.

Maggie stepped back, giving the men room.

When Callum released his hold, Ewan spun his cousin around. "Never hit one of my people, ever again."

Rory's shoulders sagged, and he shook his head. "They'll kill me."

"That's your problem," Ewan said.

"Yeah, but now it's yours as well," Rory said.

"Then you better start talking," Ewan said.

"Who are these people?" Maggie asked.

"I don't know." Rory pushed a hand through his hair. "When I ran out of money at the casino in Edinburgh, a man loaned me more and said that when I made it back, I could make good on my loan. I was playing craps and was winning...until I wasn't. I lost everything and the money the man had loaned me. I didn't see the man who'd loaned me the money as I left the casino, but I had a personal visit from some of his collectors. They came to my flat and threatened to remove parts of my body if I didn't pay my debt. When I said I had no way of coming up with that much money immediately, they told me to get it from my family." Rory met Ewan's gaze. "They specifically mentioned you. They knew your father had recently passed and that you had inherited his estate."

"They expect me to pay your debt?" Ewan snorted. "Bloody hell."

"Did you notify the police?" Maggie asked.

"They said it would do me no good to go to the police," Rory said. "They have members of their organization embedded with the police."

"You don't have the name of the organization?" Callum asked.

"No," Rory said. "Although the man who loaned me the money had a slight Russian accent, and their collectors spoke to each other in what sounded like Russian."

"Brilliant," Ewan said. "You have our family at the mercy of the Russian mob?"

"I think so." Rory shook his head. "The only way to get them to leave all of us alone is to pay them."

Ewan shook his head. "And what happens when you take money from gangsters again to gamble it away. You've placed our family at risk through your actions. I don't trust that you won't do it again. For now, you have to leave."

"But I need that money, or they'll kill me and come after you."

"Then you had better leave the country and get as far away as you can," Ewan said. "I don't want you anywhere near me or my family."

"But—" Rory started.

"Enough," Ewan said. "You're not staying here."

"What about the money?"

"You're not getting any from me or anyone else in this family." Ewan turned the man toward the door. "Leave on your own, or I'll throw you out myself."

Rory squared his shoulders. "I'm leaving. But mark my words, even if they kill me, none of you will be safe until they have their money."

"We'll handle it," Ewan said. "And before you go, apologize to Fiona and Gregory."

Rory drew in a breath and said, "Fiona, please, accept my apologies."

Fiona nodded. "Apology accepted."

Rory turned to Gregory.

Gregory stood as straight as he had when he'd welcomed Maggie to Drummond Manor, his face a solid mask.

"Gregory, I'm sorry I hit you."

The butler gave Rory a hint of a nod, turned on his heel and led the man out of the dining room to the front entrance.

Ewan's gaze followed them. When he turned to Callum, he held out his hand. "Thank you."

Callum gripped Ewan's. "Sounds like you have a bigger problem than an unwanted guest."

Ewan nodded, his gaze going to Maggie. "I wonder if the man at the train station and the four intruders in Edinburgh were part of the collection committee Rory spoke of."

Callum's lips pressed into a line. "If so, they could come looking for any one of your family."

"Should you have sent Rory away?" Maggie asked.

Ewan's brow descended. "He should never have taken money from a stranger and then gambled it away. He put my family in danger. The bastard can rot in hell for all I care."

Callum's gaze shifted to Maggie and the candlestick holder she held like a weapon. His lips curved into a smile. "Glad to see you had my back."

Her cheeks flushed a pretty pink. "I couldn't stand by and do nothing." She set the candlestick holder on the dining table and returned to Callum's side.

He slipped his arm around her and pulled her close. "Tough as well as beautiful." He brushed his lips across hers in a brief kiss, then straightened and addressed Ewan. "What do you have in the way of security on the estate?"

Ewan shook his head. "If Rory is to be believed, not enough. My father had cameras installed at the gate and the entrances of the manor, but that might not be enough to stop an army of Russian mobsters."

"I have a friend who might have connections to look into this mobster organization and find out what exactly you're up against," Callum said.

"Any help would be appreciated," Ewan said. "In the meantime, we need to stay close to the manor." He turned to Fiona. "That means keeping Bryce inside unless accompanied by me, Gregory or..." He turned to Callum.

Callum nodded. "You can count on me."

"And Alastair, our chauffeur," Fiona said. "He takes Bryce to the stables to ride his horse."

"And Alastair," Ewan said with a nod.

"I'll contact my friend and see what he can do to help," Callum said.

"Good." Ewan glanced toward the table. "Shall we finish our meal?"

Maggie shook her head. "If it's all the same to you, I've had enough, and I'm tired and want to sleep."

"I understand," Ewan said. "Please, treat the manor as your home. In fact, it's as much your home as mine."

"Ewan, I didn't come all the way to Scotland to take your inheritance," Maggie insisted. "I'm more interested in getting to know you and now Bryce. I never had siblings growing up. I can't tell you how thrilled I am to know I'm not alone."

Ewan gave her a soft smile. "You won't be alone as long as we're here."

Maggie's brow twisted. "Let's hope we all live long enough to get to know each other."

"I'll do my best to ensure the safety of my family and the employees of the estate," Ewan said.

"As will I," Callum promised.

"Thank you," Ewan glanced around the room. "If we're all finished, I'll call it a night. I want to go through more of my father's accounts."

"Let me know if we can help in any way," Callum said. "Otherwise, we'll retire for the night."

"I'll let you know." Ewan offered his arm to Fiona. "Would you like to join me for a glass of port in the sitting room before you retire for the night?"

Fiona shook her head, her face pale and pinched. "I want to check on Bryce and turn in. I've had enough excitement for the night."

"Fiona, do you mind if I go with you to check on Bryce?" Maggie asked softly. "He's such a sweet little boy."

Fiona's brow dipped. For a long moment, she didn't respond.

"If you don't want me to, I'll understand," Maggie said.

Finally, the older woman's frown faded. "I guess it will be okay as long as you don't disturb his sleep."

"I won't," Maggie said.

Ewan and Fiona led the way out of the dining room and up the staircase to the second floor. They turned in the opposite direction from Maggie and Callum's room and walked down a long hallway, stopping at a door on the right.

Fiona turned the knob and peeked inside. "Bryce, my darling boy, why are you still awake?"

"I couldn't sleep," a small voice sounded from inside the room.

"Some people want to say goodnight to you." Fiona held the door open for Maggie, Callum and Ewan to enter.

The boy scooted up in his bed, leaning against a stack of fluffy pillows behind him. He grinned when his gaze landed on the small group of adults entering his room. "Did you come to read me a story?"

Fiona shook her head. "Not tonight. They aren't staying long. You should already be asleep."

The boy's pale face sank.

"I'd be happy to read to you tomorrow," Maggie said. "I love reading books. Do you?"

Bryce's face brightened. "I do so love books. And I'm learning to read all by myself."

Maggie crossed the room to the boy and ruffled his hair. "Then we'll read together. Good night, little man."

He frowned up at her. "Aren't you going to kiss me goodnight?"

Maggie chuckled.

The sound made Callum's heart skip several beats.

"I'd love to kiss you goodnight, if it's all right with your mother." Maggie glanced over her shoulder at Fiona.

Fiona gave a slight nod.

Maggie bent over the boy and pressed her lips to Bryce's forehead. "Goodnight, sweet prince."

Callum's heart pinched hard in his chest. This woman was so kind and caring toward a child she barely knew but wanted to so badly. She'd come all this way with a heart full of hope for finding family.

"I'm not a prince," Bryce corrected. "I'm just a lord."

Callum chuckled as he joined Maggie beside Bryce's bed. "Goodnight, Lord Bryce." He ruffled the child's hair. "We hope you'll show us your pony tomorrow."

The boy's eyes brightened. "He's not a pony. He's a real horse. His name is Montana."

Maggie's gaze met Callum's.

"Did you name your horse?" Callum asked.

Bryce shook his head. "No. It was his name when my father gave him to me for my birthday."

Though Maggie smiled at the boy, her jaw appeared tight, the smile not quite reaching her eyes. "Sweet dreams, Bryce. We'll visit Montana tomorrow."

The adults backed out of the room. Fiona was last out after dropping a kiss on her son's brow.

"I'll bid you goodnight," Fiona said and left them.

"I have some work to do in my office," Ewan said. "If you need anything, I'll be awake for at least another hour."

"I don't need anything but a good night's sleep," Maggie said. "Thank you for inviting us to stay."

"It's my pleasure," Ewan said. "Although I wasn't responsible for my father's transgressions, and I can't make up for what he did, I'm happy to meet the result of one." He grinned. "Bryce and I have a sister. That's all that matters. Have a good night."

Ewan went one direction, Callum and Maggie the opposite.

As they neared the door to their room, Maggie slowed.

Callum paused with his hand on the doorknob. "If you're worried about sharing a room with me," Callum whispered, "I can sleep on the floor."

"No. No," she said, her voice tight, her hands smoothing over her dress nervously. "I'm not worried." She gave him a smile he could swear was forced.

Callum opened the door and waved her through it.

Maggie entered, slipped out of her shoes and walked across to the French doors that opened onto the balcony. She opened the doors and stepped out.

"I'm going to call my people and let them know what's going on," he said and turned away from the sight of Maggie bathed in starlight.

As the cool night air wafted into the room, Callum placed the call to Ace, his immediate supervisor, and filled him in on the altercation with Rory and the subsequent news that the threat to Rory included all of Rory's family.

"I'll have Dmytro look into what organized mobs might be in that area. In the meantime, I'll send Atkins your way. He could be there as early as tomorrow morning. Sounds like you could be in deep trouble if they don't get what they want out of Ewan's cousin Rory."

"That's what I'm afraid of." Callum ran a hand through his hair. "I think the attacks on Maggie could have been an attempt to kidnap her and use her for ransom. When they sent the one on the train, I don't think they expected any resistance."

"But you were there, thank goodness."

Callum nodded, though Ace couldn't see his head bob. "On the second attack, they sent four men."

"Right. They meant business," Ace said. "Thankfully, they didn't find you two."

"We're all on alert for any breaches to the security here, not that there's much, other than a few cameras."

"We'll get people in place as soon as possible."

"Thank you," Callum said.

"Out here."

Callum ended the call and turned back to Maggie, admiring the view of her silhouetted in the moonlight, the emerald-green dress molded to her body like a second skin. Her hair piled high on her head, left her long, graceful neck exposed. Callum closed the distance, stopping at the threshold. Close enough he could smell her scent. Close enough that if he reached out, he could pull her into his arms.

"Do you think my father did it on purpose?" she asked softly.

Instinctively, he knew what she was talking about. "Aye," Callum said. "What other reason would he think to name a horse Montana?"

"He knew where my mother settled. He had to have known of my existence," she said.

And he never bothered to contact her or get to know her.

Maggie didn't have to say the words for Callum to know what she was thinking. "Ewan said your father wasn't a nice man. Your mother might've known that and didn't want you to have any contact with him. You were better off without him."

Maggie nodded. "I had such a close relationship with my mother, I find it hard to think someone wouldn't want to know their own child." She glanced over her shoulder. "Yet, he named a horse after the place his unwanted child lived."

Callum gave in to his need, curled his fingers

around her arms and gently pulled her back against him.

When she didn't resist, he wrapped his arms around her waist and bent to kiss the soft skin at the juncture of her neck and shoulder.

Maggie tilted her head to the side, allowing him even better access to kiss her and moaned softly.

"Tell me to stop and I will," he murmured into her neck. He gave her the option but prayed she wouldn't take it.

CHAPTER 10

"DON'T STOP," Maggie said. "That feels nice."

Callum's pulse quickened, shooting red-hot blood and adrenaline through his body. He trailed kisses up the length of her neck to her earlobe. "You smell like wild flowers." Turning her in his arms, he transferred his lips to hers in a soul-searing kiss that left him wanting so much more.

She whispered against his mouth, "Is it wrong to want more?"

Her words echoed his thoughts, threatening to send him over the edge of reason. Callum captured her cheeks in his hands. "Nothing's wrong with the way you feel. I feel it, too." He stared down into her eyes as they reflected the starlight.

She sighed. "We've known each other for such a short time."

"And lived through a lot in that timeframe."

"We have." Her hands climbed up his chest to cup the back of his neck. "And yet, that's not what's on my mind."

His lips twitched at the corners. "No?"

Her eyelids lowered halfway, her gaze lowering to his lips. "No."

His heartbeat thundered against his chest as he fought for control, not wanting to frighten her when he felt they were on the precipice of something wonderful. "What's on your mind, my bonnie lass?"

"I haven't stopped thinking about the tub in the bathroom."

He laughed out loud. "A bathtub?"

"It's selfish and maybe silly, but I can't stop wondering if it really is big enough for two." She raised her gaze to his.

"Oh, sweet Maggie, there's only one way to find out." Callum bent, swept her up in his arms and marched through the French doors and across the bedroom. He didn't stop until he was in the bathroom, standing in front of the tub in question. Slowly lowering her feet to the floor, he gathered her close and brushed a strand of copper curls back from her forehead. He kissed her mouth, her cheek and her neck just below her earlobe. "Do you know how beautiful you are in that dress?"

"You might have said something to that effect," she said, her voice breathy, as if she couldn't quite get enough air. "You also said you want to take it off me."

Maggie turned her back to him. "Could you help me with the zipper?"

Callum swallowed a groan, his engorged cock straining against the confines of his trousers. If he weren't careful, he wouldn't last two seconds with Maggie. And he wanted to last all night. He gripped the tab and eased the zipper downward, past her ribs and waist to the swell of her derriere. The fact that he could see the crease between her butt cheeks almost made him lose his tenuous hold on his control. "Bloody hell," he whispered. "You're not wearing panties?"

She shrugged. "The dress clings so close to my body, they would have presented a panty line had I worn them. Does that bother you?"

"In so many ways," he murmured as he slid one thin strap from her shoulder. When he reached for the other strap, he pressed kisses in front of the strap as he edged it off her shoulder.

The dress slid to the ground, revealing her completely naked body.

His breath lodged in his chest as his hands slid over her shoulders and down her arms to her hips.

As Maggie raised her arms to loosen the tie holding her hair in the bun on top of her head, Callum slid his hands up her torso to cup her breasts.

Silken curls fell around her shoulders. Maggie leaned back into him, her arms circling behind her to grab his buttocks and press him closer.

His hard cock nudged her bottom, eager to be sheathed inside her, but he wanted to please her first. He reached around her and turned on the faucet, adjusted the temperature and set the plug.

She turned to face him, her cheeks pink, her arms wrapped around her middle. "Just so you know, first: I'm on the pill. Second, we're two individuals from different continents. When my vacation is over, I'll be heading back to Montana. You'll be here in Scotland. I have no expectations of a lasting relationship. I won't wait by the phone for you to call. Whatever happens tonight doesn't mean anything more than two people having sex—"

Callum pulled her into his arms and kissed her hard. His tongue pushed past her teeth and caressed hers in the pulsing, thrusting rhythm he hoped to repeat in other ways and forms. When he came up for air, he brushed his lips across hers. "I won't ask you for commitment. I can't. I come with baggage I won't inflict on you. You deserve better. But I want to make love to you. Not sex. If that's not what you want, tell me now."

She stared up into his eyes, her hands rising to his chest, her fingers going to the button on his shirt. She pushed it through the hole as she said, "I want you..." her fingers moved to the next button and freed it, "... to make love..." she freed another button and looked up into his eyes, "... to me." Maggie's hands went to his belt and slipped it from the buckle.

His pulse racing, his body on the verge of exploding with desire, Callum shoved her hands aside. He unbuttoned, unzipped and shed his shoes and trousers while she pushed his shirt over his shoulders.

Once he stood naked in front of her, he lifted her and sat her on the counter, parted her legs and stepped between them.

She rested her hands on his shoulders and pressed a kiss to his forehead, his cheeks and then his lips. Her hands slid down his arms and back up again.

Callum leaned forward and kissed his way down her neck, across her collarbone and lower to capture one breast between his lips while he fondled the other with his fingers.

Aware that the water was filling the tub, he flicked her nipple with his tongue and rolled it between his teeth until it formed a turgid peak. Though he didn't want to stop, he spun, turned off the water and came back to her other breast. Without missing a beat, he laved it, sucked it into his mouth and pulled gently.

Her back arched, pressing her breast closer. He took it deeper into his mouth, his hand sliding down her belly to the juncture of her thighs, where he pushed a finger into her moist channel.

She drew in a sharp breath and threw back her head. "Yes. Please," she whispered.

After swirling around in her juices, he spread her

folds and stroked her clit. At the same time, he flicked her nipple.

Maggie clutched the back of his head, her fingers weaving into his hair.

He flicked her nipple again before abandoning her breasts and kissing a path downward.

Her hands still in his hair, she massaged his scalp in a frenetic rhythm.

Callum got down on his knees, draped her thighs over his shoulders and replaced his finger with his tongue. He stroked, flicked and laved her clit.

Her fingers dug into his scalp, and she cried out his name, "Callum!" Her hips rocked on the counter, her body tensing until she flung back her head and rode her orgasm through to the end and collapsed against him, breathing hard. "Wow. That was..." She shook her head and drew him to his feet.

He lifted her off the counter.

She wrapped her legs around his waist and lowered herself over him. With the tip of his erection pressing against her entrance, he paused, though it took a lot for him to do it. "I have a condom in my wallet."

"As I said, I'm on the pill," she said, her brow furrowing. "But yes, let's get it."

He carried her into the bedroom where he'd left his wallet on the dresser.

"What about the bathtub?" Maggie asked.

"Later," Callum gritted out.

Maggie grabbed the wallet, found the condom and dropped the wallet back on the dresser.

Callum took her to the bed and lay her across the mattress. She was so beautiful, his heart pinched hard in his chest. He shouldn't make love to her, knowing once wouldn't be enough. But he couldn't commit to her. Couldn't sleep the night with her. Not when he hadn't conquered his demons. Not until the nightmares went away.

As she stared up at him, her brow furrowed. "You're thinking too hard about this. Don't. Just feel."

AFRAID HE'D CHANGE his mind and draw away, Maggie sat up, wrapped her arms around his neck and drew him down to her. Her body still pulsing with her release, she wanted the magic to continue, to feel all of him. Inside her. Now.

When he dropped onto the bed beside her, she turned to him and pressed her lips to his, tracing the seam of his lips with her tongue until he opened to her. She thrust past his teeth and caressed his tongue with hers, pressing her body against his.

Eager to take it to the next step, she abandoned his mouth, pushed him onto his back and kissed a path along his stubbled jaw to his neck and downward, tasting him, nipping his skin and touching as much of his body as she could.

His hands captured her naked ass, his fingers

gently massaging there before sliding over her hips and waist.

She climbed on top of him, her breasts pressing into him, the nipples tight little buds, overly sensitized to the coarse hairs on his chest.

Slowly, she moved down his body, pausing to capture his little brown nipple between her teeth. After tugging it softly and then flicking it with her tongue, she moved downward, skimming her lips over his ribs and his tight belly. When she knelt between his legs, she captured his cock between her hands and ran her hands up and down his length, amazed at how hard he was and yet velvety smooth. Then she touched her lips to the tip in a kiss before taking him into her mouth.

His body stiffened beneath her. He reached for her hair, digging his fingers into her curls.

Maggie took him all the way in, then back out, again and again, increasing the pace with each pass.

His hands tangled in her hair, urging her to go faster.

She did, her hand cupping his balls, massaging them in rhythm with what she was doing to his member.

The longer she moved over him, the tenser his body grew until he dug his fingers into her hair and pulled free of her mouth.

She frowned, reaching for him.

Callum shook his head. "I want to be inside you."

She smiled her agreement. Before she knew his intentions, he flipped her onto her back, ripped open the condom and rolled it over his cock.

He came to her, settling between her legs, his staff pausing at her entrance.

"Are you still with me? Do you want this?" he asked, his voice strained.

"Yes!" she cried, grabbed his ass and brought him home.

Callum entered her slowly, carefully, allowing her channel to adjust to his girth.

She didn't want *slow*. Her body was on fire with her need. With her fingers digging into his buttocks, she urged him to fill her completely.

Once he was fully seated, he gave her a moment to ensure she could handle his thickness.

Her desire mounting, Maggie pushed him away until only the tip of his cock remained inside. As quickly as she'd pushed him away, she pulled him back.

Callum took control from there, gliding in and out, slowly at first, then faster.

Maggie wanted him to go deeper, harder and faster. She dug her heels into the mattress and met him thrust for thrust, laughing over the slapping sound their bodies made as they came together. Her laughter caught in her throat as his body tensed and hers reached that incredible peak all over again. She pitched over the edge, the electric current of her orgasm ripping through her body all the way out to her fingers and toes. Her hips rose and fell, milking every last wave of sensation until she collapsed against the bed, breathing hard.

Callum continued pumping in and out. One final thrust buried him deep inside her, his release pulsing against her channel. For a long moment, he leaned over her, his face tight, his breathing ragged, his gaze meeting hers. He collapsed on top of her, crushing the air from her lungs.

Maggie didn't care if she ever breathed again. She could die in that moment with no regrets. "That was incredible," she whispered.

He chuckled and rolled onto his side, taking her with him. "Better than incredible. It was brilliant."

"Can we do it again?" she asked, "Although I'll need a minute. My body is as limp as a noodle."

"We surely can do that again, but like you, I require time to recover." He smiled into her eyes and brushed a curl back from her cheek. "You're an amazing woman, Maggie McKendrick."

"I can say the same about you," she said, trailing a finger across his shoulder and down his arm. "I'm ready for round two whenever you are."

"Amazing and a demanding wench," Callum said and brushed a kiss across her cheek.

"I don't want this night to end," she said. "For now, I want to forget the fact that my new family is in danger. I want to live in the moment, make love to you for as long as you'll have me and worry about tomorrow when it's today."

Callum kissed her lips. "I thought you were tired."

She smiled. "I am. But I can sleep when I return to Montana. I'm here for such a short time, I want to experience as much as I can."

He gathered her into his arms, his lips crushing hers.

Maggie's heart swelled with feelings she'd never felt before meeting Callum. In a few short days, she'd be back in Montana, and he'd be on to his next assignment as a Brotherhood Protector. Most likely, they'd never see each other again. If she let herself dwell on that, she'd be sad.

It was hard to be sad when wrapped in that moment in Callum's arms.

They made love through the night, even moving to the bathtub after warming the water. It was everything she'd imagined and more. Afterward, they'd dried each other off and continued exploration of each other's bodies in the bed.

Sometime in the early, dark hours of morning, she drifted off, her body spooned against his, replete in their lovemaking and satisfied for the moment. In the back of her mind, she knew she could never get enough of Callum McCall. Leaving would be harder than anything she'd done before.

The cool light of day came too soon; muted

sunlight filtered through the French doors into the room.

Maggie stretched, feeling deliciously wicked as the sheets slid over her naked skin. When she rolled over to kiss Callum awake, she was shocked and disappointed to find the space beside her empty. She sat up, pulling the sheet up over her breasts and glanced around the room.

At first, she thought she was alone in the bedroom. A movement made her direct her search to the corner of the room where a sitting area had been fashioned out of a settee and a small coffee table.

Callum lay fully clothed on his back, his legs draped over the arm of the settee, his eyes closed, his chest rising and falling in a slow, steady rhythm. Why hadn't he slept in the bed with her? The settee couldn't be comfortable for someone as tall as Callum.

Maggie rose from the bed and padded naked across the floor to where he lay. For a long moment, she stared down at him. She didn't want to disturb his sleep, but he wouldn't be well-rested if he stayed draped over the settee.

Callum moaned and rocked side to side, his arms tight against his body. "No," he murmured. "Don't." His words, though murmured, were spoken in fear and pain. The more he rocked, the more distressed he became.

Maggie's heart squeezed hard in her chest. She

couldn't let him suffer in his dreams. She had to wake him to end the nightmare and show him it was all a bad dream.

She reached out and touched his shoulder. His hand shot out and grabbed her wrist in a punishing grip. His eyes were open, but it was as if he didn't see her.

"Don't hurt him. If you do, I'll kill you and everyone in this building," Callum said, his voice ragged, guttural and fierce.

His hand on her wrist was so tight that Maggie feared he'd snap the bone. "Callum, wake up. It's just a dream." The pain was excruciating. He'd cut off the circulation to that hand. "Callum, you're hurting my wrist. Please, let go."

"You touch him, and I'll kill you with my bare hands," he growled, pulling Maggie close, his nose practically touching hers.

"Callum, honey, it's me, Maggie. You're dreaming," she said. "Wake up."

For a moment, he stared at her, his lips peeling back in an angry sneer. "You killed the others; I won't let you kill Smudge. He doesn't deserve to die, but you do." He yanked her off her feet and threw her onto the settee.

Maggie landed hard, half the breath knocked from her lungs. "Callum!" she said more forcefully. "Wake up. You're dreaming."

Suddenly, he released her hand.

For a split second, Maggie felt relief.

That relief turned to terror when his hands gripped her neck.

She fought, kicking and squirming in an attempt to free herself.

Her attempts only seemed to enrage him further, causing his hands to tighten.

Maggie's vision grayed around the edges, the room growing darker with each passing second.

For a second, he loosened his grip.

She coughed. "Callum, I'm Maggie. Please—"

As he wrapped his hands around her throat again, he gazed down at her, his brow knitting. "Maggie?" he said.

She tried to talk but couldn't. Instead, she did her best to nod and raised her hand to cup his face.

Callum's eyes widened, the shadows clearing. He glanced down at his hands around her throat. Immediately, he jerked them back and leaped to his feet, backing several feet away. "Oh, dear God. What have I done?" His gaze went from his hands to her throat. "Oh, Maggie. Are you okay? Please tell me you're okay. Did I hurt you?" He dropped to his knees beside the settee and reached for her.

Maggie shrank back, instinctively.

Callum's hands fell to his sides, balling into fists. "I should've left. I never meant to hurt you. I should've left."

Maggie sat up, rubbing the soreness around her

neck. She reached out and tentatively touched his shoulder. "I'm—" her voice squeaked. She cleared her throat and tried again. "I'm all right," she said, her voice sounding like she was gargling gravel.

Callum pushed to his feet and moved away, the distance between them more than several feet. It felt more like a chasm.

"I'm sorry," he said. "I'll call Ace and have him send someone else. I can't trust myself." He spun away. "You shouldn't trust me."

Maggie rose from the settee and crossed to stand behind him. "I don't want someone else. I want you."

His gaze swept her naked length before he closed his eyes. "I can't do this."

Maggie wrapped her arms around her middle. "I didn't understand. Now, I do. I don't want someone else," she repeated.

He spun, started to reach for her, caught himself and let his arms fall to his sides. "Go back to bed, Maggie. What we did was a mistake. I should never—"

"It wasn't a mistake." She took a step toward him. "You didn't hurt me."

He backed away, shaking his head. "I did hurt you. I could've killed you. I can't let that happen again."

The defeat in his eyes gutted her. She knew nothing she could say would make him feel better. Not at that moment. "Okay. I'll step back now. But

Callum, you might have given up on yourself, but I haven't."

"I need some air." Callum pulled on his shoes and strode across the room. "I'll be back." He left the room, closing the door softly behind him.

Maggie gathered her night clothes, slipped into them and climbed back into the bed.

She'd gone from the best sex she'd ever experienced, to almost being choked to death by the man she might be falling in love with, to sitting in the very bed where they'd made love. Alone.

Add to that the threat of Russian loan sharks coming after her and her newfound family, the last twenty-four hours had been unforgettable.

Maggie's eyes filled with tears.

She blinked them away, squared her shoulders and tightened her resolve. Her mother hadn't raised a quitter. She sure as hell wasn't quitting now.

CHAPTER 11

Callum didn't go far for his fresh air, just outside the room he'd shared with Maggie. He paced the length of the hallway, walking quietly so as not to disturb anyone else. He was the one with the problem. They didn't have to suffer because of him.

Maggie didn't have to suffer because of his nightmares.

God, he'd been a fool. He'd thought sleeping on the settee would keep him far enough away from Maggie that he couldn't hurt her. He hadn't counted on her coming to him. Nor had he counted on his nightmare manifesting into a sleepwalking horror movie where he'd almost choked to death the woman he was growing to care about.

After several quiet passes back and forth across the upper landing, he settled on the floor outside her door, crossed his arms over his chest and closed his eyes. He didn't seem to have the dreams when he slept sitting up. Hopefully, he could catch an hour of sleep before the rest of the manor woke.

He felt like he'd barely drifted off when he was startled awake by a small giggle.

Callum's eyes flew open to find Bryce standing a few feet away, wearing the pajamas he'd worn to bed the night before.

The boy tilted his head to one side. "Why are you sleeping in the hall and not your bed?"

Callum grimaced and lied. "The bed was too soft." Actually, he couldn't remember anything about the bed but the woman in it.

The boy's brow twisted as he thought over what Callum had said. "The floor is harder. I'm hungry."

Callum pushed to his feet, noticing the hallway and landing were brighter than they'd been when he'd paced not long before. Sunlight shone into the foyer from the windows across the front of the house. "Is it time for breakfast?"

Bryce shrugged. "No one else is awake."

"If you take me to the kitchen, I might find you something to eat."

The door to the bedroom behind Callum opened. Maggie stood in the doorframe, dressed in jeans and a long-sleeve, moss-green turtleneck sweater that clung beautifully to her breasts, waist and hips.

Callum's pulse quickened, and his stomach lurched. He wondered if she was bruised beneath the neckline of the sweater. He hated himself for having nearly choked the life out of this lovely woman. "Maggie," he said with a dip of his head. "Would you care to join us in the kitchen?" He wouldn't blame her if she told him to go jump in a lake or called the police and filed charges against him.

"I'd love to join you." She met and held his gaze until he looked away before turning her attention to the little boy, bestowing one of her beautiful smiles on the child. "Good morning, Master Bryce. Do you know the way to the kitchen?"

"Of course, I do." Bryce held out his hand to Maggie. "Come. I'll show you. And you don't have to call me Master Bryce or Lord Bryce. You're my sister."

She took his hand in hers.

Bryce turned to Callum and slipped his fingers into Callum's big hand. "After breakfast, can we go see my horse?"

Maggie smiled down at the boy. "We'd need to ask your mother, and you'd need to change your clothes."

Bryce glanced down at his pajamas. "Montana doesn't care if I wear my pajamas."

"He might not care, but riding clothes help protect you," Maggie said.

Bryce glanced up at her, his eyes wide. "Do you ride?"

Maggie nodded. "I ride my friend Sadie's horses back in the United States."

"Can I meet your friend Sadie?" Bryce asked. "Would she let me ride her horses?"

"It's a long way to go to where I live in the United States. And what's super cool about where I live is that the state is named Montana."

Bryce's eyes widened even more. "Like my horse?"

"That's right," Maggie said. "Like your horse, only it's a place with grasslands so big you can't see a single tree. In other parts of the state, there are mountains with snow on top of them."

"My mother let me play in the snow one time," Bryce said. "Not for long. But I got to make a snow angel and throw snowballs. Ewan said he'd help me build a snowman if it snows enough this year."

"We get lots of snow in Montana, where I live," Maggie said. "You could build a lot of snowmen."

"I'm going to ask Mother if I can go to Montana with you." Bryce led them to one side of the dual staircases. They descended to the ground floor and the marble foyer. They turned into the hallway between the two staircases and walked toward the back of the manor, passing the dining room where they'd had dinner the night before, and continued to a swing door that led into the kitchen.

Maggie didn't speak to Callum the entire way. Though she smiled for Bryce, she didn't direct smiles in Callum's direction. Not that he expected it. But he missed those smiles and her happy optimism. She appeared subdued. God, he hoped she wasn't afraid of him, though he deserved it. He wouldn't want to be around someone who attacked people in his sleep.

Maggie found eggs in the refrigerator and a skillet in a cupboard and whipped up scrambled eggs. By the time she had the eggs cooking, a woman appeared in a white jacket, her gray hair pulled back and secured under a net.

"You must be Cook. I'm Maggie." Maggie held out her hand. "I'm sorry to take over, but Master Bryce was hungry."

Cook's eyes narrowed at the pan on the stove and the scrambled eggs cooking. She nodded her head as if approving and shook Maggie's hand. "You must be Lord Drummond's sister. It's a pleasure to meet you. I can take over if you like."

Maggie smiled and handed the spatula over. "Of course. Can I help?"

Cook tipped her head toward a cabinet. "Master Bryce prefers milk and buttered toast with his breakfast. You can find glasses in that cabinet and milk in the fridge. The bread is in the keeper on the counter. And if you want coffee, there's a coffeemaker on the counter by the bread.

While Maggie went for the milk and glasses, Callum found the bread, popped four slices in the toaster and got the coffee brewing.

Cook brought out two more skillets, turned on the stove beneath them and laid slices of bacon across the surface of one while cracking eggs into the other for fried eggs. In a saucepan, she poured a large can of beans and set it on the fifth burner. Then she deftly returned to stir the original eggs until they were fluffy and cooked through. She scraped the eggs into a serving bowl, flipped the bacon to cook on the other side and helped Callum apply fresh butter to the lightly browned toast.

Maggie found plates and cutlery and set the long table in the kitchen.

"Oh, you'll want to eat in the dining room," Cook said,

"If it's all right with you, it's much cozier in here," Maggie said.

Cook shrugged. "As you wish. It's just that the former Lord Drummond required the family to eat in the dining room."

"Since the old Lord Drummond isn't part of the family anymore, we can eat wherever we like." Ewan entered the kitchen and smiled at Cook. "And we'd like you to join us at the kitchen table."

Cook's cheeks flushed a ruddy red. "Oh, I don't know. It's never done. Alastair and I ate in here."

"Then it's about time you ate with us." Ewan touched her arm gently. "You and Alastair are as much a part of this family as I am. I remember how you'd sneak extra cookies for me when I was a boy. And I rode all over the estate with Alastair. We were like brothers." He smiled. "I'd offer my help, but it appears you have everything under control."

"Lord Drummond," Cook said as she stirred the beans, "please take a seat. I'll bring your breakfast to you."

"Nonsense." Ewan eyed the serving bowl filled with scrambled eggs. "The least I can do is help carry things to the table."

Maggie set a glass of milk at the table and went back to the cabinet for more glasses, filling each with orange juice.

Gregory appeared at the doorway, looking confused by the number of people in the kitchen. When Ewan explained they'd be sharing breakfast, the butler nodded and poured coffee into mugs for those who wanted it.

The back door opened, and Alastair stepped through. Immediately, his thick black eyebrows formed a V over his nose. "What's going on?" he muttered.

"We're having breakfast in the kitchen with you, old man." Ewan clapped the chauffeur on the shoulder.

Alastair's gaze met Cook's.

She gave him a crooked smile. "The new Lord Drummond requests it."

Still, Alastair hesitated, his gaze going to Gregory, who stood by the coffee maker with a mug in his hand.

"Take a seat." Ewan waved toward the table. "Breakfast is almost ready."

The tall, dark man moved slowly toward the table.

"You can sit by me." Bryce patted the chair beside his. "We're going to take Ms. Maggie out to see Montana after breakfast."

Alastair stood behind the chair Bryce indicated and waited for the others to take their seats before he did.

"Should we wait for Ms. Fiona?" Maggie asked.

"She doesn't eat breakfast," Cook said and passed the serving bowl of beans.

After they'd filled their plates, Callum glanced around the table and then to Ewan. "This might be a good time to talk about our discussion from last night."

Maggie frowned, her gaze going to Bryce. "Are you sure?"

Ewan nodded. "I agree with Callum."

Cook and Alastair looked up from their plates and waited patiently for Ewan to speak.

"As you might have heard, we had a visit from my cousin Rory last night."

Cook and Alastair both nodded.

Bryce frowned. "Cousin Rory? Did he stay? Will I get to see him?"

Ewan shook his head. "Sorry, Bryce. He couldn't stay, but he did have some news that I think we all need to hear."

Callum wondered how Ewan would present the threat without frightening the boy.

"He said that there are some bad men who might try to come to our home. You don't have to worry because we have some nice people who will come help keep us safe. But we need to be smart and not go outside the manor without someone with us at all times." He looked directly at Bryce. "That means you can't go outside to play unless one of us grownups goes with you. Do you understand?"

Bryce frowned. "Are they going to kill us?"

Maggie reached out and wrapped her arm around Bryce. "Of course not. We wouldn't let that happen."

"Your sister is right," Ewan said. "We'll protect you. But you have to do your part and be with one of us when you go outside."

"Even to the stable?" Bryce asked.

Ewan nodded. "The stables, the garden, the garage. Anywhere outside the manor. Can you do that, Bryce?"

Bryce nodded. "Yes, sir."

"If you see any strangers, you let one of us know," Ewan said and turned to Cook and Alastair. "That goes for you as well."

"Yes, Lord Drummond," Cook said.

Alastair nodded.

Bryce's brow was still furrowed. "Does that mean I can't show Maggie my horse?"

"Of course, you can show Ms. Maggie your horse," Ewan said. "As long as one of us grownups is with you."

Bryce turned to Alastair. "Will you go take me and Maggie to see Montana?"

Alastair nodded. "Yes, sir."

Bryce's frown disappeared. "I'm finished with my breakfast, may I be excused?"

Ewan's brow wrinkled. "You haven't eaten half of what is on your plate."

Bryce rubbed his stomach. "It makes my tummy hurt."

"Do we need to have the doctor come for another visit?" Ewan asked.

"No, I'll feel better," Bryce said. "Promise." He waited on the edge of his seat for Ewan to dismiss him.

Ewan's lips pressed into a tight line. "You may go."

Bryce pushed back from the table, carried his plate to the sink and hurried out of the kitchen.

"Does he always have a tummy ache when he eats?" Maggie asked.

Ewan's lips thinned. "Fiona said it started after my father passed. She thinks it might be the stress of losing his father. She took him to see the doctor, but he couldn't find anything wrong with him. He suggested a medication for anxiety, but Fiona wasn't keen on giving a five-year-old mind-altering drugs. We're keeping an eye on him, but he hasn't shown signs of improvement."

"He really didn't eat all that much," Maggie said.

"He might be too excited to show you his horse," Ewan said.

"Then I'd better be ready," Maggie smiled.

With the boy out of the room, Callum let the others know about his conversation with his friend, who ran a security organization, and the man's promise of more help heading their way to protect them. "A former SAS, Peter Atkins, should be here sometime this morning."

"Atkins?" Ewan's eyes narrowed. "I remember an Atkins. A little older than us. He's not with the SAS anymore?"

Callum shook his head. "He works for my friend. We'll need to let him through the gate when he arrives."

Ewan nodded. "We will. Now, if you'll excuse me, I'm still going through the ledgers. I can't believe my father kept them manually in this day and age. He has them dating back to when his father was still alive."

They finished breakfast and helped Cook clear the table. She shooed them out of the kitchen. "If you keep doing my job, you won't need me anymore."

Maggie hesitated at the bottom of the staircase. "I'm going up to brush my teeth and pull my hair back."

Though he wanted to go with her, he resisted. After what had happened, he needed some distance. As long as she stayed in the house, she should be fine.

Callum explored the ground floor, noting all

doors and windows that could be opened. Though if someone wanted in badly enough, they'd break the windows. However, that would be loud and alert the occupants. The last room he investigated was what appeared to be an office or study.

Ewan sat at a large mahogany desk with stacks of ledgers piled on either side, his head bent over another opened in front of him.

Callum knocked on the doorframe.

Ewan looked up. "Come in. Come in. My eyes are already crossing at all the entries. My father might have been an arse, but he was meticulous and his handwriting was excellent." He glanced up. "I've come across some entries that don't make sense, one of which might have a connection to Ms. Maggie. Have a look and tell me what you see." He pushed his chair back, allowing enough room that Callum could get in to look at the ledger.

Ewan pointed at an entry. "This entry is marked A.M. for two thousand pounds. There isn't a check number, but there are the letters W.T., which I assume stands for wire transfer, but he made the same entry every month for as far back as I've looked so far."

"How far is that?" Callum asked.

"At least twenty years so far." He handed Callum a ledger. "Here's one from thirty years ago. See if you find it there. I wonder if he was putting money into a secret investment account that I need to find."

Callum opened the ledger and checked through several months of entries. "None here."

Ewan frowned and pulled out the one before the ledger he'd handed Callum. "None in this one as well. Wait. Halfway through the year, he started making the entries."

Callum took the one labeled the year after. "This ledger has entries like that for every month."

"Do you have bank account records?" Callum asked. "Maybe they show where that money went."

Ewan shook his head. "There's a stack of boxes full of tax records in the attic, but they only go back several years. I could look in them."

"When was the most recent transfer?" Callum asked.

"Less than a year ago."

"You could check online and see if there's more information about where that transfer was sent."

"His accounts are still tied up in probate," Ewan said. "I'm waiting for the courts to grant me access."

Callum stepped away from the desk, his thoughts going back to what Ace and Hank had said. They had people with technical skills who might be able to access those accounts. He turned to face Ewan, a former SAS like him, a man Callum felt in his gut he could trust. But would Ewan trust him?

Callum crossed to the door and closed it softly.

Ewan looked up, his brow creasing. "Is there a problem?"

"No," Callum said. "But I haven't been completely forthcoming with you."

Ewan's frown deepened. "About what?"

"Why I'm here."

"You're Maggie's fiancé." His eyes narrowed. "Are you not?"

Callum shook his head slowly. "That was my cover. I was hired to provide her protection. The friends I've mentioned who are sending help are my teammates. We're members of the Brotherhood Protectors, an organization comprised of former highly skilled men trained for special operations. We provide services like security, protection and extraction for people who need it."

"And my half-sister thought she might need it to come to Scotland to meet me?" Ewan shook his head. "Did she think I would harm her?"

"No." Callum smiled. "Quite the opposite. She's never been out of the US. Her friend's husband is the founder of the Brotherhood Protectors, a former US Navy SEAL. He and his wife worried that Ms. Maggie was going off alone and was too naïve to know when she might be taken advantage of in transit or once she arrived here. They asked me to follow her in case she needed help."

Ewan sighed. "And she did. All because of my cousin's gambling addiction and subsequent deal with the devil."

"Which we didn't know coming here to meet

you," Callum said. "In order for her to show up with me in tow, we came up with the story that I was her fiancé."

"You had no idea who attacked her on the train or in Edinburgh," Ewan's lips twisted. "She could've been targeted by her siblings, eager to get their hands on the full inheritance, rather than having to share a portion with a child born of my father's affair with the nanny. Why are you telling me this now? You could've kept that to yourself and let me believe the people coming to help are just convenient friends."

"Because they have people with technical skills and contacts who can access information and get to data that most cannot."

"You mean hackers?" Ewan crossed his arms over his chest. "You know that's illegal. What makes you think I want to be involved in hacking into databases full of private information?"

Callum shrugged. "They could get to your father's bank information quicker than the courts can grant you access. They also have a man with contacts who might identify what organization is threatening your cousin and the rest of your family."

Ewan studied Callum for a long moment. "You've already got them looking for information on my cousin's loan shark, don't you?"

"Yes."

"Well, I'd like to know where this money was going sooner rather than later. If it's to an investment account, I'm not worried. If it's blackmail money, I need to know what my father was up to in case it comes back to haunt my family."

Callum pulled out his cell phone and placed a video call to Ace.

"I'm glad you called," Ace answered. "Dmytro has some information for you."

"You're on speaker," Callum said. "I have Ewan Drummond with me. He knows who I work for and wants your tech team to look up some wire transfers his father has made over the past twenty-eight years."

"You think he was being blackmailed?" Ace asked.

"We don't know," Callum said. "But it's better to know where that money went in case it impacts the family."

Ewan rose from his chair and came to stand beside Callum. "I'm Ewan Drummond, and you are?" he said.

"Ace Hammerson, with Brotherhood Protectors International. Callum has kept us up to date on what's going on. My tech guy, Dmytro, has some information about the organization threatening your cousin and now you."

A white-haired man appeared on Callum's phone. "Hello, I'm Dmytro. Do you have access to a larger computer screen with access to the internet?" The man spoke with a Russian accent. Or in his case, Ukrainian.

Ewan nodded. "On my desk."

In less than three minutes, Dmytro walked Ewan through granting him access to Ewan's computer. Once he had control, he popped images of men onto the monitor. "Your cousin has been working with the Kholdov Coalition, Russian mobsters who have infiltrated several casino operations in the UK, Europe and the Netherlands. They are known for loaning money to gamblers who either have lots of money or have access to money through family." Dmytro's face appeared on the monitor.

"Like my cousin," Ewan said. "How do we get them to leave us alone?"

"You can pay them what your cousin owes, though by now, interest is compounding by the second."

"If I pay them now," Ewan said, "my cousin could get right back into the same situation."

"I'm working on an alternative," Dmytro said. "My contact says the coalition is operating on the down low in territory where they shouldn't be. The Donchenko Bratva governs the Russian mafia in the UK, including casinos in Edinburgh. They might take issue with another organization moving in."

"Are you talking mob war?" Callum asked.

Dmytro shrugged. "Maybe. Depends on how much they care that someone else is shaking up their customers."

"Brilliant," Ewan said. "My family could be caught in the middle of a war between Russian mobs."

Ace appeared on the monitor. "I'm calling in all my assets. We'll be in the air within the next hour. Peter Atkins should be there anytime."

"Three-hour flight time, if you have access to a jet," Callum noted.

"And we do," Ace said. "About four hours total, by the time we reach Drummond Estate."

"While stirring up the Bratva, Monroe will check into your father's bank account and find out what he's been spending his money on."

A young woman with bright purple hair leaned over Dmytro's shoulders. "All I need is the name of the bank, your father's name and the account number." She shook her head. "Never mind, just the name of the bank. I'll have that info to you within the hour."

Ewan's brow dipped. "How old are you?"

"Don't let her taste in hair color fool you," Dmytro said. "She's almost as good as me."

The young woman snorted. "I can hack circles around you, old man."

Dmytro shook his head. "She's twenty-one but has ten years of experience."

"Twelve," Monroe called out in the background.

Ewan gave Dmytro the name of his father's bank.

Ace's face appeared. "Stay safe. We'll see you on the other side."

The call ended, and Callum stepped back. "I'll let

Maggie know what's happening and keep an eye on her and Bryce."

"I'll speak with Fiona." Ewan's gaze met Callum's. "Had I known what my cousin has gotten us into, I wouldn't have invited Maggie to visit Drummond Manor."

"You couldn't have known." Callum lifted his chin. "For now, we remain alert and hope the Russians don't make a move anytime soon."

CHAPTER 12

AFTER BRUSHING her teeth and securing her curls up in a loose bun on the crown of her head, Maggie descended the stairs and found Bryce back in the kitchen, dressed to go outside and talking nonstop.

Alastair leaned against a counter, tossing an apple in the air and catching it.

Cook had her arms up to her elbows, kneading dough.

As soon as Bryce saw Maggie, he cried, "She's here!" He raced over to Maggie, grabbed her hand and dragged her toward the door. "Let's go."

Alastair shoved the apple into his jacket pocket and reached the door before Bryce. "Slow down, little man. Montana isn't going anywhere."

"Mind if I join you?" a voice said behind them.

Maggie's pulse quickened, and a shiver of awareness rippled through her.

She turned with Bryce to look over her shoulder.

Callum entered the kitchen with a smile that melted the hard knot that had settled in Maggie's gut since earlier that morning when this man had walked out of their shared bedroom. His smile might be all for show, but it made her heart flutter. If only they could go back to the easy camaraderie they'd shared before he'd tried to strangle her, thinking she was the person in his nightmare. The man had serious PTSD. Despite that fact, Maggie wasn't ready to give up on him. She'd be in Scotland for almost two more weeks. She wanted to spend as much time as she could with him. Preferably in bed, making love.

Her core heated at the thought. What they'd shared the night before couldn't be a one-night stand. It had rocked her world so hard she wouldn't walk away.

"You can come with us." Bryce reached back for Callum's hand.

Callum strode across the kitchen, took the boy's hand and walked with them out of the manor and across the manicured lawn to the stable.

The building was constructed of wood and stone in a centuries-old architectural style. The structure had either been well-maintained or reconstructed to appear as it originally had.

Alastair flung open a door large enough to allow a horse-drawn carriage to enter and exit. Inside were ten horse stalls lining both sides.

Bryce ran to the third on the right and reached up to touch the muzzle of the horse whose head leaned over the top.

"You know the rule," Alastair said. "One for Montana and one for you." He pulled an apple from one pocket and handed it to Bryce, then another from the other pocket and waited for Bryce to take the one he held out.

Bryce took the first apple and held it up to Montana. "See? I'll take a bite, then you'll take a bite." Bryce sank his teeth into the apple, chewed and swallowed. "Now, it's Montana's turn." He held out his hand for the other apple.

Alastair laid it in the little boy's hand.

Bryce held the apple up to the horse. "Now you take a bite."

The horse nuzzled the apple with his lips and carefully took it from Bryce. He crunched the fruit between his back teeth and swallowed.

"Now, you show Montana how you can eat your apple," Alastair said, "while I get his bucket of grain. Remember, you can't grow big and strong if you don't eat."

Alastair stood for a moment longer, waiting for Bryce to bring the apple to his lips.

The boy held it up and sank his teeth into it.

Alastair nodded and turned away to get the grain he'd promised for Montana.

Bryce fumbled with the apple and dropped it to

the ground. It rolled under the door and into Montana's stall. "Oh, no," the little boy murmured.

"Don't worry," Maggie said. "We'll get another when we go back into the kitchen."

Montana bent and picked up the apple, quickly chewing and swallowing it before Alastair reappeared with a bucket of grain.

"Do you want to pour it into Montana's trough?" he asked Bryce.

"Yes, please." Bryce held out his hands for the bucket and braced himself to hold it.

Alastair opened the stall door.

Maggie frowned, a little worried about the boy entering the big horse's stall. "Want me to go in with you?"

"No, thank you." Bryce walked right into the stall and tipped the heavy bucket into the trough.

"You're so very strong," Maggie commented.

"He feeds Montana every day," Alastair said. "And every day, he builds his muscles."

Bryce carried the empty bucket out and handed it to Alastair. "Alastair taught me how to ride, and someday, he'll teach me how to drive."

"Are you going to ride today?" Alastair asked.

Bryce sighed. "I'm tired, and my tummy hurts. Maybe later. I think I'll go lie down for a while."

Maggie's heart pinched. A five-year-old shouldn't be worn out at the beginning of the day. He hadn't run circles in the playground or bounced off the walls. She held out her hand. "I'll walk with you back to the manor."

"Better yet," Callum said. "I'll carry you." He swung the boy up in his arms.

Bryce lay his head on Callum's shoulder. "I want to ride," he said, "but my tummy hurts." His red hair contrasted with Callum's short, dark beard.

Maggie laid a hand on the boy's back. "Come on. Let's get you back to the house. Does your mother have any medicine to help your tummy?"

"It tastes yucky," Bryce said.

"Better to taste yucky than for your tummy to hurt," Maggie said.

"It never fixes it," Bryce admitted.

Maggie walked beside Callum back to the manor and entered through the back door into the kitchen.

"Lady Fiona is in the dining room," Cook said from where she stood at a counter, fitting lumps of dough into bread pans.

"Thank you," Callum said and strode through the kitchen into the dining room.

Fiona rose from the table, dressed in a shirtwaist dress, a frown pulling her arched brows downward. "Bryce, my love, come to mummy." She took Bryce into her arms. "Let's get you some medicine and let you lie down for a while."

"We went to see Montana." Bryce lay his head on his mother's shoulder as she carried him out of the room.

"I'm worried about Bryce," Maggie stepped out into the hallway. "I wonder if they've taken him to see a specialist. He's five. He shouldn't be in that much pain and discomfort. He should be running and playing like most kids his age."

"Agreed," Callum said. "That's not normal."

They walked companionably several more steps, giving Maggie the courage to address the elephant in the room.

"Callum." Maggie touched his arm, bringing him to a halt. "About what happened between us. We need to talk."

Callum stiffened. "There's nothing to talk about."

Heat filled her cheeks. Not from embarrassment, but anger. "There damn sure is."

"I hurt you," he said, his voice low, guttural. He shook her hand off his arm and stepped away, widening the gap between them physically and emotionally. "I can't let that happen ever again."

"You're suffering from PTSD, Callum. You didn't know what you were doing. You didn't know it was me."

"All the more reason to stay away from you. I could've killed you."

"But you didn't," Maggie said softly. "I'm fine."

His lip curled up on one corner. "And that's why you're wearing a turtleneck? Because you're fine?"

"I'm wearing it because it's drafty in the manor."

She pulled the neckline of her sweater downward. "See? No marks. I'm okay."

He stared into her eyes, his shadowed with his own internal torture. "I can't trust myself. You shouldn't trust me. I was trained to kill. My hands worked on muscle memory."

"When you're awake, you know what you're doing. You don't have to distance yourself from me."

"We could never sleep together. Ever."

"I know now not to wake you from a nightmare."

He gripped her arms gently. "What do you want from me?"

"I want what we had before. The easy companionship, being able to talk to you like a friend." She lowered her voice. "Making love with abandon."

Callum's hands tightened, and then he released her, his face turning stony. "You're going back to Montana. I'm here until you leave. Nothing will come of anything between us. We might as well end it now. I'm your protector, your bodyguard. Nothing more."

"But there's so much more," she insisted.

"No. There isn't," he said, his tone harsh, final. "Let it go. Let me go. You're better off without me." He spun on his heels and walked down the hall, across the marble foyer and out the front door.

Maggie stood still for a long moment, moisture welling in her eyes.

What did she want from Callum? A playmate for

the time she was in Scotland? When she returned to Montana, would she be able to forget about him? Could she go back to teaching preschoolers without a second thought about the man who'd rocked her world and made her want more out of life than teaching other people's children?

No. Oh, hell no.

So, he had PTSD. Other women stayed with their men even when they suffered through the demons of their memories and the atrocities they'd witnessed. They worked through or around the nightmares.

Only Callum wasn't her man. She hadn't known him long. He might not have felt the same connection she had while making love all night long. His connection might have been no more than a physical release.

To Maggie, it had been a physical release and an emotional bonding. She could fall in love with Callum. Hell, she might already be in love with him. He was kind, caring, opened doors for her and protected her from street vendors and Russian mobsters. Their tour through London had been magical, thanks to his historical knowledge, humor and love of his country. He'd been patient and concerned with Bryce and quick to call for backup when he'd realized how much danger they could be in.

And he'd made love to her, insisting it wasn't just sex.

Her heart burned with the memory. Now he wanted nothing to do with her.

Her eyes filled and overflowed. Not wanting anyone to witness her weakness, she ran. Not knowing where else to go, she hurried up the staircase and down the hallway to her room and rushed inside. Once she'd closed the door behind her, she leaned her back against it and slid to the ground, releasing the tears in messy sobs. Afraid someone might hear her, she covered her mouth, pushed to her feet and fell across the bed she'd shared with Callum the night before.

She buried her face in the pillow that still smelled vaguely like his cologne.

When the tears stopped flowing, she moved to her side of the bed. This was how it would be back in Montana. She'd sleep alone. There wouldn't be the scent of cologne lingering on the other pillow. More tears welled in her eyes.

Maggie rolled onto her belly and buried her face in her pillow to muffle her sobs. Her fingers brushed against something hard. When she'd made the bed that morning, there hadn't been anything under the pillow.

She sat up, tossed the pillow aside and stared down at a leatherbound book with a silk ribbon tied around it in a bow.

Her fingers curled around the item. She untied the bow and opened the cover.

The first page had Lady E written in large, scrolling handwriting across the page.

It wasn't a book. This was a journal.

Maggie's heartbeat kicked into overdrive as she turned the pages one by one.

Lady E, or Lady Elizabeth Wallace Drummond, had filled her journal with major events, beginning with her marriage to Lord Douglas Drummond, a union arranged by her father after Douglas Drummond's father had passed away, leaving his oldest son all his wealth and title. She went on to commemorate the day she'd given birth to the future Lord Drummond and how it had made her marriage to Douglas tolerable despite her suspicions that her husband was having affairs with other women. She'd suspected he'd dallied with some of their female employees, but she had no proof and preferred he grace their beds now that she had produced an heir.

Maggie spent the next couple of hours reading the elegant notes penned by an increasingly bitter woman whose peers pitied her relationship with her husband. She'd felt trapped in her marriage, forced to stay because of her son and the prenuptial agreement Douglas had never failed to remind her of, that she could not claim any of the Drummond fortune if she left the marriage.

He'd flirted in plain sight with the female employees, and she'd been certain he'd "rutted" with them behind closed doors. It was even more sordid than she'd suspected when she found her son's nanny crying in the garden, half-hidden by her prize roses. The uniform Douglas required nannies to wear had been torn, her hair was in disarray and she had blood on her legs.

At this point, Maggie's gut clenched, her heart skipped several beats, and more tears welled in her eyes. She wanted to wail aloud, *Sweet Jesus, no!*

She knew, without Lady E naming it, that it had to have been her mother.

All these years, she'd assumed her mother had willingly engaged in an affair with a married man and had left when she'd gotten pregnant so as not to ruin the man's marriage. Maggie had assumed her mother had loved the man who'd gotten her pregnant. She blinked back the tears and read more.

Lady E went on to write that she'd helped the nanny into the house, cleaned her up and asked her what had happened. At first, the nanny wouldn't say anything. Lady E asked if one of the other employees had done this to her. The nanny said no. That's when Lady E knew.

She'd asked the nanny if Lord Drummond had hurt her, whereupon the nanny burst into tears and told her he'd taken her to the library under the pretext of showing her a hidden passage behind the bookshelves. The passage led to a room with what appeared to be torture equipment. He'd tied her up and forced himself on her.

By the time Maggie read this, the tears were flowing freely. Lord Drummond had raped her mother.

Lady E had asked the nanny to show her where the hidden room was. Later that evening, when Lord Drummond returned home, Lady E confronted him. She knew if the nanny spoke to the police and Lord Drummond was arrested and convicted of rape, the nanny might be vindicated, but she'd be homeless. If a child resulted from her encounter, she'd have difficulty providing for it. And if Lord Drummond knew Lady E had helped the nanny, he would divorce Lady E and take Ewan away from her. He'd do his time in jail and go back to living his usual life.

Lady E had relocated the nanny to a safe location outside the house. That evening, she told her husband that he had two choices: go to jail or pay for the nanny to relocate and hush money to keep her from turning him over to the police. He would pay support for the child, should she be pregnant from his criminal behavior. He would also rewrite his will to leave his estate to be shared equally among his children, even those spawned outside his legitimate marriage.

Lord Drummond had raged and threatened to kill Lady E. She'd told him that should anything happen to her, his victim would go directly to the police and tell them all.

A day later, Lord Drummond conceded and paid

for an airline ticket to send the nanny away. Once she was settled and had opened a bank account, he'd started making monthly payments.

Lady E had reviewed the ledger and the bank account each month for years to ensure Lord Drummond lived up to his end of the bargain. Later in her journal, she wondered if she'd done the right thing, allowing her husband to get away with rape. By not turning him over to the police, he had no criminal record. No one knew he was a rapist. He could have done it again, just not in the manor as Lady E had arranged to have the hidden doorway nailed shut.

By the time Maggie finished reading Lady E's journal, she was gutted, the shock making her shake all over. Her mother had fled Drummond Manor because her employer had raped her. No wonder she'd never said anything about him.

Maggie's stomach roiled to the point she rolled off the bed and rushed into the bathroom, where she emptied the contents of her belly into the toilet.

She lay on the cool tile until she felt well enough to stand. For a long time, she stared into the mirror at her pale complexion and curly red hair. Now that she knew how she'd come about her genetics, she wasn't proud. Her mother had had to live with the constant reminder of what he'd done to her every time she'd looked at her daughter.

Yet, Maggie knew without a single doubt that her mother had loved her with all her heart.

She washed her face, brushed her teeth and left the room.

Now she knew why her mother had left her home in Scotland to move all the way to Montana. Her feet carried her downstairs and directly to the library.

Call it morbid curiosity or whatever, she had to see the hidden passage, had to know what her mother had endured. She needed to know if the torture equipment still existed. If so, she wanted it removed and burned so that no other woman ever had to submit to that kind of terror.

Once in the library, she searched the shelves until she found a set that didn't look exactly like the others. It wasn't as flush against the wall as the others. Nobody else would have picked up on the difference if they didn't know it existed.

Lady E had said it had been nailed shut.

Maggie expected that it wouldn't move when she grabbed and pulled the shelf.

It swung toward her, no creaking metal or resistance, as if someone had oiled the hinges recently.

Despite her trepidation, Maggie pushed the shelf wide and peered into the darkness below.

Her pulse quickened, and her first thought was to go to Callum and have him go with her into the darkness.

However, he was too wrapped up in what had happened in his nightmare to help her now. Maggie couldn't take the time to find him and tell him what she'd learned from the journal before she stepped onto the stairs leading downward.

As soon as she took the first step downward, she stopped. This was a mistake. She needed a witness, someone to know where she was in case she ran into trouble.

Maggie started to turn toward the entrance.

A hand clamped on her shoulder and shoved her forward, sending her tumbling down the steps into the darkness.

CHAPTER 13

AFTER CALLUM LEFT MAGGIE, he jogged laps around the manor in an attempt to erase Maggie from his mind.

It didn't work. He slowed to a walk and extended his range to the edge of the manicured lawn and made several passes before he admitted to himself he would never walk, jog or erase Maggie from his consciousness. Having spent an incredible day and night with the woman, he knew she was different. Someone worth fighting for. Someone he could love and who could find her way to love him, despite his violent nightmares.

After an hour and a half of circling the compound, he shortened his circle, coming closer and closer to the structure and Maggie. He couldn't avoid her forever. He was there to protect her.

Circling the perimeter was counted, but having eyes on the target was better.

Having been away from her long enough, he had to see her and know she was okay.

A quick look around the bottom floor revealed nothing other than Ewan still poring over ledgers in his office.

"Have you seen Maggie?" Callum asked.

Ewan shook his head. "I've been at these ledgers all morning. Why?"

"I was out on the perimeter. She's probably in her bedroom. I'm headed that way now."

"Let me know if you need help finding her," Ewan said.

"Thanks." Callum headed for the staircase, a sudden sense of urgency making him take the steps two at a time.

When he arrived at the door, it hung open.

He frowned and pushed through. "Maggie?"

No one answered.

His heartbeat quickened as he poked his head into the bathroom.

She wasn't there.

As he passed through the bedroom again, his glance strayed to the bed where they'd made such amazing love through the night.

A book lay open on the comforter as if someone had left it there, intending to pick up where she'd left off.

He opened the pages and skimmed through the content, his heart sinking to the pit of his belly.

Callum glanced up and called out, "Maggie! Oh, sweet girl."

He stepped out into the hallway, a knot twisting his insides. "Oh, baby. I'm so sorry," he murmured as he raced for the staircase and descended so quickly that he stumbled at the bottom.

Once he'd righted himself, he looked left then right. Where would she have gone?

Then it hit him. She would have gone where it had begun.

Callum ran down the long, broad hallway and dove into the library.

It was empty. Maggie was nowhere in sight.

As he turned to look elsewhere, he heard a faint cry.

"Maggie?" he called out.

"Help," her voice sounded as if from a distance.

"Maggie, talk to me." He moved around the room, searching for the hidden entrance mentioned in the journal. "Where are you?"

"Please, oh God, please, help me," she cried.

"I want to," he said, his hand moving over the shelves, searching for the hidden doorway.

Finally, he felt a faint coolness he hadn't felt anywhere else in the room. He grabbed the closest shelf unit and pulled. When it didn't budge, he gripped the one next to it and leaned back with all his weight.

The shelf swung open like a door.

Maggie spilled out and flung herself into his arms, sobbing.

He held her close, his heartbeat hammering against his ribs. "It's okay. I've got you. You're okay."

"I couldn't get out," she said, her lips pressed against his neck, her tears soaking his skin.

"But you're out now. I've got you. I won't let anything happen to you." He leaned back and stared into her eyes. "How did you get stuck in there?"

She buried her face against his neck and wrapped her arms around his waist. "I was pushed."

He leaned her back, frowning. "You were pushed?"

She nodded, her body trembling. "I was pushed."

"Did you see who did it?"

"No." Maggie moved her head side to side. "One minute I'm standing at the top of the stairs, the next, I'm falling into the darkness." Her body shook violently.

"Are you hurt? Callum asked. "Do I need to take you to the hospital?"

"Just bruised," she said.

"Did you hit your head?" He set her at arm's length and stared into her eyes.

She shook her head. "No. I managed to break my fall going down." Maggie pushed the sleeve up on her arm, exposing a red mark that would be black and blue in hours.

"Oh, baby," he said and gently kissed the spot. "I'm so sorry."

"Why?" she asked, frowning. "You didn't push me, did you?"

He gave her a tight-lipped grimace and pulled her close again. "I should've been with you. Had I been here, no one would've pushed you down the stairs."

"Who would've thought someone inside the manor would attack me? Does that mean the Russian mobsters have infiltrated Drummond Manor?" Her eyes rounded, and she tried to free herself from Callum's embrace. "Bryce—has anyone checked on the boy?"

Callum slipped an arm around Maggie's back. "No, but let's do that now."

Maggie hurried alongside Callum as they climbed the stairs and rushed to Bryce's room.

Not wanting to wake the child, Callum twisted the knob and stuck his head inside the door.

Maggie pushed it wider and peered inside the darkened room.

Bryce's small figure lay still in his little bed, the blanket pulled up beneath his chin.

A movement to the left made Callum tense and push Maggie behind him.

Maggie touched his arm and leaned up on her toes to whisper, "Fiona."

Bryce's mother sat in a wooden rocking chair, her head leaning back, her eyes closed, a foot pushing against the floor, causing her to rock back and forth in her sleep.

Maggie tugged on Callum's arm, pulling him out of the room.

He closed the door gently and turned to pull Maggie into his arms.

She wrapped her arms around his waist and rested her cheek against his chest. "What's happening here?"

He held her close, not wanting to release her or leave her for a single second by herself. "I don't know. If a Russian mobster is inside the manor, none of you are safe. We need to let Ewan know."

Maggie looked up into Callum's eyes. "What if he's the one who pushed me?"

Callum couldn't imagine Ewan as the attacker in this case. He'd welcomed Maggie with open arms as the sister he'd always wanted, a bonus family member with whom he was willing to share his inheritance. He'd been SAS. Callum trusted the men who'd gone through the training. Only the best, physically, mentally and morally were selected. He'd trust his life with a man like Ewan.

Would he trust Maggie's life with Ewan?

With no answers and no clues, Callum couldn't trust anyone with Maggie's life. Not even himself. With too many attempts already, he couldn't bring himself to trust anyone with the woman he was falling so quickly and hopelessly in love with. God, he wished he wasn't such a screw-up. If he could wipe away the demons powering his dreams, he would. Then he wouldn't have to worry that he'd wake up with his hands around Maggie's throat. Though he couldn't trust himself to sleep with her, he could be in the same room as long as he kept his distance when he slept. Couldn't he?

He'd only tried to choke her because she'd gotten too close when he was in the throes of his nightmare. His other choice would be to have one of his teammates with the Brotherhood Protectors International take over the protection of the pretty redhead. He could step back and ask for a different assignment.

If she were attacked while he was on another assignment, could he forgive himself for not being there?

No.

Was he a danger to her?

Yes.

Inside, Callum warred with himself on his decision to stay. He would stay with her at least until they neutralized the Russian mobster threat.

His arms around her, holding her tightly, he knew he didn't want to be anywhere else.

Slipping his arm around her waist, he walked with her to their bedroom and pushed the door open.

Her gaze went to the book on the bed, "You read it?" she asked.

He nodded. "I skimmed." Callum shook his head. "I'm sorry,"

"My mother was—" She swallowed hard, her voice choking on a sob.

"I know."

"Makes me want to shave my head."

Callum chuckled. "Why?"

"You heard Ewan. We look like him." Maggie shoved her hands into her thick coppery curls and pulled hard. "I hate them. I hate him. Why couldn't I look like my mother?"

"Ewan wasn't a fan of his father either. He's not shaving his head. And how would that make Bryce feel if you and Ewan hated your red hair?" Callum swept a curl back from her forehead. "I don't care where you are in your genetic lineup, but not all Drummonds are bad. I can't hate Douglas Drummond completely because what he did with your mother created you." He cupped her cheek and brushed his thumb across her lips. "I'm sorry your mother was treated so badly. No woman should have to go through what she did. But she chose to keep you when she had alternatives."

Maggie nodded. "I loved her so much, and she loved me."

"Red hair and all," Callum said softly. "Your red

hair is what I loved about you from the first moment I saw you at the airport."

She sniffed. "You're just saying that to make me feel better."

With his thumb, he tipped her chin up. "Is it working?"

Maggie smiled, her lips trembled, and a single tear escaped from the corner of her eye. "A little."

"Good. Because I don't want to kiss a woman with a dreadfully damp face." Despite his words, he did kiss her. He knew it was a mistake and would only make him want to continue kissing her, but he couldn't resist. When he hadn't been able to find her, briefly, he'd thought she was lost, and he'd almost lost his cool. He would have ripped the entire house apart looking for her.

"I'm not the right man for you, Maggie McKendrick, but you're stuck with me until we figure out who is targeting you."

She gave a shaky laugh. "You don't hear me complaining."

"Just don't get used to me. I'm serious. You deserve better."

"I'll take what I can get for as long as I can." Maggie pushed up on her toes and pressed her lips to his.

Callum dragged her up closer to him and claimed her mouth in a crushing kiss that stole his own breath away.

When he finally broke away, he knew he would have a hard time walking away from her, but he couldn't think about that now. Someone in the house had pushed her down the stairs of the hidden room.

"We can't do this all day."

"No?" Maggie drew in a deep breath and let it out slowly. "Why not?"

"Because someone tried to hurt you. I assume it's someone in the manor." Callum took her hand and led the way to the bed. Once there, he grabbed the journal. "Where did you get this?"

Maggie shrugged. "I found it under my pillow when I came back to the room."

"Did you see anyone coming or going from the room?"

She shook her head. "No."

"Whoever left it might have followed you to the library."

"I was alone in the library," Maggie said. "Or at least I thought I was until I was pushed."

With the journal in one hand, he took Maggie's other hand and went back downstairs and into Ewan's office.

"Lord Drummond, we have a problem," he said without excusing himself.

Ewan glanced up from the stack of ledgers. "We do. I heard from your computer hacker, Lucie. She traced the money and found that it was being deposited into a bank in—"

"—Montana," Callum finished.

Ewan's brow twisted. "How did you figure that out?"

"Because someone conveniently left this journal under Maggie's pillow. It explains a lot about your father."

"Whose journal is it?" Ewan asked.

Maggie's mouth pressed into a thin line. "Your mother's, Lady Elizabeth."

Ewan's frown deepened. "My mother's? I never knew she kept one. You say someone left it under your pillow?"

Maggie nodded. "That's where I found it."

"You have to assume whoever put it there knows the manor and knows where you are inside it. So, we need to be alert at all times." Ewan shook his head. "Who would have kept my mother's journal?"

"I don't know, but I suspect it was the same person who shoved me down the stairs to the secret torture room," Maggie said.

"Torture room?" Ewan stared at Maggie as if she'd lost a few marbles. "What are you talking about?"

"Were you not aware of the secret room hidden behind a bookshelf in the library?" Maggie asked.

Ewan shook his head. "As a child, I was all over the manor. I would have found it. You say it's in the library?"

Maggie nodded. "I found it and then someone pushed me down the stairs and shut the door, effectively locking me inside. If Callum hadn't come along when he did, I'd still be there."

"The depths of my father's treachery astounds me." Ewan shoved a hand through his hair. "How did you know where to look for this hidden room?"

"It's in the journal you're holding in your hand. Your mother said that your father—" Maggie swallowed hard. "That your father raped the nanny in a secret torture room hidden in the library. You mother forced your father to pay for the nanny to find a new home and provide child support for her child."

Ewan's mouth formed a thin, tight line. "Bloody bastard." He shook his head. "I take it that nanny was your mother. There's no excuse for rape. None. We can only hope he's rotting in hell for what he did." He glanced toward the ledgers and back to Callum. "That all lines up with the information I just received from your purple-haired techie. The mystery money my father was wire transferring went to a bank in Eagle Rock, Montana."

"The money your mother made him pay in child support," Maggie said.

"I wasn't here when my mother died. When I returned from my deployment, her room had been cleared of all her belongings." He met Maggie's gaze.

"Who would've cleared her belongings?" Maggie asked. "Your father?"

Ewan snorted. "I doubt it. He'd have had Mrs.

Jones do it, and she would've turned the journal over to my father. In which case, he would've burned it. I can ask Mrs. Jones about it."

"Ask me what?" a voice called out from the door to the study.

Callum turned to find Mrs. Jones carrying a tea tray.

"Your afternoon tea, sir," Mrs. Jones set the tray on a table in front of a Victorian settee. "You wanted to ask a question of me?" Once she'd divested herself of her burden, she straightened and faced Ewan.

"Yes, Mrs. Jones." Ewan held up his mother's journal. "Did you leave this in Ms. McKendrick's room today?"

The woman's brow dipped. "No, sir."

"Do you recognize it?" Ewan asked.

"No, sir." Mrs. Jones's eyebrows rose. "What is it?"

"My mother's journal."

Her eyes widened. "In all the years I knew Lady Elizabeth, I didn't know she kept one." She tilted her head. "Is there a problem?"

Ewan shook his head. "No, Mrs. Jones. Thank you for the tea."

"You're welcome." She glanced at the people in the room. "If you don't need me for anything else, I'll be in the kitchen helping Cook with dinner." Mrs. Jones left the study, closing the door softly behind her.

Callum waited enough time for Mrs. Jones to be

well out of earshot before asking, "Do you believe her?"

Ewan's gaze had followed the housekeeper out of the room. He still stared at the closed door. "I have no reason not to. She's been with the family for a very long time."

"She spoke with me about my mother," Maggie said. "I would think she'd have shared the journal or knowledge of it with me at that time. She knew my mother was pregnant when she left, but she didn't seem to know who the father might have been."

"Or she didn't want to tell you what happened to your mother," Callum suggested. "Maybe she put the book under your pillow so that you could read it for yourself."

Maggie stared at the journal Ewan still held. "I didn't get that feeling when Ewan asked if she knew what the book was. She appeared genuinely clueless. But you could be right."

A knock sounded on the door.

"Enter," Ewan called out.

Gregory stepped in. "Lord Drummond, your guest, Mr. Atkins, has arrived."

"Show him in," Ewan said.

Gregory opened the door wider.

A man entered wearing dark slacks, a white button-down shirt and a tweed blazer. His gaze moved from Ewan to Callum. "Callum McCall?"

Callum raised hand. "I'm Callum."

The man nodded. "I'm Peter Atkins. Hammerson said you might need a little assistance on this assignment."

Callum moved forward and gripped the man's hand. "Thanks for coming." He turned to Maggie. "This is Maggie McKendrick."

"Ah, the client," Atkins said and shook her hand. "Pleasure to meet you, Ms. McKendrick. We'll do our best to keep you and your family safe. I have a daughter, a little younger than you, who was kidnapped. Hammerson and his team helped me get her back. Alive."

"That's reassuring," Maggie said. "Thank you for coming."

Atkins turned to Ewan and grinned. "I'd recognize this man anywhere. Ewan Drummond. We served together in Afghanistan back when you were a young pup fresh out of SAS training."

Ewan shook the man's hand. "You saved my bloody arse when I almost stepped on an IED."

"If I recall, you covered for me when my weapon jammed." Atkins clapped Ewan on his back. "Good to see you again. Wish it were under better circumstances."

"Me, too." Ewan waved toward the settee and armchairs on the opposite end of the room from his desk. "Please, have a seat."

As if on cue, Mrs. Jones appeared with another tray, this one filled with more teacups, a second teapot and a stand holding muffins, finger sandwiches and pastries. She set the tray next to the first one she'd brought and left the room.

For the next thirty minutes, Callum, Ewan and Maggie brought Atkins up to date on what had occurred thus far.

"Hammerson is on his way and should be here within a couple of hours. Have you seen any signs of the Kholdov Coalition thus far?"

"No," Ewan said. "My staff is on alert. Should they see anyone enter the property, they're to inform me immediately."

Atkins glanced from Ewan to Maggie and back. "There is no mistaking you for a Drummond, Ms. McKendrick."

Maggie's lips pressed together, but she didn't say anything.

Callum reached for her hand and held it while the men talked through security and weak points on the property.

"All the doors and windows are secured," Ewan said. "No one leaves the house without one of the menfolk for protection."

A soft knock sounded on the door.

Before Ewan could grant entry, Bryce poked his head inside. "I want to ride Montana. Will someone come with me?"

"Montana is his horse," Ewan said and glanced around at the adults surrounding him.

"Is your horse in a barn or stable?" Atkins asked.

"In the stable," Bryce responded.

Atkins turned back to Ewan. "I wouldn't mind seeing the stable and any other outbuildings there are, as well as viewing the perimeter," Atkins said.

Ewan waved the boy closer. "Bryce, this is Mr. Atkins. He's come to visit for a few days. Mr. Atkins, this is my brother, Bryce."

Bryce entered the room and reached out to shake Atkins's hand. "Nice to meet you, Mr. Atkins."

Callum was amazed at the boy's manners and decorum. He was like an old man in a little body.

"The pleasure is mine, Bryce," Atkins said as if speaking to an adult, not a child. "I'd love to see Montana."

Bryce beamed up at the newcomer. "He's a horse, not a pony."

"Of course he is," Atkins said and held out his hand. "Lead the way."

Callum, Ewan and Maggie followed Bryce and Peter Atkins through the house and down to the stable.

Ewan opened the large barn doors and held them while the others entered.

Bryce ran forward. "Montana! We're going for a ride." When he reached the horse's stall, he stopped. "Montana?"

That morning when they'd visited the horse, Montana had poked his head over the top of the gate as soon as Bryce had approached. He didn't this time.

Bryce pulled back the latch, opened the stall gate and screamed, "Montana!"

Ewan and Callum rushed forward.

Ewan pulled Bryce back from the stall.

Maggie pulled the boy into her arms.

Callum turned to find the horse lying on its side, its breathing labored.

Ewan, Callum and Atkins entered the stall.

Callum looked for any possible injuries. When he found none, he shook his head.

"We need to get Alastair in here," Ewan said. "This horse is sick. He might know what to do. I'll notify the local veterinarian, as well."

Callum looked up to check on how Bryce was taking it.

Bryce wasn't standing outside the gate. Neither was Maggie. She'd probably taken him back to the house to his mother.

With Ewan on the phone, Callum started back toward the house.

Alastair came running across the yard. "Master Bryce and Ms. McKendrick said Montana's down."

"Where are Bryce and Maggie?" Callum asked.

"They were heading into the manor," Alastair said. "Show me the horse."

Callum led Alastair back into the barn, where Ewan and Atkins were standing inside the stall. Ewan was on the phone describing the horse's symptoms to the veterinarian.

With Alastair there and Ewan on the phone with the veterinarian, they didn't need Callum. He needed to get back to Maggie and Bryce.

Callum left the stable and jogged back to the manor. Cook let him in through the kitchen door. "Have you seen Bryce and Maggie?" he asked.

She shook her head. "They were headed out to the stable with you the last I saw them."

Callum hurried out of the kitchen and down the hallway, peering into open doorways in case they'd stopped in a sitting room or the study. When he found no sign of them, he headed up the stairs and ran for Bryce's room. Maggie and the boy weren't there. He ran toward the room he'd shared with Maggie. It was empty.

By that time, his heartbeat hammered against his ribs. He stepped out onto the landing where he found Fiona coming out of Bryce's room.

"Have you seen Bryce?" he asked.

Fiona frowned. "I thought he was with you."

"He's not. His horse is sick. I assumed Maggie brought him back to the manor." Callum started down the stairs.

Fiona followed, her voice rising. "I haven't seen either of them. Are you sure they didn't go back to the stable?"

"I didn't see them. I'll go back and check."

"I'm coming with you," Fiona said, running to keep up with Callum as he raced through the manor and out through the back door.

When Callum was halfway across the yard, Ewan and Atkins emerged from the stable.

Ewan frowned when he saw Callum running toward him.

"Are Bryce and Maggie inside the stable?" Callum asked, knowing the answer before Ewan spoke.

"No. I thought they would be with you."

"They aren't. As far as I could tell, they're not in the manor."

"What's wrong?" Alastair asked from the open stable door.

"Bryce and Maggie are missing," Callum said.

Alastair shook his head. "I just saw them. They were heading to the manor."

"They aren't there," Callum said, a terrible weight settling low in his gut.

"We need to spread out and check the garage, the garden and the grounds," Ewan said.

"I'll check the garage," Callum said.

Ewan pointed to Atkins. "Go wide, check the perimeter. Alastair, check the garden on the south lawn. Bryce likes to play there."

"I'll look through the house again," Fiona said and hurried away.

The men took off at a run.

Callum raced to the garage, where one of the

overhead doors was up and the long, black car was backed into the bay. "Maggie?" he called out. "Bryce?"

No one answered.

He searched inside and all around the building and found nothing.

Ewan, Atkins and Alastair met him at the entrance to the manor. Gregory, Mrs. Jones, Cook and Fiona came out, frowns pulling their brows downward.

They hadn't found them.

Callum pulled out his cell phone and hit Ace Hammerson's number before he remembered the man was on a plane headed his way. He called Dmytro instead.

"McCall, this is Dmytro. Did Atkins make it?"

"He's here," Callum replied. "But we've lost Maggie and Bryce."

CHAPTER 14

Maggie chased Bryce all the way to the garage. For a sick kid, he moved fast, especially when his horse's life depended on it.

A delivery van was pulling up to the garage at the same time as Alastair emerged. He glanced toward the van.

"Alastair!" Bryce called out. "Help. Montana is sick. You have to help him." The boy raced up to Alastair and wrapped his arms around the man's legs. "Please. Help Montana."

Alastair patted the boy's copper curls. "I will. I will. You and Ms. Maggie should head for the house and let your mama know to call the veterinarian. I'll go now and check on Montana. Don't worry. I'll take care of him." He met Maggie's gaze. "The delivery driver might need a signature, could you tell them to wait before you head inside?"

Maggie nodded.

"Go," Bryce begged. "Help Montana."

"I'm going." Alastair pried Bryce's arms loose from his legs. After one last glance at the delivery van and Maggie, he took off toward the stable and disappeared around the side of the four-car garage.

The delivery van swung close to the garage in a one-hundred-and-eight-degree circle and came to a stop. The back doors opened, and two men in dark clothing jumped out wearing black jumpsuits and baseball caps pulled low on their foreheads.

Maggie frowned. They weren't carrying any packages. Perhaps they were supposed to pick up something…? When they headed straight for her, her gut told her this wasn't a delivery. She grabbed Bryce's shoulders and spun him toward the manor. "Run!" she said. "Run, Bryce."

The little boy took off. Maggie was right behind him.

Neither one of them got far before the two men in black caught up with them.

One man caught her from behind, trapping her arms at her sides. "Run, Bryce. Don't look back!"

Her captor loosened one arm.

Maggie kicked and yelled, trying to remember all the self-defense training she'd taken back in Montana.

The man holding her slapped a rag over her mouth and nose.

His buddy snatched Bryce up in his arms. The kid gave it all he could, wiggling, kicking and biting.

Don't give up, Bryce! she wanted to yell, but couldn't.

Maggie held her breath and turned her head side to side, trying to shake free of the cloth. Her lungs ready to burst, she had to release the breath she'd been holding and inhale as the man carried her toward the back of the van. Within moments, her body went limp, and darkness closed around her.

* * *

How long she'd been out, Maggie had no idea. Minutes, hours, days? She couldn't tell. When she opened her eyes, she could see nothing but darkness. She was lying on her side on a hard metal surface. She tried to move her arms and couldn't. Her wrists had been secured behind her by what felt like a hard plastic zip tie. Her ankles were bound as well.

The last thing she remembered was being carried toward the delivery van. She was probably still in it. But it wasn't moving and, if the silence was any indication, the men who'd captured her weren't in the van at that moment.

A slight movement in front of her made her freeze.

A soft, high-pitched moan pierced the darkness and almost broke her heart. The men who'd captured her had taken the boy as well. She fought back a sob, angered by the cruelty. No child should have to be so terrorized. "Bryce?" she whispered.

"Mmm," he murmured, probably still under the effects of whatever they'd used on the rags they'd held over their mouths.

"Hey, sweetie, are you awake?" she asked softly.

"Mummy?" his small voice said into the dark void.

"No, sweetie, it's me, Maggie."

"I can't move my hands," he said.

"Me either," she said, trying to manage a calm, soothing tone when her heart was racing. "The bad men tied us up. Can you move your legs?"

"I can move them."

"Good. Now all we have to do is figure out how to get free." A slightly hysterical laugh slipped free. She clamped her lips shut and reminded herself she had to be strong for Bryce.

"I want my mum." Bryce's voice wobbled. "I'm scared."

"Honey, I'm scared, too. But you'll be back with your mother before you know it. First, we have to find a way out of here."

"Where are we?" he asked.

"I'm not exactly sure," she said.

"Why is it so dark?"

"I think we're in the back of that delivery van." Where the van sat was an entirely different question, along with how anyone would find them.

"Where are the bad men?" he whispered.

"I don't know, but while they're not here, let's find a way out."

"How? I can't move my hands."

"We need to find something sharp to cut these ties." She inched-wormed across the metal floor until her back and wrists bumped into the sidewall. Moving all the way around the back of the van, she could find nothing sharp she could use to break the ties.

"We need something sharp," Maggie murmured.

"I once bit a plastic straw in two," Bryce said.

"Oh, honey, this is harder than a plastic straw. I would hate for you to break a tooth on it."

"My mum says I'll lose my front teeth next year. They're baby teeth, and I'll get new ones."

He had a point.

"Let me break yours first to see if it's even possible." Maggie snaked across the floor until she was behind Bryce. He raised his wrists to get closer to her.

His tiny wrists were cinched tightly together, making it hard for her to get close enough to sink her teeth into the plastic. Once she was able to bite into the plastic, she didn't let go. It would take too much time to get back into position.

Maggie tried biting with her front teeth, but it didn't seem to make much of a dent in the hard plastic. Using a combination of biting and a back-and-forth sawing motion, she started making headway until suddenly it snapped in two.

Bryce immediately wiggled around. "Let me get yours."

Maggie rolled over, giving Bryce her back and her wrists.

Using his hands, Bryce felt along her side and found her wrists. Then his little forehead pressed against her back as he bit into the zip-tie.

Maggie had adult teeth. How would a five-year-old with baby teeth be able to break through the hard plastic?

While he continued to bite into the tie, Maggie did her best to pull it tight, hoping that keeping tension on the binding would help.

Voices sounded outside the van.

Bryce lifted his head.

"Don't stop," Maggie whispered. "But if they open the door, drop down, pretend you're sleeping and hide your hands behind your back. Got it?"

"Yes, ma'am," Bryce said and went back to biting her zip tie.

As the voices moved closer, Maggie tensed, ready to tell Bryce to drop.

Then her tie snapped, and her hands were free. She quickly slipped out of her shoes and wiggled and pushed until she was able to slip the ties off her ankles. Then she slid her feet back into her shoes.

Footsteps sounded near the back door.

"Get down and close your eyes," Maggie said softly.

Bryce lay down beside her.

She wanted to pull him into her arms and shield him, but they had to appear as if they were still asleep. Instead of holding the boy, she lay on her side, her arms behind her back, her ankles crossed together as if still secured.

At the screech of a metal door handle being turned, Maggie closed her eyes almost all the way, giving herself just enough of an opening to peer through her lashes.

Dim light eased the darkness from overhead lights in the distance.

"We got the brother and the sister," said a man with what sounded like a Russian accent. The beam of a flashlight bounced against the door and then shone into the interior of the van.

Maggie closed her eyes to the light, careful not to squint. She needed her captors to think she and Bryce were still under the influence of whatever they'd used to put them to sleep. If they thought they were awake, they might drag them out and learn they'd broken free of their bindings.

Maggie prayed Bryce wouldn't open his eyes or move.

"You must negotiate the ransom with your

cousin," the Russian said. "Tell him he has four hours to transfer money. If he doesn't pay, his family dies and you with them."

"Oh, he'll pay," a familiar voice said. Maggie recognized it as Ewan's cousin, Rory. "Look, I'm not going anywhere. Is it necessary to keep me tied up?"

"No, but then I don't want you to try anything."

"I'm surrounded by your men, each one of whom is armed. I'm not stupid."

The Russian snorted. "You take a loan to gamble."

"Okay, I'm not smart when it comes to gambling. But I'm not stupid when it comes to men with guns. Besides, I'll need my hands to use my phone."

"I'll take it under consideration," the Russian said.

A shout echoed across what sounded like a large warehouse. Another shout followed.

The man holding the door called out in Russian and then said something that sounded like a curse. He slammed the van door shut. Footsteps pounded as people ran. The shouting grew louder, more voices joining in.

With the door closed, Maggie released the breath she'd been holding. "You okay?" she whispered.

"Yes." Bryce moved closer. "Are those bad men going to kill us?"

"Not if we can help it, sweetie." Maggie hoped she was right. She'd do the best she could to get them out of the van, but from what Rory had said, they were surrounded by Russian gang members, and they were armed.

Maggie prayed Callum's other friends had arrived, that they'd come armed and that they knew where to find them.

CHAPTER 15

As soon as Callum realized Maggie and Bryce had gone missing, he'd notified Dmytro and Lucie. They'd promised to get back to him as soon as they knew anything. Dmytro had insisted his contact had something in the works.

With no idea where to start looking for Maggie and Bryce, Callum was forced to stand fast and wait for further information. He paced in Drummond's study, then down the hallway and out the front door, where he stared down the drive leading off the estate.

While waiting for Dmytro to come up with a location, Ewan spent the time in the stable working with Montana in an attempt to save the horse for his little brother. The veterinarian was with him and Alastair.

Since Callum and Peter Atkins were only in the

way, they returned to the manor and awaited the information they needed to stage a rescue.

An hour passed.

Callum was ready to climb a wall. He was a man of action. The wait was killing him, one minute at a time.

Ewan appeared in the doorway of the study, drying his hands on a towel. "We think Montana will make it. The veterinarian thinks he has come into contact with a toxin. He gave him something to counteract it. Time will tell if he pulls through."

"The horse is in a stall. How would he get hold of something toxic?" Callum asked.

"I don't know. Maybe a mouse that had eaten rat poison got into his stall, and the horse ate the mouse...?" Ewan shrugged. "We've done what we can. The vet will stay with him until he either dies or shows signs of improvement. What do you know about Maggie and Bryce?"

"Not a damn thing." At that moment, Callum's cell phone chirped. Dmytro's name flashed across the screen. Callum answered. "What have you got?"

"I have good news and bad news," Dmytro said. "The good news is that I know where they've taken them."

A rush of relief washed over Callum, followed quickly by a sense of impending doom. "And the bad?"

"You know how I said the Kholdov Coalition was operating in Donchenko Bratva territory?"

"Yes," Callum bit out impatiently. "So?"

"You might want to get to where they have taken them before the men of Donchenko Bratva arrive. They were angry to learn the Kholdov Coalition were operating on their turf. They are armed and likely to kill everyone in that warehouse. It will be a blood bath."

Callum met Ewan's gaze. "Where are they?"

"In Edinburgh, at a warehouse along the wharf. Sending coordinates now."

Callum's phone pinged an incoming text.

"We're on our way." Callum motioned for the others to follow as he ran for the door.

"Wait," Ewan said.

Callum stopped halfway out the study door.

Ewan went to a panel on the wall and pressed his finger to something. The panel slid back, exposing a large safe. He quickly rolled the tumbler right, then left and then right again, slowing to a stop. He cranked the handle and pulled open the door. Inside the safe was a collection of handguns in shoulder holsters, neatly hung on the back wall.

Ewan handed one to Atkins, one to Callum and took one for himself. He reached into a metal ammunition box and extracted several magazines filled with bullets and handed four to each man.

Callum slammed one magazine into the handle of

his pistol and shoved the spares into his pockets. He shrugged out of his jacket, slung the holster over his arms and buckled it in place and then slipped his jacket over the holster and gun.

Once they had their weapons, they left the study.

Fiona stood in the foyer, wringing her hands. "I'm going with you."

Ewan shook his head. "No."

"But he's my son," she said. "He'll be scared."

"You'll be more of a liability to this mission, putting Bryce at further risk," Ewan said sternly. Then his tone softened, "We'll let you know as soon as we get him safely away from his abductors."

She clutched Ewan's arm, her eyes filling with tears. "Please, bring back my little boy."

"We will." Ewan hugged the woman briefly while Callum and Atkins passed him in the hallway and ran toward the rear of the house.

"We'll take the big car," Ewan said. "Alastair can drive."

"If it's all the same to you, I'll take my rental. I would explode letting someone else drive," Callum said. "Besides, Alastair should stay with Gregory to protect Fiona and Cook in case the Russians circle back while we're gone."

Ewan nodded. "Agreed. Besides, he's not combat-trained. I don't even know if he can handle a gun, other than for hunting rabbits like we did when we were children."

The three men ran for the garage and climbed into Callum's rental car. Within minutes, they were out of the gate, racing for Edinburgh and the wharf where a Russian mobster was holding Maggie and Bryce.

Twenty minutes into the travel time to the coordinates, Ewan's phone chirped.

"It's from Rory," Ewan said. "Bloody hell."

Callum's breath caught and held. "What?"

"He says, *You must transfer five hundred thousand pounds to a specified account in two hours or they will kill Maggie, Bryce and me. If you try to find us, they will kill us. If you involve the police, they will kill us. Just transfer the money.*"

"That's not enough time," Ewan said. "I can't get to that much money. It would have to come from my father's estate. The bank won't release the funds since it's still in probate."

Callum's jaw tightened. "Then we have to find Maggie and Bryce and extract them before any harm comes to them."

"And the cousin?" Atkins asked.

"That bastard is on his own," Callum said through his teeth.

Clouds blocked the setting sun, making the day turn to night earlier. As they neared Edinburgh, light rain fell, making the roads slick and the traffic move at a glacial pace, forcing Callum to slow as well. Zipping in and out of traffic wouldn't get him there faster, but could cause him to wreck. He couldn't risk that.

Callum's cell phone rang; he handed it to Ewan. "Answer and put it on speaker."

"It's Hammerson," Ewan said as he received the call and hit the speaker button.

"Just landed," Ace said. "We have the coordinates to the warehouse and are loading into a car now. We'll be there in twenty minutes."

"Good, that's about what time we'll get there," Callum said. "If the traffic keeps moving. We can't park close to the warehouse. The kidnappers threatened to kill Maggie and Bryce if we tried to find them."

"Got it. Will ditch the car a couple of blocks from the warehouse and go in on foot. We have weapons and comms. Whoever arrives first, wait for the rest to get outfitted. We're tracking your phone location so we'll know where you are."

Callum prayed they'd arrive at the same time. He'd be hard-pressed to wait for the other, knowing the clock was ticking for Maggie and Bryce.

Two blocks from the coordinates, Callum pulled into an alley.

Moments later, another vehicle pulled in behind Callum's.

No sooner had the vehicles stopped than everyone leaped out. A tall man with dark hair and dark eyes approached Callum, Ewan and Atkins.

Atkins stuck out his hand to shake the other man's. "Ace, glad you made it." He turned to Callum. "Callum, Ace Hammerson, Regional Director of Brotherhood Protectors International."

Callum quickly shook hands with the man he'd spoken with on the phone a number of times but hadn't met in person until that moment. "Thanks for coming."

Ace nodded and quickly turned to the man beside him, who looked vaguely familiar and a little taller than the others. "You might know former SAS operative, Fearghas Gordon. He was the one who recommended you for our team."

"Good to see you, mate," Fearghas said with a decidedly Scottish accent, as he shook Callum's hand. "Heard about your last mission. I'm sorry it ended the way it did. We lost some of our best."

Callum gripped the man's hand hard, his heart constricting in his chest. He remembered serving with Fearghas on several missions early in his career with SAS. The man had known the men who'd died on Callum's last mission. "Good to see you," Callum said, a lump forming in his throat.

Fearghas backed a step and waved toward the man beside him, "This is Jack Collins, a former US Army Ranger. He met us at the airport, having flown over from Dublin."

Ace moved to the side and waved a hand toward the man on his left. "This is Dax Franklin, former

Marine Force Recon, and last but not least is Bennett Ramsey, former SAS, another one of our new recruits. Glad to have you both aboard."

Callum quickly shook hands with the men.

Introductions over, Callum helped Ace lift a duffel bag out of the trunk and lay it on the hood of their car. Inside were three semi-automatic rifles, a submachine gun, ammunition, bulletproof vests and a bag filled with communications devices and an assortment of knives.

Each man took a radio headset. One by one, they tested them. All the while, a clock ticked in Callum's head. He needed the ability to communicate with the team, but all this was taking time they needed to assess the situation, get in and extract Maggie and Bryce.

He shrugged out of his jacket and the shoulder holster, the heavy drizzle quickly soaking his shirt before he could slip into the bulletproof vest. Once he had it in place, he settled the shoulder holster over the vest, adjusting the straps, and slid two of the extra magazines into the vest pockets.

Dax took one of the semi-automatic rifles. Callum grabbed the submachine gun, and Jack commandeered the last semi-automatic. Each man clipped a sheathed knife onto his belt, locked and loaded their magazines and gathered close for instructions.

"I'll take Ramsey, Dax and Jack around the front of the warehouse," Ace said. "Fearghas, go with Callum, Ewan and Atkins and approach the building from the back. Report what you see: number of sentries, doors, windows we might sneak through, anything relevant. They can't know we're there until we get to the hostages."

They moved out, clinging to the shadows of the buildings. Callum led the way around the back. During the day, the area was busy with forklifts, booms and trucks moving cargo from ship to shore. At night, most dock workers and longshoremen went home, leaving the area in a ghost-like hush.

The men moved silently from building to building, ever closer to the one containing the Kholdov Coalition and the woman Callum could fall in love with, if he let himself. Hell, he was already well on his way there, despite his vow to stay away from relationships until he could control his nightmares.

But his feelings weren't important. What mattered was freeing the woman and child before they were harmed. They deserved a chance at a long, healthy life. He'd do his bloody damnedest to see they got that.

Callum stopped when the warehouse came into view. He peered into the shadows, searching for any guards positioned on the back side of the building.

A movement caught his attention. A shadow

moved as a figure detached itself from the dark side of the building. A man holding a rifle stood straight and still as if listening.

Callum froze, afraid he'd made a sound that had alerted the man.

Then the guard turned away from where Callum pressed against the corner of a building with Ewan, Atkins and Fearghas behind him.

Another guard stepped out of the shadows at the far corner of the building. He waved to the other and started running toward the guy at the center.

"We have a guard standing in front of a large overhead door," Callum reported. "Another on the far corner, moving quickly toward him."

"Three bogies on the front," Ace said. "They were leaning against the building. Now they're alert, weapons at the ready. Makes me wonder if they saw us coming. No. Wait. Headlights are coming toward us and the warehouse. They're moving fast. Damn."

"What?" Callum asked.

"They skidded to a stop in front of the building. It's a truck, and men are pouring out."

The pop, pop, popping sound of gunfire erupted.

"I believe the Donchenko Bratva gang has arrived," Ace said. "Any chance of entering through the rear?"

"Yes, if we move quickly. Right now, there are only two guards back here, and they're heading into the building. We're moving in."

"Jack and I will back up, swing around and cover you from the rear," Ace said. "We're leaving Ramsey and Dax to cover the front in case someone makes a run for it with the hostages."

"Ewan, Atkins, Fearghas, let's go." Callum led the way, submachine gun poised and ready.

The guards who'd been outside moments before had disappeared through a smaller door next to the overhead doors. The muffled sound of gunfire inside the building made Callum's gut roil. He hoped Maggie and Bryce were lying low, out of the line of fire.

As Callum reached the smaller door, the two guards who'd gone in burst through it. When they saw Callum, they raised their rifles.

Too late. Callum released a short burst of rounds from the submachine gun. The men jerked, dropped their rifles and fell forward.

Callum stepped past them, ducked low and slipped through the door, moving quickly to the side.

A man hiding behind a stack of wooden crates, leaned around the corner every so often to pop off a round with his handgun. He didn't notice Callum as he slipped up behind him, hooked his arm around the man's neck and squeezed tightly.

The man fought, but without air, he couldn't call out.

Fearghas grabbed the gun from the man's hand as Callum dragged him out the back door.

"Where are the girl and the little boy?" Callum asked. He loosened his arm enough for the man to respond.

He coughed and said something in Russian.

"He just called your mother a whore," Atkins said.

Callum tightened his hold around the man's neck and lifted him off his feet. He kicked his feet and clawed at Callum's arm, but Callum didn't relent, adrenaline pumping through his veins, his temper growing shorter.

As the man's attempts to escape slowed, Callum loosened his hold barely enough to allow the man to breathe. "Last chance," Callum warned him.

"In the van," he gasped in heavily accented English.

Callum shoved him toward Fearghas. "Shoot him, stab him, turn him over to Donchenko Bratva, I don't care. Just don't let him leave until I get Maggie and Bryce out." Callum entered the door again and took up the position the Russian had held long enough to study the dimly lit interior of the warehouse, where a turf war was in full swing, bullets flying indiscriminately. When he spotted the van, he let out a quiet curse and spoke into his radio headset. "I've spotted the van Maggie and Bryce might be in. It's halfway across the building. It appears the two gangs are divided in the building, shooting at each other. The van is near the middle of the battle."

"Getting to that van would be suicide," Fearghas said. "What's your plan? I'm in."

"You're right, there's no way a sane person could get to the van by just walking over to it. But it's faced forward, with an overhead door directly in front of it. If we could get to the van, we could ram it through the door and out into the street."

"Callum, you're not getting to the van," Atkins said. "There are so many bullets flying, you'll have lead poisoning before you can get inside it and drive it through the doors."

"I might not have to get inside it."

"How else will you crash it through the doors?"

Callum stared at a giant forklift near the back overhead door. "All the rest of you have to do is cover me while I get to that forklift."

"Callum, you're fucking crazy," Ewan murmured through the headset.

"You got a better idea?" Callum asked. "I'm listening."

"You know how to drive one of those things?" Atkins asked. "If you don't, I do."

"I worked in my uncle's bottling company for three summers and on weekends," Callum said. "I know how to drive a forklift. Cover me."

"We've got your six," Ace's voice came through the headset. "We're right behind you."

Callum glanced right, then left and then aimed for another stack of crates across an empty space.

Hunkering low, he sprinted, tucked the submachine gun into his belly and dove behind the crates as bullets splintered the wood over his head. He came up on his knees and aimed toward the source of the bullets, letting loose a burst of fire.

Behind him, his team added to the gunfire, giving Callum the chance to make it to the next stack of crates, several feet from the forklift.

"Moving forward. Right behind you," Fearghas said. "Keep going." His guys laid down suppressive fire.

Callum ran for the next stack of crates and ducked behind them.

A man dressed in black leaned around the stack.

Callum was ready. He unloaded another burst of bullets.

The Russian slid to the floor.

Callum burst out into the open, running full tilt for the forklift.

Gunfire rattled around him, the sound so loud it was almost a roar echoing off the rafters of the warehouse.

Bullets ricocheted off the metal casing of the forklift as Callum leaped up onto a ledge and dove into the driver's seat. He ducked low, his hands feeling around the controls in the semidarkness to find the key. He twisted it, and the engine chugged for a second and died.

"Start, you bloody pile of junk," he yelled and twisted the key again.

The engine chugged and then roared to life.

Callum shifted the gears, sending the forklift lurching forward. He dared to look up long enough to aim the tines of the machine toward the van at the center of the conflict and moved slowly forward.

His team had moved close enough to provide some suppressive fire as the forklift closed the distance to the van.

As he neared, he slowed even more and slid the tines under the chassis right before the forklift bumped into the back of the van. He increased the speed, pushing the van faster and faster toward the overhead door. If he could get it going fast enough, the weight of the van, combined with the speed at impact, should allow it to burst through the sheet metal out into the open, free of the showdown between the warring Russian mobsters.

That was his plan. It wasn't a great plan, but it was all he had. A bullet whizzed past his head, bounced off the metal roll bar and hit his shoulder.

Callum barely winced. Hyped up on adrenaline, he had one goal in mind: get the hostages out of the middle of the Russians' gunfight.

He glanced up in time to see that the van was nearing the overhead door. He increased the speed for one final burst of velocity before he'd have to stop the forklift to let the van smash into the door and push through with its own forward momentum. If he tried to push the van through with the forklift, he risked smashing the back of the van where Maggie and Bryce were likely held, killing them in the process of an attempted rescue. For a split second, doubt consumed him. He quickly brushed it aside and continued moving forward.

Suddenly, a man appeared near the overhead door. He slammed his palm against a big button on the wall, and the overhead door rose upward. The man who'd hit the button jerked, twisted and fell to the ground as bullets cut him down.

Though the door continued to rise, it wasn't quite fast enough for the van to clear it. The front of the van slammed into the door, catching it in the middle of the windshield and shattering the glass, but not crushing the body of the van.

The sheet metal of the overhead door crumpled, allowing the van to keep moving forward.

Callum stayed with it all the way out into the street, even managing to turn it slightly, taking it further away from the warehouse and closer to where they'd parked their cars.

Ramsey and Dax jogged alongside the forklift, weapons at the ready.

When Callum was far enough away from the firestorm, he slowed to a halt, backed the forklift away from the rear of the vehicle and shut down the engine.

Sirens sounded nearby, growing louder.

With Ramsey and Dax providing cover, Callum dropped down from the machine and ran toward the back of the van. The rear door was smashed in enough that he couldn't open it. He pounded his fist against the metal. "Maggie! Bryce! Please tell me you're in there." He leaned his forehead against the cool metal and prayed.

"Callum?" Maggie's muffled voice sounded through the door. "Callum? Oh God, Callum. I knew you'd come. I knew it."

"I want to go home," Bryce called out.

"The door is smashed. I'll need something to pry it open."

"Are you safe?" Maggie asked. "We heard gunfire. Some of the bullets came through the sides of the van."

Callum's breath caught. "Were you hit?"

"No," Maggie said.

Fearghas, Jack and Ewan arrived. They tried opening the door with all of them pulling hard with their hands. It didn't budge. A minute later, Ace showed up with a tire iron in his hand.

Callum wedged it in between the doors and pulled hard, leaning all of his weight into the metal bar. The door burst open, and Maggie fell into Callum's arms.

He dropped the tire iron to the ground and gathered Maggie close to him. Ewan swept Bryce up in his arms and held him close as the boy buried his face against his brother's chest. "I was scared, but I tried to be brave," he said with a catch in his voice.

Maggie leaned over and touched Bryce's arm. "You were very brave. You broke my zip tie. I couldn't have done it without you."

"We were brave together," Bryce reached for her hand, "because we're family."

As he stared at the three redheads holding each other, Callum's heart swelled. "Like family," he whispered, a family he'd love to be a part of. Though Douglas Drummond had been a bloody bastard, his children had turned out all right despite him.

"What about Rory?" Ewan asked. "Did you see my cousin in there?"

Callum placed a hand on Ewan's shoulder. "I'm pretty sure he was the guy who opened the overhead door." He shook his head. "He didn't make it."

"I'm sure we'll get the call later this evening." Ewan hugged Bryce closer. "As angry as I was that he put our family in danger, I didn't wish for him to die that way."

"He got us out of the warehouse," Callum said. In his eyes, the man had redeemed himself at a heavy cost—his life.

"As well-meaning as the rescue effort was," Ace said, "I'm not sure the Scottish police will look the other way at the weapons we brought into the country."

Behind them, the truck that had brought the Donchenko Bratva to the warehouse spun in the middle of the road and took off in the opposite direction. No one else emerged from the building.

Callum looped his arm around Maggie's waist and hurried her to where they'd parked the cars. They tossed the weapons into the trunks, climbed in and took off down a back alley, not emerging onto the main road until they were well past the incoming police cars.

Maggie sat in the front seat, holding Callum's hand all the way back to Drummond estate.

When they arrived at the manor, Bryce was reunited with Fiona, who cried as she held her little boy.

They gathered in the kitchen where Cook had prepared food for all of them. After Fiona took Bryce up to his bed, the others stayed up late, talking about the mission until the adrenaline waned and they wandered up to the bedrooms Mrs. Jones had prepared for the additional guests.

Callum walked Maggie to the door of the bedroom they shared.

"You're staying," Maggie said.

He pulled her close and kissed her gently. "I thought I'd lost you, and it nearly broke me."

"I thought I'd never see you again. Bryce and I

were working on finding our way out when the bullets started flying. I didn't think you'd find us in time. All I could think about was that I wanted to be with you."

He leaned his forehead against hers. "But I can't. I don't trust myself."

"We can make love and then sleep in different beds. You'll be close, but far enough away you won't hurt me."

"I can't ask you to live like that."

"You don't have to ask me." She wrapped her arms around his neck. "I'm telling you it's what I want."

"You deserve a better life. A better man. One who doesn't try to kill you in his sleep."

"Do I get a say in this?" she asked.

He kissed the tip of her nose. "No." Callum knew what he had to do. He had to walk away, though every fiber of his being wanted to stay. "I'll sleep on one of those fancy sofas in the sitting room downstairs. I'm leaving with Ace and his crew tomorrow."

Maggie's eyes widened. "That's it? You're going to leave?"

He nodded. "I have no choice. I'm not fit for a relationship with anyone."

"I get it." Maggie backed away. "You aren't as into me as I'm into you, but you can't just come out and say it." She squared her shoulders. "Thank you for coming to my rescue. You did your job. Making love with me was probably just a perk, or worse...a responsibility to keep the client happy. Either way, you're off the hook. I won't bother you anymore. You can go on with your life, and I'll go back to Montana."

Maggie stepped into the room Callum had shared with her and made the sweetest love with her. She met his gaze. "Goodnight and goodbye." Then she closed the door.

CHAPTER 16

MAGGIE LAY AWAKE ALL NIGHT, stewing over Callum's rejection. As much as she wanted to stay the rest of the two weeks and get to know her brothers, she couldn't remain in the house where she'd made love to Callum and fallen in love with the big jerk.

He was leaving with Ace the next day. She couldn't stay in a house filled with memories of him after he left. She'd be so depressed she'd be horrible company for Ewan and Bryce. They had gone through enough that they didn't need to have her hanging around, making them sad, too.

She might as well go home. If she could leave before Callum, she wouldn't have to experience that empty, lonely feeling of a place that had been full of him and suddenly wasn't. Okay, that sounded crazy, but it was a thing.

Rather than lie in bed, crying over a man who

obviously didn't feel the same about her as she felt about him, Maggie gave up, got up and packed.

By the time dawn peeked over the horizon, she had gathered her belongings and showered and changed into her travel clothes—a pair of leggings, a stretchy T-shirt and a long, warm sweater. She draped her overcoat over her arm and carried her suitcase down the stairs, careful not to make a noise and wake anyone in the house.

Rather than exit through the front door, she decided to go through the kitchen and out the back to avoid running into anyone.

As she passed the sitting room, she paused and peered into the darkened interior.

Callum sat on the sofa near the fireplace, his feet propped on the table in front of him and his head leaned back against the carved wood frame of the seat as if he'd fallen asleep sitting up, trying to stay awake.

Were his nightmares so bad he didn't want to go to sleep?

Maggie pressed a hand to her chest, feeling his pain, knowing she could do nothing to ease it. Not as long as he pushed her away, refusing to let her help him in any way.

She couldn't help him if he didn't want to be helped. It wasn't as if they'd known each other long. He hadn't committed anything to her. He'd said from the beginning that nothing would come of a relationship between them.

Then why did she feel like she was abandoning the man? That she was running away from helping him work past the PTSD that plagued his dreams.

Maggie had to remind herself that he didn't want her help and that he would be leaving that day anyway, probably going with Ace to Zurich, where the Brotherhood Protectors International was based.

She'd always wanted to go to Switzerland. Maggie sighed. She'd have to save her money and make that trip alone. Callum wasn't interested. He wouldn't be waiting for her.

Hiking her backpack over her shoulder, Maggie gave Callum one last, longing glance then moved on, down the hall, heading for the back door.

As she passed through the kitchen, Cook stepped out of the pantry, nearly scaring her to death. She pressed a hand to her chest and laughed. "I didn't think anyone was awake yet."

Cook eyed Maggie's suitcase. "Are you leaving?"

Heat filled Maggie's cheeks. "I need to go home to Montana."

She gave Maggie an accusing look. "Lord Drummond and Master Bryce will be disappointed you didn't stay long enough to say goodbye."

"I left a note on the dresser in my room. It explains everything. I don't like long, drawn-out goodbyes."

Cook crossed her arms over her ample chest. "What about Mr. McCall? He went to the trouble of rescuing you from the Russians. Doesn't he deserve a face-to-face goodbye?"

Maggie's mouth twisted into a grimace. "Didn't he tell you? He's leaving today. I'm just leaving sooner. He won't miss me."

Cook's eyes narrowed. "You're running away."

Maggie shook her head. "No. I just know when I need to go home. I don't belong here. My life is in Montana, teaching preschool children. This was just a nice vacation where I got to meet my brothers." Her eyes filled with tears. "I really hope Bryce feels better soon. He's such a beautiful and brave little boy. And I hope Ewan gets through the probate period without any issues. I told him in my letter that I want nothing from the estate and that it should go to the rightful heirs: Ewan and Bryce. I only wanted to meet them, not take anything from them."

"Ewan never wanted any part of his father's estate," Cook said. "He was so very happy to know he had a sister. One more person to share the burden of his father's legacy. He was really happy when you arrived. And Master Bryce...he loves having a sister. Even if she's a grown woman. You're one more person to love. That little boy has a heart so big, he fills it with all the people he loves without running out of room." Cook sighed. "Please reconsider and stay."

Maggie's eyes filled with tears. "I love Ewan and Bryce. I always wanted siblings, and I'm happy to know I have them, but I can't stay. I don't belong here. I belong in Montana. I'm sorry, but I have to go." *Before I fall apart and beg Callum to love me.* She wanted to say that and almost did.

Instead, she adjusted her backpack on her shoulder, lifted her suitcase and smiled. "Thank you for everything, Cook. Tell everyone I love them."

"Them or him?"

Maggie's heart skipped several beats. "Goodbye, Cook. Thank you for everything," She turned and left the manor.

The sun had just risen on the horizon as she made her way to the garage, hoping to find Alastair awake and able to take her to the Edinburgh airport. Once she got there, she'd have the airline change her ticket and find her a flight leaving that day, heading back to Eagle Rock, Montana, and the only home she'd ever known. A home empty of family. Her mother was gone. Her brothers would be here in Scotland, and the man she was falling in love with would be on his way to Zurich.

She had nothing to keep her in Montana. Now that she knew she had family in Scotland, she couldn't bring herself to stay with the memory of Callum lingering everywhere she turned in the manor.

As she approached the garage, she called out

softly, "Alastair?" She hoped she didn't have to wake him, but she really wanted to leave before Callum woke. He'd rejected her the night before. She couldn't go through that again. Her heart already hurt so much.

"Alastair," she called out again.

"Ms. McKendrick," a voice said behind her. "Can I help you?"

Maggie spun to face the tall, dark-haired man. "Yes, please. Could you give me a ride to the airport? I need to go back to the States sooner than I'd expected." *Because I foolishly fell in love with a man who doesn't love me in return.*

"Of course," Alastair said. "Give me a minute to wash my hands. I was working with Bryce's horse this morning."

"Is he feeling better?"

"He is." Alastair gave her a brief nod. "I'll be back in a moment." The man hurried away. A couple of minutes later, he returned, his hands still damp from having washed them. He held the back door of the big black car open. "I'll get your suitcase," he said.

"Thank you," Maggie said, glad he would handle it. She slid into the back seat. Alastair closed the door, then carried her suitcase to the trunk and stowed it there.

Maggie sat in the back seat, her hands in her lap, her heart a sore, aching lump in her chest.

Alastair slid into the driver's seat, started the car and drove out of the garage.

When they passed through the gate, Maggie made the mistake of looking back.

Was she making a mistake? Should she have tried harder to convince Callum that his PTSD wasn't insurmountable, that she could love him no matter what?

As it was, he didn't know that she'd gone from greatly attracted to the man to loving him so fast that her head was still spinning.

She was in love with him.

Maggie leaned forward and called out, "Alastair, turn around. I forgot something." She forgot to tell Callum that she loved him. She was more than willing to work with him or wait for them to share a bed throughout the night as long as they could be together through the day and into the night when they were making love together.

Alastair didn't slow or turn around.

Thinking he might not have heard her, she raised her voice a little louder. "Alastair, I need to go back to the manor. I forgot something very important."

Still, Alastair didn't slow, stop or turn around.

"Can you hear me?" she asked.

"Oh, I hear you," Alastair drove out onto the highway and headed toward Edinburgh. "I just don't choose to turn around."

Maggie met Alastair's dark eyes in the rearview

mirror. "What do you mean, you don't choose to turn around? Don't you work for the Drummonds?"

Alastair snorted. "You think I don't know why you came to Scotland and Drummond Estate? You want your share of the inheritance. You think a bastard child of Douglas Drummond is entitled to inherit an equal portion of his estate? You're wrong. You read the journal. You know he was forced to put that wording into his will. His wife blackmailed him, or he never would have agreed to that wording. Each child of lord Drummond shall inherit equal shares of his estate." Alastair laughed. "The old man knew that wording would destroy his heritage by diluting it across all the children he spawned should they discover their connection to the bastard." Alastair shifted his gaze to the road ahead. "Drummond wanted his oldest son to take an interest in his estate, to follow in the old man's footsteps. Ewan hated his father and never wanted to join the family business. He couldn't wait to get as far away from the man as possible. What Lord Drummond didn't know was that his oldest son never left—because his oldest son wasn't Ewan."

"Ewan isn't his oldest son." Maggie's gut clenched. "You are."

"Ding, ding, ding! Give the bright girl a prize." Alastair met her gaze in the mirror again. "Ewan isn't the oldest child of Douglas Drummond. I am. Like your mother, he raped mine, too. Only Lady E didn't find my mother crying in the garden. My mother didn't have Lady E stand up to Lord Drummond and demand he do right by the woman he raped. Because my mother loved my father, the man who raised me, so much, she didn't want him to lose his job and didn't want him to know what had happened, so she let my father believe I was his child."

Alastair's anger burned through his gaze into hers.

Maggie pressed a hand to her chest, suddenly afraid of the man who'd seemed to be a loyal servant to the Drummond family.

"Unbeknownst to Daniel Boyd, he raised his boss's son as his own. My mother, the assistant to Lady E, kept that secret through my childhood, through the death of Lady Elizabeth and to her own deathbed, where she confessed the truth to my father. Several months later, I knew he was dying of a broken heart, but not just because my mother had left us. He was also heartbroken that they never had children together, as he'd thought for all those years. He told me he couldn't stand to look at me, knowing I was Lord Drummond's son, not his. He died hating Lord Drummond and hating me."

"I'm so sorry that happened to you. But I didn't come to Scotland to claim an inheritance. I came to meet my brother, only to learn I actually had two. Now, make that three."

"And there's no telling how many more half-brothers and sisters we have if my father continued in his penchant for adultery. For the longest, I thought I only had to get rid of two to claim what is rightfully mine as the oldest son. Not a portion of the estate, but everything. All the things my mother and I didn't get that you got when Lady E tried to make right what our father did to your mother. My mother didn't have that advantage. And when she died of cancer, Douglas Drummond didn't even visit her in the hospital or send her flowers. He shrugged her off the moment she got sick."

"You want the entire estate?" Maggie asked, shocked at Alastair's confession.

"Everything down to the horses in the stable. I'm the oldest son. I should inherit everything, not Ewan. I stayed and cared for the horses. I drove the old man around wherever he wanted to go. He never thanked me, never acknowledged me other than as someone who could do his bidding. I deserved more."

All the while Alastair was talking, he drove further and further away from the estate. Based on the landmarks, Maggie could tell that they were at least headed in the direction of the airport. She leaned forward and studied more of the signs. Yes, they were headed toward Edinburgh. She slipped her cell phone out of her purse. Holding it low on her lap, she looked for Callum's number.

"You are taking me to the airport, aren't you?"

Maggie asked as if nothing was terribly wrong when she knew things were about to get bad.

Alastair shook his head. "I told you, I only had two Drummonds to get rid of until you showed up. Now, I have three."

"Get rid of?" She glanced up. "What do you mean? I'm going back to Montana. Isn't that what you want?"

Just when she found Callum's number, Alastair slammed on the brakes.

Maggie jerked forward, the seatbelt catching her.

Alastair pivoted, reached over the back of the seat and plucked her phone from her hands. He rolled down the window and tossed her phone out." Then he resumed driving. "Even in Montana, you can inherit a portion of the Drummond Estate. It's mine. Not yours, not Ewan's and not Bryce's. It's mine, and I'm going to make sure no one else gets it."

"The apple..." Maggie's heart sank into the pit of her belly. "The apple you gave to Bryce made him sick after one little bite. Did you know it rolled into Montana's stall?"

Alastair shot a narrow-eyed glance at Maggie. "You lie."

She shook her head. "Bryce dropped it. Before he could pick it up, it rolled in with Montana. He ate all but the tiny piece Bryce ate for your benefit." Maggie's brow furrowed. "It was poisoned, wasn't it? That's why Montana was so sick. You've been giving

Bryce apples laced with poison. Haven't you? That's why he's been so sick." She covered her mouth with a hand. "I can't believe you did that. Are you so greedy that you'd poison a child?"

Alastair's mouth formed a tight line across his face. "I want what's mine. All I have to do is eliminate the competition." He stared straight forward, continuing to drive down the country road toward Edinburgh.

As they came to a slow-moving river along the way, Alastair cast a quick glance toward Maggie in the back seat, hit the child locks on the back doors and then he veered off the road and drove the car toward the river.

Maggie screamed as the vehicle bumped down a short hill toward the river.

At the last second, Alastair opened his door and flung himself out onto the bank.

The car continued forward and plunged into the dark waters of the river.

Maggie scrambled to unbuckle her seatbelt as water quickly filled the interior of the vehicle. Her seatbelt refused to release. When she tried to open the back door of the vehicle, the child locks had been engaged. To make them release, she'd have to climb over the front seat, find the release button, disengage the child lock and then get the hell out of there.

Cold water swirled around her, chilling her to the bone. Was this the end of a good run? Would she never see her home in Montana again? She wouldn't have the pleasure of watching Bryce grow into a handsome man like his brother Ewan. She wouldn't see Callum again and tell him she wouldn't give up. When you found someone so perfect for you, you stuck around and showed him how right you were for each other.

Maggie fought with the buckle, determined to return to the manor and tell Callum all the reasons why he should get over himself and let her love him.

Damn it! She refused to die.

The water filling the interior of the car had other plans.

CHAPTER 17

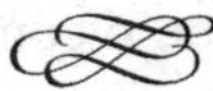

Tap. Tap. Tap.

Callum brushed away something small tapping against his shoulder. He hadn't slept so soundly since the mission from hell. He wanted to continue sleeping.

Tap. Tap. Tap.

"Mr. Callum, are you awake?" a soft, high-pitched voice whispered in his ear.

Callum lifted an eyelid.

Bryce stood beside him, his face inches from his.

Callum jerked awake and sat up.

Holy hell. If he'd been in the middle of one of his nightmares, he could have killed the kid.

His heart racing, he shoved his hands through his hair.

Then it dawned on him that he hadn't had a

nightmare. He'd slept the entire night without a dream.

He straightened and focused on young Bryce. "You're up early."

Bryce nodded. "I want to go see Montana. I thought Ms. Maggie would come, too, but she isn't in her room. Do you know where she is?"

Callum frowned. "Is she in the kitchen?"

Bryce shook his head. "No. Only Cook."

Callum pushed to his feet. "I'll go look for her. While I do that, you should have Cook fix breakfast for you."

Bryce nodded. "When you find Maggie, can you tell her I want her to come with me to see Montana?"

"Will do," Callum said. The boy must have bonded with Maggie over their shared adversity, having been kidnapped together.

While Bryce went off to the kitchen, Callum climbed the stairs and knocked on Maggie's bedroom door. When she didn't answer, he went in, thinking she might be in the bathroom and hadn't heard his knock.

The bathroom door was open with no sign of Maggie.

As he looked around the room, he noted the neatly made bed and a clean, pristine room with absolutely no sign of the woman who'd been there. No clothes were draped across a chair, no roller bag lay unzipped and open on the floor. No backpack.

His own backpack lay beside the door where he'd set it the first night there, but everything that had belonged to Maggie was gone. It was as if she'd never been there.

His heartbeat quickened as an empty feeling settled like lead in the pit of his belly.

She's gone.

One last glance at the room was all the verification needed. She'd packed up and left.

As he turned back toward the door, something caught his eye. An envelope lay propped against a pillow on the bed. He crossed to the bed and noted his name scrawled across the front in Maggie's handwriting.

His hand shook as he lifted the flap on the back, extracted the single sheet of paper inside and read.

Dear Callum,

I couldn't stay and watch you walk away again, so I'm leaving before you have the chance.

You think your PTSD makes you dangerous to me, but what you don't understand is that I could have loved you—every piece of you, even the broken ones—if only you'd let me. We all carry trauma. We all have scars. That doesn't mean we're unworthy of love.

I wanted the chance to love you. Truly, I did. I would have taken you any way you came—nightmares, darkness, and all—because those things don't define you. They're only a part of your story, not the whole of you. Together, we could have found a way through the violent dreams and the shadows. But you have to let someone in. You have to let me in.

I'm returning to Montana. If you decide you're ready—if you decide you want to give me that chance—I'll be there. The next move is yours, Callum.

Ready to love you,

Maggie

Callum read the letter a second time through a haze of moisture in his eyes. She wanted to love him.

God, he wanted to love her. Could he let her in? Would the risk to her life be too great? He could never live with himself if he hurt her.

Though they hadn't known each other long, he knew deep in his heart that he could love her. Yes, he could live without her, but he'd be the miserable, lonely shell of a man he'd been since losing his team. He wanted the chance to love and be loved.

He wanted Maggie.

Now, she was gone.

Callum frowned. How far could she have gone? To get to Montana, she had to catch a flight. Surely, she'd have to wait to catch that flight at the airport. If he hurried, he might catch her before she left Scotland. Even if she had left Scotland, he could follow her all the way back to Montana. And he would because she was the best thing that had ever happened to him, and he couldn't let her leave without a fight. He'd get the therapy he needed, work through the trauma and bad dreams with the ultimate goal of spending the rest of his life with a woman so warm, caring and beautiful inside and out as Maggie.

Spurred by determination, he ran from the room and descended the stairs two at a time. She would have had to get a ride into Edinburgh. Alastair, the chauffeur, would have taken her.

Callum ran down the hallway toward the back of the manor.

Before he reached the back door, Cook stepped out of the kitchen and blocked his exit. "She left less than twenty minutes ago. If you hurry, you can catch her."

Callum grabbed Cook and pulled her into a quick hug. "Bless you."

"No need for that," Cook murmured, her face flushing a ruddy red as she smoothed her hands over her apron.

With a bark of laughter, Callum grinned and spun. As he ran for the back door, he called out over his shoulder, "Let Ace Hammerson know where I'm headed. Hopefully, I'll be back soon with Maggie."

He sprinted for the garage, arriving within seconds. The overhead door where the big black car was usually parked was rolled up. The space was empty.

Callum opened the door behind which his rental car was parked, jumped in, started the engine and raced out of the garage. He skidded sideways on loose gravel as he turned onto the driveway and floored the accelerator.

A twenty-minute head start wasn't insurmountable if the roads were dry and traffic didn't get in the way. He could be at the airport before she had a chance to check in with the airline.

Feeling hopeful, he floored the accelerator on the straight stretches and slowed on the curves. When the road straightened, following along a slow-moving river, Callum pressed his foot all the way to the floor. The rental car picked up speed. With no other vehicles on the road, he flew.

Suddenly, a man with soaking wet clothing scrambled up the bank bordering the river and stumbled into the road.

Callum slammed on the brakes and turned slightly to avoid hitting the man. He didn't have time to stop until after he passed the man. Several yards further, he was able to pull the car to the side of the road. As much as he wanted to get to Maggie, the drenched man appeared to be in trouble, and there was something familiar about him.

Callum shifted into park, jumped out of the car and ran back to the man who was heading his way.

As he neared, Callum recognized the man as Alastair Boyd, the chauffeur and the man transporting Maggie to the airport.

Alastair staggered toward him. "I don't know what happened... Everything was fine, and then the car veered off the road. I couldn't stop it and was barely able to get out."

Callum gripped the man's arms. "Where's Maggie?"

"I couldn't open the door. I couldn't get her out. It's too late." Alastair fell against Callum.

No. It couldn't be too late. Alastair was just coming up from the river. He pushed Alastair to arm's length and shook him. "How long ago did the car go under?"

"Too long. She's gone, I tell you. It's too late."

"It's not too late. She's not going to die if I can help it," Callum said through gritted teeth. He tried to push Alastair away.

The big man wrapped his arms around Callum and wouldn't let go. "It's too late. She's gone. You'll only put your own life at risk."

"Let go. She might have found an air pocket. I have to try."

Alastair tightened his hold around Callum. "I can't let you do that."

A rush of rage boiled up inside Callum. "The hell you can't." What the hell was wrong with the man? Why was he holding him back from saving Maggie? Desperate to get to her, Callum slammed his heel onto Alastair's instep.

Alastair grunted in pain and loosened his hold just enough that Callum was able to bring his hands up between them and knock the other man's arms away. Once free of Alastair, Callum started for the river.

The chauffeur swept out his leg, tripping Callum. He came down hard on his knees. Alastair jumped on the man's back and tried to pin him in a wrestler's hold.

Fear for Maggie's life gave Callum the adrenaline and determination to roll Alastair over and break free of his grip, but the man was like an octopus. As soon as Callum freed himself of one hold, Alastair pinned him in another.

Beyond frustrated, Callum roared, doubled his fists together and swung them at Alastair's jaw. The force of the hit knocked the man backward and over the side of the road. Alastair tumbled down the embankment and crashed into a tree, headfirst. He lay still, unmoving.

Callum spotted the rear end of the black car, the only part of the vehicle that hadn't sunk below the surface. If he wanted to get her out, he would have to break a window. He ran back to the rental car, popped the trunk and grabbed the tire iron.

His heart in his throat, Callum slid down the embankment, dove into the river and swam for the car and Maggie, the tire iron weighing him down and making it hard to fight the current. At last, he reached the car, dragged himself up onto the rear end, almost losing his grip on the tire iron in the process.

Then he knelt close to the rear window and yelled, "Maggie, if you can hear me, move away from the back window. I'm going to break it." Without waiting another moment, he slammed the tire iron into the window.

The glass shattered where the metal bar hit it, but it took several more hits before the window was sufficiently broken. Using the tire iron, he swept the jagged edges loose.

The interior of the car filled the rest of the way with river water. In the murky swirls, copper curls floated to the surface.

Callum's heart squeezed so painfully, he couldn't breathe. He reached for the curls, tangled his hands in them and started to pull Maggie up by her hair. She didn't budge.

Callum reached deeper for her head, ran his hands along her shoulders and found that her seat-belt held her in place. He dove headfirst into the frigid water and followed the belt to the buckle. After several failed attempts, the buckle came loose. He pushed the shoulder strap aside.

His lungs about to burst, Callum hooked his arms beneath Maggie's and hauled her through the rear window onto the trunk of the car. She lay limp and lifeless, her face pale, her chest still.

"No, no, no. You said you wouldn't give up on me." Callum pinched her nose, covered her mouth with his and blew breath into her lungs. Then he performed chest compressions, alternating between them, repeatedly.

A shout from the top of the riverbank made him glance up for only a second. Two men stood there waving and then disappeared.

A few minutes later, the wail of a siren came screaming to a stop somewhere nearby.

Still, Callum didn't stop. Couldn't stop. Maggie wouldn't have given up on him. He wasn't giving up on her. "You have to live. I have to tell you." He breathed into her mouth and then whispered against her lips. "I love you, Maggie McKendrick. You have to live."

Resuming the compressions, Callum glanced across to the bank where emergency rescue personnel were shoving a paddleboard into the water. Two of the men, dressed in wetsuits and life jackets, swam the paddleboard toward the car. The men on shore held onto a line attached to the board.

The vehicle shimmied beneath Callum. "Don't go down on us now," he said. "Maggie needs you to hold on just a little longer."

The rescue team made it to the car as it shook violently beneath Maggie and Callum.

They grabbed Maggie's shoulders and were lifting her onto the paddleboard when the car moved forward and sank beneath the surface.

"Take my hand," one of the rescuers called out, reaching for Callum.

Callum shook his head. "Get her out. I'll make it on my own."

The two men shoved Maggie onto the board.

Their team on shore pulled the line tight and reeled in the swimmers and the paddleboard with Maggie.

Callum swam behind them, anxious for them to continue CPR on Maggie. He came ashore several feet away, giving the rescue team the space they needed to maneuver.

As they dragged the paddleboard up onto shore, Maggie's body jerked. She rolled her head to the side and coughed up water.

Callum's legs buckled beneath him, and he fell to his knees.

Maggie's eyes opened. "Callum," she croaked.

He crawled through the mud as close as he could get. "I'm here, my bonnie lass."

"You came for me?"

He gave a laugh that sounded more like a sob. "I did. I want you to give me another chance. You believed in me when I didn't believe in myself."

"I hadn't gone very far—" Maggie coughed before she could continue. "I asked Alastair to take me back to the manor." She reached for his hand.

He took it and held it gently.

"I wasn't going to give up on you. I couldn't," she said, her voice gravelly and weak. "You're worth fighting for."

"I was following you to the airport to stop you before you got on the plane. I couldn't let you go. I love you, Maggie."

Maggie lay back and closed her eyes, a smile curving her lips. "That's all I need to hear. The rest, we can work on." Her eyes popped open again. "Alastair?"

One of the rescue team leaned close to Callum. "Is Alastair the guy we found nearby, crashed into the tree?"

Callum nodded.

The man's lips pressed together. "I'm sorry. He must have died on impact."

Maggie sighed. "The world is a better place without him." Her gaze locked with Callum's. "He deliberately drove the car into the river to kill me—and he was poisoning Bryce."

Callum swore.

"Montana ate the apple meant for Bryce. It almost killed the horse. Bryce would be dead had he eaten more than a tiny bite."

"Why would he do that?" Callum asked.

Maggie closed her eyes. "The inheritance. He was another one of Lord Drummond's bastard children. He was our brother. The difference was that he wasn't willing to share."

The emergency medical technician carried Maggie up to the road and loaded her into an ambulance. Callum climbed in with her and held her hand all the way to the hospital in Edinburgh.

"You know, we have some decisions to make," Callum said.

"We do?" she asked. "As in, you and me? Or do you have a mouse in your pocket?"

Callum chuckled. "We, as in me and you."

"What decisions?"

"Montana or Scotland, for one."

Her brow furrowed. "My head is full of water. I don't understand."

"Are we going to live together in Montana or Scotland. I'm game for either location. I've always wanted to ride western and wear a cowboy hat."

"If I have a choice, I'd like to stay in Scotland near my brothers."

"I think Ewan and Bryce would be amenable to that. We could get a place close to the manor."

"The manor has a lot of rooms," Maggie mentioned. "And I think Ewan would make another great addition to the Brotherhood Protectors International team."

Callum grinned. "I was thinking the same. I'd almost bet Ace has started that discussion while we've been busy swimming."

"You know," Maggie said, "if what's happening here goes to the next step, will you wear a kilt to our wedding?"

Callum laughed. "I'd wear a pink polka-dotted

tutu if it made you happy." He leaned forward and kissed her forehead.

"You two are nauseatingly cute." The medical technician adjusted Maggie's IV line. "If you don't end up together, it would be a bloody shame."

Maggie grinned at Callum.

The medical technician added, "And definitely, wear the kilt."

EPILOGUE

STANDING in front of the full-length mirror, Maggie adjusted the tartan sash of the Drummond clan. She'd draped it over her strapless white wedding dress with its fitted sweetheart bodice and slim skirt. A strand of curls had escaped the pin holding it in place in the elaborate updo the hairstylist had created. She turned around and looked over her shoulder at the medium-length soft train that would trail gracefully down the aisle as she walked the length of the church aisle to meet her fate with the amazing man she would marry that day. The dress was perfect.

Sadie sighed. "You're absolutely stunning."

Maggie smiled. "Coming from the beautiful, famous actress Sadie McClain, that's a huge compliment." She frowned as she looked at her reflection in the mirror. "It's just that my hair..."

Sadie studied her with her head tilted slightly. "It's lovely, but..."

"Not me," Maggie finished,

"You should wear it down," Fiona said as she walked into the anteroom, carrying the bouquet of flowers Maggie would carry down the aisle. "You have such lovely curls. I'm sure Callum fell in love with you when you had your hair down around your shoulders. It reflects you as the warm, generous—"

"Wildly free and loving person you are," Sadie finished. "Fiona is right. Wear it down."

"But the stylist spent so long getting it all pinned in place."

"And it will take no time at all to pull all the pins out," Fiona said. "Sit."

Maggie grinned. "Yes, ma'am." She sank onto the chair in front of the makeup mirror.

Sadie and Fiona went to work pulling the dozen or more pins from her hair. Then Sadie fluffed her curls, tucked a few locks back on each side of her face and pinned them in place.

"Perfect," Fiona said. "You look like a wild Highland lass."

Maggie stood and smoothed her hands over her belly. "I'm just glad the dress fits. If I'd waited any longer, I'd be getting married wearing the wedding tent, not the dress."

"Oh, don't be silly," Sadie said. "You're hardly showing at four months. But then this is your first baby. When I was pregnant with my second, I looked five months pregnant when I was only three months along."

Mrs. Jones, wearing a pretty green mother-of-the-bride dress, poked her head through the door. "I checked with the preacher. Everything is ready."

"That means it's showtime," Sadie said with a grin.

Mrs. Jones held out her arm. "Then let's show them how it's done."

Maggie hooked her hand through the older woman's arm. "Thank you for agreeing to walk me down the aisle. My mother would've been happy it was you."

"It's my pleasure entirely." Mrs. Jones sniffed and wiped a tear that had slipped from the corner of her eye. "I wish I'd been able to help your mother more. She was such a beautiful young lady with a big heart. Though you didn't take after her in looks, your personalities are so very much alike. She'd be proud of what you and Lady Fiona have accomplished with the children in the village."

"I didn't need all the money I inherited as much as the village needed a preschool for the children," Maggie said. "And I'm doing what I love best."

"Working with children." Fiona nodded. "Even Bryce has been a big help, working with the little ones. He likes pretending he's a big brother."

"When are you going to marry Peter Atkins and

give that boy a sibling?" Mrs. Jones asked as they walked out of the room.

Maggie glanced over her shoulder at Fiona.

The woman's face had flushed a pretty pink. Maggie had suspected Peter Atkins was hanging around more for Fiona than to help Ewan and Callum remodel what had once been the basement torture room into a war room for the UK satellite office of the Brotherhood Protectors International. Maggie thought it fitting to convert it from a place where bad things had happened into one where they could work to help others.

Fiona had blossomed under Peter's attention. After her marriage to the horrible Lord Drummond, she'd been hesitant to get involved with another man. Peter proved to be patient and had given her the space and time to come around. Now, they were often sighted walking through the gardens holding hands or holding Bryce's hands as he swung between them.

"I'm glad Ewan agreed to work with the Brotherhood," Fiona said. "He's much happier with a bigger purpose in life other than managing the estate. All that training with the SAS shouldn't go to waste."

"And it won't. He's already been on one mission and Ace has him lined up for another that kicks off soon," Maggie said. "He's in his element, just like Callum."

"Speaking of Callum," Mrs. Jones smiled. "He's

waiting for you at the end of the aisle." She stepped out of the anteroom with Maggie on her arm.

Sadie and Fiona hurried ahead of her to take their seats.

As Maggie entered the sanctuary, everyone seated in the pews stood.

She didn't see anyone but the man standing beside the preacher at the end of the aisle.

As promised, he wore a kilt in the McCall colors, with the pleated fabric draped around his legs. The white shirt he wore with the kilt had full sleeves and made him look like a swashbuckling pirate. The ornate leather pouch, or sporran, added function and flair to the look. He'd even grown his hair out a little. With his neatly trimmed beard and mustache, he had a rakish air that made Maggie's heart flutter with excitement.

He'd come a long way from having nightmares every night to only restless sleep on occasion. When he slept with Maggie, he was more at peace than at any other time.

Over the past few months, Maggie had fallen deeper in love with this Scotsman who'd saved her twice. With love in her heart and their baby in her womb, she held her head high, wearing a smile she couldn't tame and marched to her future with her kilt-wearing protector, glad he hadn't opted for the pink polka-dotted tutu.

FRANCE FACE-OFF

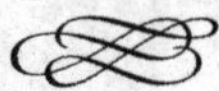

BROTHERHOOD PROTECTORS
INTERNATIONAL BOOK #6

New York Times & USA Today
Bestselling Author

ELLE JAMES

BROTHERHOOD PROTECTORS
INTERNATIONAL
FRANCE FACE-OFF
New York Times & USA Today Bestselling Author
ELLE JAMES

CHAPTER 1

WHAT THE HELL had he gotten himself into?

Dane "Striker" Ryan adjusted the bowtie at his throat and stared around the *Baie des Anges* reception hall of the Hotel Le Negresco in Nice on the southern coast of France. He'd never worn a bowtie in his life, never been to Nice and sure as hell couldn't afford to pay the room rates at the hotel. If he'd had any other choice, he wouldn't be a fish out of water, dressed in a monkey suit walking into a highly publicized event attended by world leaders from all over the globe.

No, he'd be with his SEAL team, training or performing vital missions in some of the most godforsaken locations in countries these world leaders hailed from.

His chest tightened into a hard knot.

The only reason he was in France and not homeless on the streets of San Diego was because he'd been given what he hoped was a second chance, an airline ticket and a wad of cash he couldn't refuse.

The offer couldn't have come at a better time. On the verge of being evicted from his apartment because he couldn't pay the rent, he'd been desperate. His job flipping hamburgers for a mom & pop burger joint hadn't earned enough money to keep a roof over his head. His years of training with the Navy SEALs meant nothing in the civilian world. The only jobs he was suited for required a clean record.

His record was shit. Dishonorably discharged from the military, he couldn't get employment washing dishes on a military base or in any government facility. He sure as hell couldn't get on with any security firms, providing armed escorts to diplomats or the rich and famous.

What else was he good for? He'd never held a desk job, his truck had been repossessed and he'd been facing homelessness. He'd been sitting at McP's pub, nursing a beer in the middle of the day while the rest of his team was gainfully employed, probably training for the next mission, when he'd gotten the call.

That fateful call.

It had come through as an unknown caller on his cellphone. Usually, he ignored such calls. But he'd applied to a number of establishments, hoping for more lucrative employment. He hadn't been able to afford to ignore a single call. He'd used his last few bucks to buy a beer, which wasn't nearly enough to drown the pain of his unwarranted disgrace and subsequent removal from the only job he'd ever known and loved.

"Dane Ryan?" a female voice had addressed him as soon as he'd hit the receive button.

"Speaking," he'd said.

"I understand you're being evicted from your apartment at the end of the week."

He'd frowned and almost hit the button to end the call, but curiosity stayed his finger.

"Who's this?" he'd demanded.

"Someone who knows what you did to lose your job, and the people who gave you the order to do it and then let you take the fall for them."

That had his attention.

His eyes narrowed. "What do you know?"

"That you can't get work because of the black mark on your record, you barely have two nickels to rub together, you need a job that pays more than minimum wage to afford an apartment in San Diego, and your team called you Striker because you were the best sniper in the Navy SEALs."

"You seem to know a lot about me," Striker had said.

"I do," she'd said. "I know you grew up in the foster care system, joined the Navy at the age of seventeen and made something of yourself."

"Who is this?"

"Someone who cares. Someone who knows the value of your training and commitment to doing what's right."

"Yeah, yeah. Whatever. Do you have a name?"

"You can call me Lucie," she said.

"Okay, Lucie," he'd said. "Why are you calling me, telling me things I already know?"

"Because I have a job for you."

Striker leaned forward in his seat in the corner of the bar. "I'm listening."

"Good. Be looking for a packet to be delivered to your apartment. You'll receive instructions in that packet. Money has been deposited to your bank account. You'll receive another payment upon completion of your mission."

"What kind of mission?"

"You'll receive further instructions." And she'd ended the call, leaving Striker with more questions than answers. Immediately following the call, he'd received a text from his bank that a wire transfer had been made to his account.

When he'd logged into his account, he'd found that thirty-thousand dollars had been deposited into his checking account. He had no idea what the woman wanted him to do for that money, and it worried him. Did she want him to kill someone? He'd killed before, but never for money and only the enemies of his country. If the woman knew him at all, she'd know that he wouldn't commit murder, no matter how desperate he might be.

That had been the beginning of this wild ride.

He'd hurried back to his apartment to find the packet that had been delivered. It contained a passport with his image and a fake name on it, a first-class airline ticket to France and the address of a hotel. It had also contained a wad of cash, the name of a men's clothing store and a note to buy himself some nice clothes for the trip. More instructions awaited him at his destination. At the bottom of the packet was a burner phone.

Thousands of dollars, airline tickets to France and a fake passport couldn't be good.

Striker had almost bailed at that point.

The burner phone rang. He'd answered, ready to say he was out and she could take back all the money and stuff.

"You're wondering if all this is legit at this point, aren't you?" the woman's voice sounded in his ear. "You're probably thinking this isn't an honorable mission and wondering if I'm setting you up to put a hit out on someone. Am I right?"

"Yes, ma'am," he said. "This kind of money can only mean trouble."

"Or it means what you're being tasked to do is

very important."

"I'm leaning toward trouble."

"I know you were tasked to assassinate the Russian in charge of Internal Affairs. The man responsible for the corruption of their police force and the deaths of a number of American diplomats and tourists."

Striker's grip on the burner phone tightened. How did she know? The mission had been top secret. "I don't know what you're talking about."

She chuckled softly. "Would you consider a mission to possibly save the world for a second chance at your career in the Navy SEALs?"

"You can do that?" On second thought, he shook his head. "No one can do that."

"I have connections," she stated. "As a show of faith, look out the window of your apartment."

"Are you going to show your face?" he asked as he walked across the bare room to the window and opened the blinds. Below, in the parking lot, sat a black four-wheel-drive truck with knobby tires, tinted windows and a decal of a frog on the back windshield. "My truck? You got my truck?"

She laughed. "It's yours, free and clear, no debt associated with the vehicle, if you agree to perform this mission."

Striker frowned. "Still feels like a hit, especially with as much money as you're throwing at it."

"It's not," she said. "I'm not asking you to kill anyone."

"What *are* you asking me to do?"

"Take the ticket, buy the clothes, go to France. You'll receive further instructions from there."

"But what if—"

She'd ended the call.

Striker had had three choices. One, he could ignore the woman and keep the money and his truck. Two, he could ignore the offer, return the money and truck. Three, see where the mission was going, save the world and keep the money and truck.

He'd followed the instructions, reluctantly, knowing he didn't have much of a choice. The money in his account and his truck could just as easily disappear as it had appeared. The woman had said she didn't want him to kill anyone. How hard could this mission be?

And here he was, dressed like someone important, inside the reception hall of a fancy hotel in France, rubbing elbows with world leaders and awaiting orders.

When he'd arrived at the hotel, the clerk had been expecting him—at least the man on the fake passport. He'd handed Striker the keys to a suite in the hotel on the fifth floor. The bellman had led the way up, carrying the new suitcase containing his new clothes. Once inside the room, he'd found a tuxedo hanging in the closet, dress shoes in his size, an invitation to a reception in the hotel and a note.

Wear the tux, go to the reception and receive your orders there. Good luck.

Lucie

Before he'd gone down to the reception, he'd spent time reading up on the web about the reception, the attendees and the political issues they were facing.

The reception was the beginning of a two-day energy summit. The biggest issue up for debate would be the natural gas pipeline scheduled for expansion from Russia to Germany. Striker had studied the players involved from Sergei Baranovsky, the Russian diplomat heavily involved in the negotiations for the pipeline, to the German Federal Minister of Economics and Energy, Hans Sutter. Japan's representative was a small man with salt-and-pepper hair, Hikosaburo Kono. Other representatives hailed from the United Kingdom, France, Italy and the European Union. The one person who had him most intrigued was the man who'd replaced the assassinated leader of Russian Internal Affairs.

The man Striker had terminated while still a SEAL.

His replacement, Anatoly Petrov, had a reputation as an aggressive negotiator and a ladies' man. He liked women, and he liked getting his way, even if it meant turning his back and walking away from the table.

Striker wasn't sure what he had to do with the Energy Summit, and he wasn't sure how he was supposed to receive his next instructions unless the instructions had only been to wear the tuxedo and show up at the reception.

Surely, that wasn't all of it.

Lucie seemed interested in his skills as a Navy SEAL.

Navy SEALs weren't normally dressed in tuxedos, attending diplomatic receptions with leaders of foreign countries. When he'd taken out the Russian in charge of Internal Affairs, he'd done it from the top of a building over a hundred yards away. He'd had his rifle packed up and moved out of the building before anybody really knew what had happened. He'd never been this close to a bunch of politicians, and he sure as hell didn't fit in.

Along with the tuxedo and the shoes, he wore the earbuds Lucie had given him in his first packet of information back in the States. He carried the burner phone in his pocket and awaited some clue as to what he was supposed to do at the reception.

He stood near the entrance, having arrived early to watch as the guests entered. Based on the pictures from the internet, he'd picked out Hans Sutter, the German, the Russians Sergei Baranovsky and Anatoly Petrov, the Japanese representative, and

Lorenzo Ricci, the Italian. Richard Weddington, the United Kingdom representative, had yet to put in an appearance.

Movement at the door caught his attention. The UK representative and his wife stepped through the entrance, showed their invitations to the security guard manning the door and crossed the room to the bar where they ordered glasses of wine.

A raven-haired woman entered next, wearing a long silver gown that clung to her curves and rippled like mercury with every step she took. She smiled and handed the security guard her invitation. He frowned down at it for a moment, and then glanced up with narrowed eyes. She laughed and smiled more broadly, pointed at the invitation and said something Striker couldn't quite hear from where he stood. The security guard tapped his ear and spoke into his microphone. A moment later, he gave the woman a nod and she entered the reception hall.

"Striker, can you hear me?" a voice said in his ears, startling him.

He hadn't realized how focused he was on the woman who'd just walked in until Lucie's voice sounded in his ear. The comm device was a two-way radio which meant Lucie had to be there in France and was close enough for the signals to come through.

"Roger," he said.

"Are you ready for your mission?"

Irritation flared. "Depends on what the mission is," he said. "Although, the use of my combat training seems irrelevant in this monkey suit."

Her chuckle filled his ear. "It all will become clear momentarily," she said. "And by the way, you look stunning in that tuxedo."

Striker glanced around the reception hall, searching for a female possibly standing alone who was talking to no one in particular. There were several women who had accompanied their husbands to the event. Most of them were older, and all of them seemed to be occupied with other people, except for the one in the silver dress. She stopped to snag a glass of champagne from one of the waiters circulating through the room, smiling to thank him.

"Your mission tonight..." Lucie said into his ear.

The woman in the silver dress turned at the same time, her mouth still forming a smile across her lips.

"—is to keep an assassination from happening," Lucie concluded.

No, the woman in the silver dress did not move her lips. The elusive Lucie couldn't be her. Somewhat disappointed, Striker looked around the room. "Whose assassination am I supposed to stop? And by the way, I recognize the irony."

"Good. I know you did your homework on this event," Lucie stated. "If you've been following the energy struggles between Russia and Germany, you know how important this summit could be. I received intel indicating an assassination attempt will be made on one or both of the Russian diplomats. An agreement must be reached at this summit, or the energy needs of Europe could be at risk. Climatologists indicate the coming winter could be one of the harshest in decades. Without the additional capacity the new pipeline could produce, and with the growing population in Europe, it could spell disaster if an accord is not reached."

"Any idea who the assassin might be?"

"Therein lies the problem. My intelligence reports it's the same assassin who has eliminated four of the five diplomats with connections to the Russian mafia. No one has seen the assassin to know who he is. I know that's not much to go on," she said. "The targets are the Russians. Have you located Sergei Baranovsky and Anatoly Petrov?"

"Yes, ma'am," he responded. "This summit concludes in two days. Do either of the Russians know that I will be looking out for them?"

"No, and they are not to know. We hope that in the process of protecting these two men you might reveal the identity of the assassin."

"And my cover for this operation?" he asked.

"You're an escort for Natalya Zotin, a United Kingdom citizen of Russian descent, who speaks fluent Russian and translates for the Russian Minister of Energy and the Russian in charge of

Internal Affairs. She should be entering the reception hall at this moment."

A woman with auburn hair and wearing a green dress stepped through the entryway, handed her invitation to the security guard and looked out across the room. When her gaze met his, she smiled.

"Red hair?" Striker asked, careful not to move his lips too much.

"That's her," Lucie said. "I'll leave you to it."

"Does she know why I'm here?" he asked.

Lucie didn't respond.

Great. He didn't know if this Natalya woman was another one of Lucie's agents or if he was supposed to pretend to be a male escort. How he was supposed to keep an eye on the Russians while entertaining a translator was a mystery to him. With the Russians in his peripheral vision, he moved toward the redhead in the green dress.

As they converged on the floor of the reception hall, she held out her hands. "Ah, yes. You must be Daniel Rayne. I was told to expect a handsome man as my escort this evening."

"You must be Natalya." He took her hand in his and lifted it to his lips, pressing a kiss to the backs of her knuckles. The name she'd addressed him by was the one on the fake passport he'd received in his packet from Lucie.

She arched a perfect eyebrow. "You're American?"

He nodded. "Yes, ma'am."

She spoke perfect Queen's English with only a slight Russian accent. The fine lines around her eyes and mouth were a subtle indication of her age. She had to be in her late forties or early fifties and aging well.

"Do you speak any Russian at all?" she asked.

He shook his head. "Sadly, no."

Natalya sighed. "Up to that point, you were almost perfect."

"I shall take that as a compliment." He offered her his elbow.

She slipped her hand through the crook and turned toward the other guests in the reception hall.

Striker spotted the two Russians standing with the German.

"I suppose I need to work," Natalya said. "Shall we?"

Following her lead, Striker stepped out across the floor and headed toward the Russians.

"I know they speak fluent German, and the German speaks fluent Russian. So, I only have to be close by in case someone else wants to enter the conversation. Which means, I won't be completely tasked all evening. I had hoped to dance. You do dance, don't you?"

Striker grimaced. "My dancing has been strictly limited to country western music. My dancing skills are in the form of the two-step and the waltz. I'm good for those."

She smiled. "I'll keep that in mind. I am not familiar with the two-step, but the waltz...it is beautiful, no?"

Once again, *Great,* he thought. How was he supposed to keep track of the Russians while he was dancing as an escort for the translator? At that moment, he wished he had a handgun, a rifle or a knife. At least, then, he'd feel like he was in his element.

The reception got into full swing. Natalya made her rounds, following the Russians around the room. Striker quickly realized the woman could translate in a number of different languages, including Italian, French, English and German.

"I'm learning Japanese," she said, "But I'm not proficient yet." The music started from the string quartet in the corner. Several songs were played before Natalya smiled and said, "That's a waltz, would you like to dance with me?"

He frowned. "Are you sure you can take a break from translating?"

She laughed. "Yes, for at least one song."

He nodded and held out his arms.

She stepped into them and placed a hand on his shoulder, the other hand in his palm and he led her across the floor in a waltz. The music was different but the dance was the same, and he managed not to make a fool of himself in front of all the important diplomats. As they whirled around the floor, he took the opportunities he could to keep an eye on the Russians. In one turn around the floor, he noticed the woman in the silver dress approaching Petrov and Baranovsky. When she spoke, they turned and responded, stern faces softening into smiles.

"The woman speaking with Petrov and Baranovsky, who is she?" Striker asked. He spun Natalya around so that she could see the woman.

His dance partner's brow furrowed. "I do not know this woman, though I might have seen her before at another event involving Russian diplomats. She seems to be holding a conversation with my two Russian charges. It appears my translations services are not needed."

The woman in the silver dress laughed and laid a hand on Petrov's arm. She turned to the side and, as she did, Striker noticed a long slit in the side of her dress that exposed her leg from the ankle to halfway up her thigh.

His groin tightened.

She had a stunning figure and an equally stunning leg. When she moved again, he noticed something odd about the tone of her skin just below the slit's opening. Maybe it was a trick of the lighting in the huge hall, but there seemed to be a discoloration just below the top of the slit. Perhaps the discoloration and the flesh tone of her leg was an undergarment she used to smooth her shape, as he was aware many women did. Or could it be a strap holding a weapon against the inside of her thigh…?

He stiffened. Thankfully, at that moment, the waltz came to an end.

The woman in the silver dress hooked her hand through the crook of Petrov's arm and walked with him toward an arched passageway.

On Striker's initial inspection of the reception hall, he had followed different hallways and corridors to determine where they led. The one the woman in silver was headed down led out to a tropical garden. The beautiful woman could be going with Petrov for a private assignation surrounded by lush, flowering bushes and palm trees. Or she could be carrying a knife beneath her dress with the intention of assassinating the Russian in the darkness.

"If you'll excuse me, ma'am," Striker said. "I need to visit the water closet."

"By all means," Natalya said. "I need to powder my nose, as well."

He indicated the direction in which the ladies' room was located.

Fortunately, the men's room was on the opposite side of the hall, conveniently positioned along the same corridor that led to the hotel garden.

"One moment, please." Natalya tipped her head toward the taller of the two Russians. "It appears Sergei might be leaving the reception hall and Anatoly already has."

All the more reason for Daniel to hurry and catch up with Petrov and the woman in the silver dress. However, he stood steady and gave Natalya his attention.

"Since they're leaving the reception, there is no need for me to stay to translate. I find myself fatigued. I too shall retire." She patted his cheek with the palm of her hand. "Your services are no longer required."

He captured her hand in his and touched the backs of her knuckles with his lips. "The evening has been my pleasure."

"Mine, too," she said with a smile. "And you're quite good at the waltz. The escort service did well in sending you."

"You'll have to look into country western dancing to learn the two-step for next time." He smiled and waited for her to turn away. Once she did, he headed out across the floor toward the corridor leading into the garden. With no other doorways leading off the corridor, he didn't wait or check to see if they'd stopped along the way.

When he stepped out into the hotel garden, he waited for his eyes to adjust to the darkness. His ears perked as he listened for sounds at the other end of the dimly lit area.

Once his night vision adjusted, he eased away from the chateau and followed a pathway, walking as lightly as he could in his patent leather shoes. He followed the sound of voices.

Before he'd gone more than twenty yards, he saw the two silhouetted against the stone wall at the rear of the garden.

Striker stopped within twenty feet of them. He could reach them quickly, if needed. Instead of rushing the couple, he paused and watched. For all he knew, it could be a lovers' assignation. A tryst in the garden, away from prying eyes.

Petrov turned and gripped the woman's arms.

She reached up in an attempt to pry his hands loose from her arms. Her voice turned from a conversational tone to a higher pitched, strained nature.

"*Nyet,*" she said and rattled off something in Russian. She tried to break free of the man's grip on her arms.

When Petrov still hadn't released her, her tone dropped low, the intensity increasing. A flash of movement brought her hands up through the middle of his arms, breaking free of his grasp. She grabbed his head, turned her back and flipped him over.

Petrov landed flat on his back.

In the next second, the woman had a knife pulled, the blade glinting in the moonlight.

Striker raced forward.

The silver-clad woman said something fast and

furious in Russian as she held the knife over the man lying splayed out on his back.

Striker reached the woman before she could plunge the knife into the Russian's neck. He grabbed her wrist and yanked it up behind her back.

"Damn it, let go of me," she muttered.

Striker put his lips near her ear. "Ah, my dear, I found you finally. I believe they're playing our song. Shouldn't we be dancing?" He pretended to just take notice of the man on the ground. "What's this?" He frowned down at the Russian. "Sir, have you fallen?"

The Russian grunted and struggled to get to his feet.

With his free hand, Striker reached down and gave the man a hand up.

The woman he held with the arm up behind her back stood straight, unmoving, her chin tipped upward in defiance.

As the Russian stood, he brushed leaves from his suit and glared at the woman in silver.

"Are you okay?" Striker asked. "Do I need to call for medical assistance?"

The Russian shook his head. "*Nyet,* I am quite fine," he said in his stilted English. "Is this your woman?" He jerked his hand toward the woman in silver.

"Why, yes," Striker said. "I came to get her because I'm ready to leave. Are you ready to depart, my dear?"

She gave him a narrow-eyed glance out of the corner of her eye.

Using her body as a visual barrier, Striker removed the knife from her hand, folded the blade and slid it into his pocket. He lowered her arm to her side and slipped a hand around her waist, his grip firm. "Please, sir, allow us to see you back to the reception hall."

The Russian adjusted his suit. "I do not need assistance to find my way back." He turned and walked back toward the building.

Striker guided the woman in silver behind the Russian, giving him several yards of distance between them. Once the Russian reached the reception hall, Striker came to a halt, stopping just short of the building. He turned the woman around and lightly gripped her arms. He stared down into eyes as black as the night, the only light in their dark depths that of moonlight reflected off their liquid surface. "Who are you and why were you trying to kill the Russian?"

She spoke in Russian.

He shook his head. "English."

Again, she spoke in Russian.

"I heard you curse in English. Talk, before I turn you over to the security guards."

She stared up at him through narrowed eyes. "He attacked me. I was only defending myself."

"Sure, and you always carry a knife to diplomatic

receptions? How did you get that past the security guards and metal detectors?"

She lifted a narrow shoulder. "A woman has to defend herself."

Her English held no trace of an English accent; it was American.

"You speak American English. Are you American?"

The woman crossed her arms over her chest, tipped back her head and stared down her nose at the man. "What's it to you?"

"Let's just say that I like to know my enemies."

"Am I one of your enemies?" She arched a black wing of a brow.

"I don't know. Are you?"

Her eyebrows dipped. "Only if you've done something to hurt me or my family."

"And is that what Petrov has done to you?"

Her mouth firmed into a thin line. "Perhaps."

"Do you make it a habit of trying to kill those who hurt you or your family?"

"No, but if he hurts me again, I will defend myself."

"In this case I will give you the benefit of doubt. In what capacity are you here?"

"I could ask the same of you."

"I'm here as a paid escort. And you?" He waited for her response.

"Translation services."

"Your name?"

She lifted a narrow shoulder and let it fall. "Alexa Sokoloff."

The name didn't ring a bell. None of the people who were attending the reception that were in the news had gone by that name. He'd have to put Lucie to work discovering all there was to know about the raven-haired beauty. In the meantime, he'd do well to watch his back lest she plunge a knife in it.

ABOUT THE AUTHOR

ELLE JAMES also writing as MYLA JACKSON is a *New York Times* and *USA Today* Bestselling author of books including cowboys, intrigues and paranormal adventures that keep her readers on the edges of their seats. When she's not at her computer, she's traveling, snow skiing, boating, or riding her ATV, dreaming up new stories. Learn more about Elle James at www.ellejames.com

Website | Facebook | Twitter | GoodReads |
Newsletter | BookBub | Amazon

Or visit her alter ego Myla Jackson at
mylajackson.com
Website | Facebook | Twitter | Newsletter

Follow Me!
www.ellejames.com
ellejamesauthor@gmail.com

ALSO BY ELLE JAMES

Stealth Operations Specialists Series

Saint Nick (#1)

Rogue (#2)

Crusher (#3)

Draco (#4)

A Killer Series

Chilled (#1)

Scorched (#2)

Erased (#3)

Brotherhood Protectors International

Athens Affair (#1)

Belgian Betrayal (#2)

Croatia Collateral (#3)

Dublin Debacle (#4)

Edinburgh Escape (#5)

France Face-Off (#6)

Brotherhood Protectors Hawaii

Kalea's Hero (#1)

Leilani's Hero (#2)

Kiana's Hero (#3)

Casey's Hero (#4)

Maliea's Hero (#5)

Emi's Hero (#6)

Sachie's Hero (#7)

Kimo's Hero (#8)

Alana's Hero (#9)

Bayou Brotherhood Protectors

Remy (#1)

Gerard (#2)

Lucas (#3)

Beau (#4)

Rafael (#5)

Valentin (#6)

Landry (#7)

Simon (#8)

Maurice (#9)

Xavier (#10)

Jacques (#11)

Papa Noel (#12)

Everglades Overwatch Series

with Jen Talty

Secrets in Calusa Cove

Pirates in Calusa Cove

Murder in Calusa Cove

Betrayal in Calusa Cove

Raven's Cliff Series

with Kris Norris

Raven's Watch (#1)

Raven's Claw (#2)

Raven's Nest (#3)

Raven's Curse (#4)

Brotherhood Protectors Yellowstone

Saving Kyla (#1)

Saving Chelsea (#2)

Saving Amanda (#3)

Saving Liliana (#4)

Saving Breely (#5)

Saving Savvie (#6)

Saving Jenna (#7)

Saving Peyton (#8)

Saving Londyn (#9)

Brotherhood Protectors Colorado

SEAL Salvation (#1)

Rocky Mountain Rescue (#2)

Ranger Redemption (#3)

Tactical Takeover (#4)

Colorado Conspiracy (#5)

Rocky Mountain Madness (#6)

Free Fall (#7)

Colorado Cold Case (#8)

Fool's Folly (#9)

Colorado Free Rein (#10)

Rocky Mountain Venom (#11)

High Country Hero (#12)

Brotherhood Protectors

Montana SEAL (#1)

Bride Protector SEAL (#2)

Montana D-Force (#3)

Cowboy D-Force (#4)

Montana Ranger (#5)

Montana Dog Soldier (#6)

Montana SEAL Daddy (#7)

Montana Ranger's Wedding Vow (#8)

Montana SEAL Undercover Daddy (#9)

Cape Cod SEAL Rescue (#10)

Montana SEAL Friendly Fire (#11)

Montana SEAL's Mail-Order Bride (#12)

SEAL Justice (#13)

Ranger Creed (#14)

Delta Force Rescue (#15)

Dog Days of Christmas (#16)

Montana Rescue (#17)

Montana Ranger Returns (#18)

Brotherhood Protectors Boxed Set 1

Brotherhood Protectors Boxed Set 2

Brotherhood Protectors Boxed Set 3

Brotherhood Protectors Boxed Set 4

Brotherhood Protectors Boxed Set 5

Brotherhood Protectors Boxed Set 6

Iron Horse Legacy

Soldier's Duty (#1)

Ranger's Baby (#2)

Marine's Promise (#3)

SEAL's Vow (#4)

Warrior's Resolve (#5)

Drake (#6)

Grimm (#7)

Murdock (#8)

Utah (#9)

Judge (#10)

Delta Force Strong

Ivy's Delta (Delta Force 3 Crossover)

Breaking Silence (#1)

Breaking Rules (#2)

Breaking Away (#3)

Breaking Free (#4)

Breaking Hearts (#5)

Breaking Ties (#6)

Breaking Point (#7)

Breaking Dawn (#8)

Breaking Promises (#9)

Hearts & Heroes Series

Wyatt's War (#1)

Mack's Witness (#2)

Ronin's Return (#3)

Sam's Surrender (#4)

Hellfire Series

Hellfire, Texas (#1)

Justice Burning (#2)

Smoldering Desire (#3)

Hellfire in High Heels (#4)

Playing With Fire (#5)

Up in Flames (#6)

Total Meltdown (#7)

Take No Prisoners Series

SEAL's Honor (#1)

SEAL'S Desire (#2)

SEAL's Embrace (#3)

SEAL's Obsession (#4)

SEAL's Proposal (#5)

SEAL's Seduction (#6)

SEAL'S Defiance (#7)

SEAL's Deception (#8)

SEAL's Deliverance (#9)

SEAL's Ultimate Challenge (#10)

Cajun Magic Mystery Series

Voodoo on the Bayou (#1)

Voodoo for Two (#2)

Deja Voodoo (#3)

Texas Billionaire Club

Tarzan & Janine (#1)

Something To Talk About (#2)

Who's Your Daddy (#3)

Love & War (#4)

Billionaire Online Dating Service

The Billionaire Husband Test (#1)

The Billionaire Cinderella Test (#2)

The Billionaire Bride Test (#3)

The Billionaire Daddy Test (#4)

The Billionaire Matchmaker Test (#5)

The Billionaire Glitch Date (#6)

The Outriders

Homicide at Whiskey Gulch (#1)

Hideout at Whiskey Gulch (#2)

Held Hostage at Whiskey Gulch (#3)

Setup at Whiskey Gulch (#4)

Missing Witness at Whiskey Gulch (#5)

Cowboy Justice at Whiskey Gulch (#6)

Boys Behaving Badly Anthologies

Rogues (#1)

Blue Collar (#2)

Pirates (#3)

Stranded (#4)

First Responder (#5)

Cowboys (#6)

Silver Soldiers (#7)

Secret Identities (#8)

Warrior's Conquest

Enslaved by the Viking Short Story

Conquests

Smokin' Hot Firemen

Protecting the Colton Bride

Protecting the Colton Bride & Colton's Cowboy Code

Heir to Murder

Secret Service Rescue

High Octane Heroes

Haunted

Engaged with the Boss

Cowboy Brigade

An Unexpected Clue

Under Suspicion, With Child

Texas-Size Secrets

Made in the USA
Las Vegas, NV
13 February 2026

41905409R00203